ACCIDENTAL SIBLINGS

ACCIDENTAL SIBLINGS

FAMILY CONNECTIONS

HELEN M. CROSER

Matchstick Literary
1-888-306-8885
orders@matchliterary.com

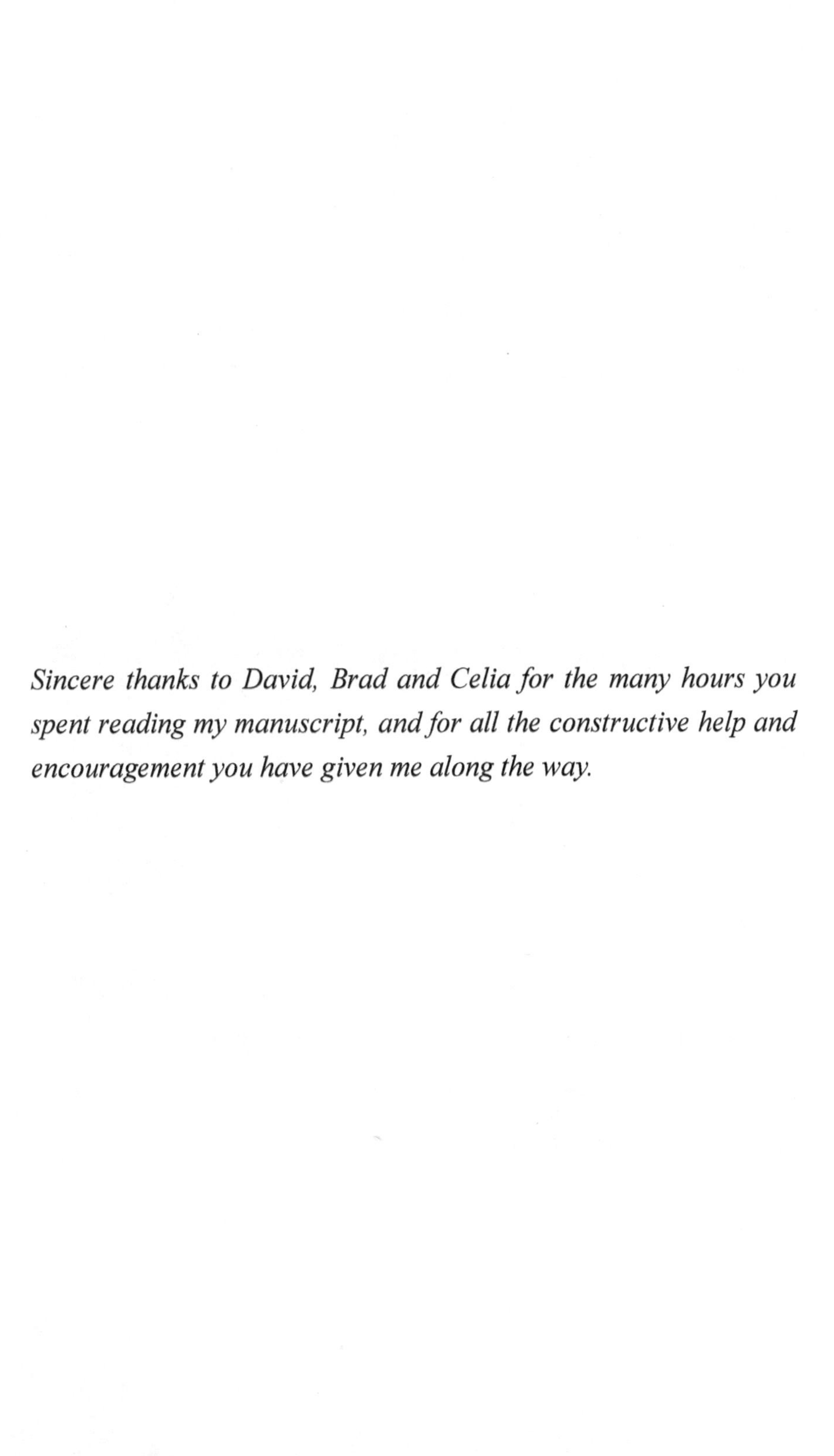*Sincere thanks to David, Brad and Celia for the many hours you spent reading my manuscript, and for all the constructive help and encouragement you have given me along the way.*

CHAPTER 1

Shivers skittered down Felicity's spine as she surveyed the scene below the clifftop. Her breakfast was regurgitated as she recognised Jack, her husband's father, sprawled face down in a shallow tidal inlet of Clapper's Cove. His body appeared battered and bruised, tangled in a long-forgotten, partly buried roll of barbed wire. The churned-up sand around his body indicated he'd been involved in a struggle.

Although seasons fluctuated and advanced as usual, farm life proved very different after Jack's death. Jack's large imagined funeral, featuring respectful crowds of townspeople overflowing from the town hall and on to the footpath, didn't eventuate. Although he didn't have any enemies in the town, his real friends were minimal, and many people only came to see who else attended. Some were there to enjoy chatting with friends and acquaintances or for the afternoon tea destined to be served by the CWA afterwards. Some of the locals— and Jack had been one of them—rarely missed a funeral in their later years, knowing they'd be given a plate of goodies to take home for their evening meal if they stayed to help pack up the venue.

A funeral service carefully crafted by family members frequently showcases a whitewashed account of the deceased person's life. Family tensions can be almost palpable at some funerals as warring factions try to present a united front. Sometimes families even remain separated by their differences by only attending either the church or the graveside service.

Jack's funeral service was possibly presented more honestly than most. His family loved him but could see no reason to gloss over the fact he'd been excessively stubborn and controlling.

He could be the life of the party at family gatherings, amiable and agreeable, but with all things pertaining to the running of the farm, he'd laid down rigidly immovable laws! His quirky sense of humour often contained barbed innuendoes that made listeners cringingly uncomfortable. The family didn't elaborate, but the townspeople had all experienced or observed these traits in him. They'd registered how his domineering pomposity had affected his only son and his son's marriages. They'd seen his daughters gladly move away from home as soon as they left school and how his need for total control had shaped his own marriage.

Inside the Uniting Church at Jack's funeral service in the nearby township of Wattle Flat, a series of photos depicting his life was projected on to a large permanently mounted screen. There were pictures of him as a small boy, a young married man, and recent frames of him as a proud farmer. Some of his favourite fifties music played quietly in the background during the slide show. The officiating clergy eventually wrapped up the church service by utilising well-worn Bible readings and hymns about being 'at peace now' and 'in a better place'.

With the eulogy taken care of in the warmth and relative comfort of the church, the presiding minister knew little would be gained by having a lengthy graveside service where family grief overflowed, causing everyone to feel uncomfortable.

They buried Jack in the Wattle Creek cemetery, the nearest to their closest town of Wattle Flat. It wasn't a place to linger in contemplation. Apart from the undertaker catering for the needs of close relatives, the cold and windy graveyard had no seating for elderly attendees, and toilet facilities were non-existent.

Except for the appearance of the coffin, the brief service followed a conventional pattern. Jack, having spent most of his life farming, had felt no personal need to be involved in outside activities unless they provided him with benefits. In his younger days, he'd been a champion cricketer and a respectable swimmer but was always too busy when called upon to coach the younger generation, even when his own children were growing up.

Modern technology enabled 'wrapped' reproductions of photos depicting Jack's farming life to enhance the coffin's appearance— photos of his header, his tractor, his cattle and crops, and his dogs that so often balanced on the back of the ute or Agricultural trike. Appropriately, due to Jack's lack of interest in gardening (either vegetables or flowers), instead of floral tributes being left at the graveside to blow away in the wind, the family suggested donations be made to the Royal Flying Doctor Service. Although situated less than three hours from Adelaide, the RFDS frequently answered calls from Wattle Flat to fly sick or injured people to Adelaide for specialist care.

After a much-loved local fisherman and family man failed to be resuscitated after being swept out to sea by a freak wave at Rohan's Rocks, donated land several miles out of town meant the town obtained a permanent landing strip.

An RFDS helicopter safely flew Jack directly to Flinders Medical Centre after he'd suffered a heart attack several years previously. If he'd travelled to Adelaide by road, his survival might have been in jeopardy. There were many other instances when adults and children's lives were saved by being able to access the Royal Flying Doctor Service. On average, transportation of one patient to the city from Wattle Flat occurred each week.

Australian history fascinated Felicity, and she readily absorbed any information remotely linked to Clapper's Cove or Wattle Flat township. She learned the Royal Flying Doctor Service was founded in Cloncurry in Queensland, way back in 1928. First called the Australian Inland Mission Aerial Medical Service, it was the brainchild of Rev. John Flynn, a Presbyterian minister. He dreamed of providing health care to people who were unable to access a hospital or general practice due to the vast distances of the Outback.

Felicity read that the first RFDS flight happened in a single-engine fabric-covered biplane, and in the late 1930s, the service expanded into South Australia. She would have found it incomprehensible that in little over eighty years, the RFDS in South Australia would be using Pilatus PC-12 jets, fitted out with state-of-the-art equipment and housed in modern facilities adjacent to Adelaide Airport. The RFDS had steadily grown to become one of the largest and most comprehensive aeromedical organisations in the world, providing twenty-four-hour emergency service to people over an area of approximately three million square miles.

*   *   *

The townspeople all knew that Barry and Felicity could have multiple reasons for not being grief-stricken when Jack died.

'How did Jack die? Was he attacked? Did he trip and fall?'

'Was he pushed over the crumbled cliff edge, or were his injuries caused by his efforts to free himself from the tangled barbed wire?'

'Were Barry or Felicity responsible for his death? Would they be investigated as prime suspects?'

All these questions provided fodder for the ever-active group of local gossips.

Felicity had tried very hard to be liked and accepted by Jack. After all, she respected the fact he was her husband's father. She'd always wanted to live in the country, and when she met Barry, she was bowled over by his gentle nature, as well as his tall well-proportioned body topped off with the mass of curly red hair he kept mostly imprisoned under an old well-worn Akubra. She'd always been partial to men with facial hair, and Barry had rebelled against his father's control and nurtured a well-cared-for, neatly trimmed moustache and beard. Felicity loved the way he looked.

'Why do you want to hide behind face fungus? It's unhygienic. Moustaches harbour germs, and beards are dribble catchers! The world doesn't need to have you advertising the fact my only son is too lazy to shave!'

Barry didn't bother trying to tell his dad that a moustache and a neatened beard also needed regular attention. It would have been a waste of breath, as he knew Jack wouldn't have listened to his explanation anyway once he'd formed his own opinion.

Barry's hair colouring differed from both of his parents and twin sisters but clearly resembled that of his maternal grandmother. Her glorious deep-red hair kept its vibrancy right up until she died. He also inherited his dark-brown eye colour from his father. Altogether, he was a very pleasing male package.

Jack, her new father-in-law, wouldn't listen to her if she expressed any ideas at odds with his because Felicity was a female, came from the city, and had a mind of her own. When she'd asked him on one occasion if she could present some thoughts to him, he'd replied, 'By all means, you can have your say, girlie. But I won't listen to you!'

He didn't come to their interstate wedding—said someone needed to mind the cattle and sheep, the farm dogs, the ducks and chickens, and their heavily pregnant cat—even though there were offers from neighbours to help out. Secretly Felicity felt pleased. She'd seen him in action at a family wedding she'd attended a month prior to their marriage. He'd frequently interjected comments during the speeches at the reception and ended up taking over and telling inappropriate stories about the bride's family!

At first, Felicity felt confident about adjusting to being Barry's wife and living on his family farm. Moving to the country and becoming the wife of a farmer fulfilled the dream she'd had ever since early childhood after going with family friends to stay on their farm near Horsham.

She remembered feeding the chickens and harvesting vegetables and fruit from the large fenced-off area adjacent to the farmhouse. She could visualise the wheat turning golden as it ripened and being frequently admonished not to climb on the tractor!

But life had taken Felicity in different directions until she'd met Barry, aged forty-three, soon after she'd turned thirty-eight. From then onwards, her world changed in more ways than she could ever have imagined possible.

The Wattle Flat locals fought to keep the controversy over Jack's death away from the national media. The well-nourished grapevine frequently refreshed as everyone expounded different theories. They didn't want Australia-wide publicity. They were mostly respectful of Jack's memory despite the fact he'd often been privately referred to as that 'pompous controlling bastard.' But Felicity hadn't envisaged the hostile kaleidoscope of reactions directed her way from Wattle Flat locals.

The people of Wattle Flat fiercely protected the reputation of their small town and district. They solidly banded together to preserve the illusion that nothing bad ever happened there. They firmly denied they weren't like another nearby small town where decaying bodies were found in a bank vault, or where there were frequent suicides, or episodes of domestic violence or where young teenagers met untimely deaths associated with bullying, speeding and drunk driving, or drug-taking. All manner of theories had circulated. Some pointed fingers at Felicity, while others suggested Barry had finally become tired of waiting to take over the farm. Occasionally there'd been a murmur linking Jack's death with his loneliness since Louise died, questioning whether he'd been suicidal.

Felicity learned over time that it would take many years to be accepted as a local. Because she'd been an independent woman running her own business prior to meeting and marrying Barry, the understanding of her previous lifestyle reached beyond the comprehension of many people in the local farming community.

*　　*　　*

The sheep Jack freed from the tangle of barbed wire soon rejoined her mob. She hadn't waited to see her rescuer being found face down in a shallow tidal pool, which filled at high tide.

*　　*　　*

When Jack's faithful old crossbred kelpie limped home alone in the middle of the afternoon from the direction of the clifftop, Felicity had a horrible premonition something bad had happened. Since Louise had passed away, Jack spent some part of every day keeping an eye on things at the farm. He'd been lonely and hadn't previously realised how well Louise had cared for him.

Felicity knew Jack might have run out of fuel, so she anchored a spare can of petrol on to the back of the ute. In case she would need to treat an injury, she made sure the first aid kit and some woollen blankets were also on-board. She contemplated calling Barry on her mobile phone. He'd told her he intended to spray weeds on the 'away' farm several miles up the road after he'd repaired the fence along the clifftop cut by shooters who'd been illegally hunting kangaroos. (Permits were needed to cull kangaroos that had multiplied alarmingly in recent years.)

With kangaroo meat becoming increasingly popular, shooters appeared to have less regard than ever for a farmer's property. Sheep had sometimes been slaughtered as well. Felicity decided to search for Jack first, taking Kimba with her on the back of the ute, hoping there would be no cause to worry Barry. But deep in her gut, she didn't feel good.

She discovered Jack's trike parked on the clifftop like a silent sentinel with the ignition turned on, the motor no longer running, and the fuel tank empty. Minutes later, she saw Jack tangled in barbed wire, lying at the bottom of the cliff face down in the tidal pool. She slithered and slid down the cliff face, dislodging clumps of grass and gazanias as she descended. Even after rolling him away from the water and freeing him from the coiled wire, her frantic searching failed to find his pulse. There was no doubt Jack was dead—and his mobile phone sat safely in the carrier on the front of his trike!

Would the outcome have been different if I'd been able to persuade him to always carry his phone on his person? she wondered.

Felicity had argued with Jack on more than one occasion about his tendency to leave his phone in the vehicle he'd chosen to drive. Barry also tried to convince him of the importance of always carrying his phone instead of leaving it safely in the front carrier of the quad or trike or under the seat of his ute. Explaining that because of his advancing years, he may be more likely to need assistance from time to time, fell on deaf ears.

Apparently their combined persuasiveness had failed to break through his stubbornness.

CHAPTER 2

There'd been a few strange happenings around the paddocks prior to Jack's death, apart from trespassers and illegal shooters stirring up the stock and damaging fences. Only the immediate family knew that Jack had been suffering from depression. Jack felt overwhelmed and wouldn't acknowledge the existence of his condition to anyone outside the family. He'd refused to see a professional about his weird thoughts or inappropriate actions and didn't tell the family how often he'd considered taking his own life. He couldn't understand why he kept dwelling on suicide and felt frightened and ashamed. Previously, he'd always managed to remain in control. Being in control was an integral part of his being.

Barry had worried and was puzzled when one day Jack asked him where the key to the gun cupboard was kept. Jack hated guns ever since a neighbour returned from a tour of duty during the Vietnam War with half his face shot to pieces. From then on, he'd insisted Barry take charge of the gun cupboard key and tell no one of its whereabouts. One day, when Jack asked for the key, he'd muttered something about an increase in rabbit numbers, but when Barry ignored his request for access to the cupboard, Jack didn't ask again. Another time, Barry noticed Jack leaving the garage furtively with a jerrycan of fuel, putting it on the carrier of the quad bike, and carefully covering it with his work jacket before driving off in the direction of some thick scrub. He returned sometime later without the fuel can.

'Where's the jerrycan from the garage?' Barry asked hesitantly, not wanting Jack to think he was being watched, giving him ample space to supply an answer.

'Which jerrycan are you asking about?'

'The jerrycan that usually sits on the second shelf of the high cupboard near the back.'

'What are you talking about? I haven't taken any fuel can from the workshop. You must be imagining things!'

Although Barry took the ute over to the scrub later in the day, he failed to find anything out of place except the boxthorn puller he'd misplaced two seasons ago. He wasn't surprised to find the fuel can back in the workshop later on—soon after his father had been out on the ag. trike 'to check the fences near the scrub'.

At other times, Barry discovered ropes in inappropriate places. He'd found one underneath the huge mulberry tree in the orchard and another coiled under a bush on the clifftop. Once, when he went looking for his longest and strongest rope (used for towing), he'd found it looped over a rafter in the machinery shed.

Jack seemed to believe he was invincible and would always be in control of his life until Louise left him for good. While Louise was alive, he'd mainly used his phone to call home to say when he would be home for dinner. As acceptable with his generation, because he physically worked outside on the farm, he expected to be waited on when he returned home.

From Jack's perspective, until Louise's illness, he'd had a good life. He had a capable wife, a son who'd only ever wanted to be a farmer and would one day take over the running of the farm, and beautiful twin daughters who both had promising careers after doing well at school in Adelaide. However, his world turned upside down when Louise, his talented, supportive wife, took ill and died.

The deterioration in her health advanced insidiously and relentlessly. When she learned that a collection of seemingly unrelated minor health conditions were connected, she already had advanced breast cancer with secondaries in her spine and brain. Her subsequent mental confusion meant she'd be safer spending her final months in palliative care.

Louise grew up living in the country, so when she married Jack, she'd slotted easily into her role of traditional farmer's wife. They'd met at a cricket match and were engaged within three months. They married soon after Jack demobbed from the army at the end of the Second World War. Louise had always been grateful her man had survived that terrible part of history, which had ultimately achieved very little in the way of world peace. So many husbands and boyfriends never came home. Some returned so haunted by the horrors they'd seen or so physically changed they were unable to slot successfully back into civilian life.

Jack had been lucky. He'd spent the war driving trucks up through Alice Springs in Australia's dead centre, taking supplies to the railhead at Larrimah in the Northern Territory. These were then railed to Darwin before being shipped overseas to Australian troops. (In later years, he'd lamented the fact he hadn't been overseas, as a service person required this criteria to enable them to obtain a Gold Card to cover medical expenses.)

He was very proud, and it was well known throughout the district that he had wrestled the farm back from the bank at the end of the war, after his father wasn't able to meet mortgage payments. Jack's father had been ill for several months, and with a shortage of labour and an unwillingness to have women help out, he lost the whole wheat crop to severe winds and torrential rain—right at the end of the growing period. (However, Jack would never acknowledge he'd been so gung-ho about doing his bit by joining the army with his brothers, that he'd ignored the fact he could have been exempt if he'd stayed to work with his father, providing vital manpower to keep the farm productive.)

All three brothers joined the army. Only Gordon went overseas, and when his death in New Guinea was announced via a dreaded telegram, it linked them with other grieving families in the district. Arthur served alongside Jack, transporting food and fuel in trucks on miles of unsealed roads towards the port of Darwin for shipping overseas to Australian troops.

Over the years, there were many times when Louise made excuses for Jack's need to control every detail related to management of the farm. She knew how close his family had come to losing it forever years ago. However, although she saw and understood what was happening to her family and had tried many times to intervene, she finally gave up battling against Jack's autocratic control.

Louise spent her pre-teen years living on her family's farm near Clare in South Australia but went to boarding school in Adelaide for her final years of schooling to learn to be a young lady. In an era when women rarely worked outside the home, she learned to be a skilful cook and housekeeper and excelled at many handicrafts, especially dressmaking and crocheting.

Many friends envied her when she married Jack Clapper. He came from a well-established family who'd settled on Yorke Peninsula soon after farming land first opened up. Although Jack had two brothers, being the eldest son, he knew he'd eventually inherit the family farm. At the time of his marriage, Jack, tall and stocky, with dark-brown eyes and a shock of curly dark-brown hair, contrasted against Louise's pale complexion, blue eyes, and blond hair.

They made a striking couple. Her only lifelong regret was that Jack's stubbornness to be the sole provider had blocked her ambition to open a dressmaking shop. This could have been a boon when poor crops meant lean years of limited farm income. Just the same, with her sewing expertise, she supplied the family with treats on special occasions with money she earned altering or making clothes for neighbours and friends.

Losing Louise had been devastating. Being ten years older than her, Jack had expected her to be around to care for him in his old age. In preparing for Barry and Felicity's marriage, they'd moved out of their farmhouse to the house in town they'd owned and rented out for many years. Before moving, they had the rental house extensively renovated and added fittings to make their old age together more comfortable. They replaced linoleum with non-slip tiles, fitted shutters to exposed windows, and built-in cupboards in all bedrooms.

They added a dishwasher and a tumble dryer and installed ducted air conditioning—appliances Louise had always longed to own. But without Louise, Jack found the house to be empty, cold, and gloomy.

Belinda and Rebecca, Barry's twin sisters, two years his junior, had grown up being discouraged to learn about the workings of the farm. Following the tradition in Louise's family, the girls were sent to boarding school in Adelaide when they entered their teen years. Both girls earned excellent qualifications, which led them to successful careers. Belinda owned a successful catering business, while Rebecca qualified with distinction as an emergency nurse and took up a responsible position working with the RFDS. (Jack told them at an early age that they wouldn't be supported by the farm after they left school, and their legacy would be the house he and Louise owned in town.)

In the final weeks before her death, Louise received loving care in a hospice in Adelaide. Mercifully, she appeared unaware of the seriousness of her plight and often commented she would soon be home again. Jack didn't cope well with her deteriorating condition and made very few trips to the city to visit. It seemed that once Louise couldn't pander to his needs, he wrote her off and set about building a life without her.

'What's the point in going to see her? She's zonked out on painkillers most of the time. I can't handle seeing her fading away. I don't know how I'll manage without her, but I guess I can get Meals on Wheels and employ someone to clean the house.'

As usual, his thoughts were all about himself and about his difficult situation since Louise had become unwell.

The fact that the mother of his children lay dying seemed to have totally eluded him, and his children relied on comfort from each other and from their friends.

Barry was greatly distressed by his mother's illness and visited as often as he could be freed from farm duties, often fabricating reasons for his increased trips to Adelaide. As Jack knew very little about the workings of farm machinery, Barry cited saving freight by collecting a tractor or header part, as justification for his more frequent trips to the state's capital. Belinda and Rebecca visited together whenever they could, providing each other with much needed reassurance and support.

Jack chose an elaborately carved coffin for Louise, but Rebecca and Belinda insisted on a simple, respectful church service reflecting their mother's gentle nature. They draped the coffin with mauve and white fabric and flowers. A slide show accurately depicted her life, her creativity, and all things she loved. The female officiating clergy had attended the same boarding school in Adelaide with Louise.

Funerals have changed over the years. No longer are they only attended by menfolk clad in sombre suits or their Sunday best, meeting together to mourn the dead. Womenfolk and related children are now welcome to celebrate the life of a departed relative. It's now less usual for a minister to harangue his captive audience to repent and believe. In fact, the clergy's role in many funeral services has altered to mainly keeping the 'celebration' running in an orderly manner and later holding a suitably pious expression at the graveside while the attendees dropped a sprig of rosemary—for remembrance—an ear of wheat or barley, or some other appropriate item on to the coffin in the open grave.

Modern clergy appear to be more in touch with their congregations and, after a short service, may be heard urging them to leave the cemetery where the dead reside and join living relatives and friends back in town for refreshments. Tea and coffee, sandwiches, and cakes replace the traditional beer and spirits of wakes in previous years and probably help those who travel great distances to arrive home safely.

When Louise died, Jack's anger surged because plans for his old age had been disrupted and now needed to be revised. After her passing, when faced with fending for himself, he finally acknowledged what a wonderful cook and housekeeper she'd been and soon had irrefutable evidence of his own domestic incompetence. In his era, men worked outside, and the women cared for the home and family.

Jack had never wanted to alter this tradition. He liked to do things the way they'd always been done, and remained stubbornly oblivious to any facts that may have influenced him to think otherwise.

The family wondered whether Jack would give up on life with Louise's passing, but Jack joked he would soon be able to find a suitable housekeeper from among the many widows in the district. However, the widows who'd been at the beck and call of their husbands all their married lives vowed they wouldn't give up their wonderful new freedom to keep house or marry again. Barry and his sisters were relieved. They didn't particularly want a stepmother married to their father for all the wrong reasons. And Barry certainly didn't want any newcomer in the family who might make some claim on his right to inherit the farm.

*　*　*

Jack's farm wasn't one of the most prosperous in the district, although he'd often been heard pompously boasting about his assets, saying he could 'buy up anyone in the district!' The mediocre soil had begun to suffer from years of being treated each year with the same fertiliser to nourish the same type of crop. Worms were rarely found in the sandy alkaline soil that held water on the surface instead of allowing it to soak through to give deeper-rooted plants a chance at living.

The surrounding countryside looked best when the crops were coming out in head. The different-coloured greens of wheat and barley contrasted with the brilliant yellow of paddocks of flowering canola. Other crops such as peas and beans were distinguished by their leaves and height.

As summer approached, the whole countryside changed colour except for the paddocks of hardy saltbush and stunted roadside trees. Sheep stripped all reachable leaves from the saltbush, exposing their naked branches until the leaves renewed with the next season. Native trees and plants mostly flourished without attention, while farm gardens managed to produce a wide selection of fruit and vegetables.

Coastal plants, if unchecked, soon invaded the paddocks, and a brilliant display of gazanias in various shades of gold edged the clifftop. Paddy melons spread rapidly through adjoining paddocks if not pulled out before the birds accessed the seeds from the fruit trampled by cattle. Boxthorn bushes required frequent eradication, and more recently, prickly lettuce infiltrated the paddocks of crops or pasture.

Jack doggedly refused to look at implementing the use of barley, peas, legumes, or canola as a rotation for the wheat crop he sowed religiously each year the week after Anzac Day, at the opening of the sowing season. He kept sheep for many years, but with the wool price at an all-time low, he'd reluctantly added Brangus cattle to bolster up yearly returns. This proved to be necessary for with older machinery requiring frequent repairs, much of the wheat profit often evaporated paying repair bills. In some years, the sale of cattle had been their main source of income. But even when breeding cattle, Jack's reluctance to listen to advice about introducing a new strain of bull to his herd had resulted in poorer returns than what could have been achieved if he had listened and acted on knowledgeable advice.

Farming was never predictable. With crops producing excellent yields, the market could be flooded with grain, often resulting in lower prices when it reached the silos. Wind and rain at the wrong time of the year frequently caused havoc, and when machinery broke down, repairs were costly and from time to time resulted in crop losses. On the surface, Jack was a successful farmer, but his stubborn control had severe repercussions in many directions after his death.

CHAPTER 3

Jack had grown up on the family farm and attended the two-roomed Rocky Beach school. (The reason for naming it Rocky Beach proved to be a mystery, as over five miles of farmland separated it from the nearest coastline.) He'd left school as soon as he could, for he never wanted to do anything other than work on the farm. In those days, there were no wage agreements or legal regulations, but it was accepted as normal for family members to work for their keep, and were given a bonus if crops yielded a profit over and above expenses.

Like Barry (his only son), farming ran in Jack's blood. Fortunately for Jack, his father would have been happier as a journalist, rather than working the farm he'd inherited. Gladly he'd allowed Jack to make most of the decisions. But Jack missed out big time with his own son by being blind to Barry's potential and not tapping into his enthusiasm and passion for farming. His relationship with his son could have been very different. As a youngster, Barry doted on his dad and couldn't wait to leave school. Jack always hoped to have a family of boys to share all the work on the farm.

Until the twins went away to boarding school, no family member had advanced beyond eighth grade, and Louise had hoped Barry would stay longer at school to give him more life options. He'd always been the smallest boy in class, and when he left school, Jack often ridiculed his efforts as he struggled to be involved in heavy lifting jobs around the farm. But Barry became resourceful, soon devising ways to overcome his small size. Although Jack never told him, he secretly admired Barry's passion for all farm activities. Barry didn't object to doing mundane or less appealing jobs such as picking up rocks or cleaning out grain bins or the header after harvest. Being his hero back then, Barry had happily followed all of Jack's instructions. However, as the years passed and he wasn't allowed input into the running of the farm, Barry's view of his future and his father, with his dogmatic ideas and a need to totally control, began to sour.

When Barry left school, plans for his future on the farm should have been put in place. It wasn't long before he noticed he was being treated with less respect than the occasional hired help employed at harvest time. At least they were receiving a wage! (The itinerant worker was more commonly referred to in the district by what Felicity considered was the less respectful or derogatory title of working man.) Jack's grandfather had been forty-two when he died. His father inherited the farm and lived until fifty-eight. However, Jack was seventy-six and still running the farm when he passed away. He'd hoped to live at least another ten years.

'There's no need to talk about the future or draw up fancy legal papers. The farm will go to you when I'm good and ready, and I don't want to hear any more about this. I don't want to retire yet, and there's no reason why I can't stay farming for many more years. It's the way things have always been done, and that's the way it will continue,' Jack told Barry when asked about his future plans for the farm.

He couldn't, or wouldn't, see Barry's point of view—that Barry had earned a right to have a say in farm management. Barry desperately wanted to run the property he'd been promised, where he'd worked ever since he left school. He didn't want to reach retirement age without ever being able to do what he'd always wanted.

*   *   *

Barry had been married before, briefly, to a local girl who'd previously left home to see the world. They'd courted for two years while she'd worked in the local milk bar while still living at home with her parents to save as much money as possible. Then with their savings program well on schedule, she'd decided she wasn't ready to settle down and wanted to go overseas first.

'I want to go to England and visit Paris and Venice—all those places we read about in school. I'm only nineteen, much too young to get married and settle on an isolated farm, a long way out from any neighbour and the nearest town.'

'I love you, Jane, and I have been looking forward to settling down and having a family with you.'

'I don't want to have children yet. It seems there are many things we need to sort out. I have to go overseas, Barry, or I may resent not taking the opportunity while I was young to explore the world.'

'Jane, Dad won't live forever, and one day, I'll own my own farm, be prosperous, and be able to take you and our children on overseas holidays. Can't you imagine how wonderful it would be to all go to America and visit Disneyland?'

'I'm sorry, Barry, I'm not prepared to give up my dream to travel. I need to go overseas first before I settle down and marry anyone.'

Barry didn't live like a monk while Jane travelled. He oscillated between wanting to wait to see if she would come back home and wanting to move on with his life. They corresponded a few times but wrote less and less as time went by. When Jane returned, she thought fate smiled at her when she found Barry still single. After her absence of seventeen months, their relationship resumed, and they were married twelve months later.

Jane's parents relocated to Melbourne while she journeyed overseas. Although Jane missed them, Louise helped bridge the gap, and she and Jane were soon firm friends. They often went shopping together or bought a cup of coffee at the bakery, and Louise also helped her make new curtains. Town gossip would have declared Jack's control over his son had a lot to do with the breakup of his first marriage, and although Louise could see what was happening, she'd felt powerless to alter the situation. When Jane finally left Barry to battle for his farm on his own, she wrote him a Dear John letter, packed up her belongings, and loaded them into her Ford sedan. She thought she'd been ready to settle down and adjust to living on the farm, and maybe if they'd been able to start a family, everything would have been all right. When he finally went to see a fertility professional, Barry was mortified to find he was the major contributor to their not having children. He found it astonishing to learn that about 15 per cent of couples were probably infertile, and about half of the instances could be attributed to the male. When his sperm had finally been assessed, he learned that his count was low and his sperm were sluggish.

'Jane, there must be something wrong with you as well!' he'd declared on more than one occasion, but her medical report declared everything in her reproductive system appeared in tip-top order.

'Sounds as though your sperm would rather watch television than get to work,' quipped Jack when Barry told him about how both he and Jane had undergone fertility testing.

'Are you sure there's nothing wrong with Jane? There's never been any problem with fertility on our side of the family before.'

Jane was incensed that Barry had told his father about the tests and the subsequent results without discussing it with her first!

'Stop giving your parents a blow-by-blow account of our life together. There are things that only concern us. We are not children, having to run to Mum and Dad with progress reports of our daily activities. I'm your wife, and I hate having private things discussed with your parents without you at least consulting me first!'

'Stop making a fuss about nothing! They care about us, and besides it's what I've always done. I've always confided in them.'

'Oh, for goodness sake. We are adults, and we have a right to some privacy. I don't want them knowing everything we do. Maybe you would rather be single again and living back with your parents!'

They'd hoped that a course of hormone injections given to Barry over several weeks would bring about the desired results, but a whole year passed without any sign of a pregnancy. Jane loved her husband but hated Jack's continual intolerable control over their lives. Having travelled extensively in Australia and overseas and capable of managing her own affairs, she didn't take kindly to being treated like a child. When Jane suggested they move away and live somewhere else, Barry adamantly rejected the idea. He'd invested too much of his life in the family farm to give it all away now. She'd tried to be patient, knowing her husband would inherit the farm one day and Jack wouldn't be around forever, but for the sake of her health and sanity, she knew deciding to leave was the correct move for her to make.

Jane was unaware of her pregnancy when she left Barry. When she missed her first period, she thought the stress of finally leaving Barry had caused an upset to her usually regular ovulating cycle. Then when her breasts started feeling slightly uncomfortable, she assumed her period would probably arrive in the next day or two. Having made the decision to leave, she decided she couldn't go back to him just because her situation had changed. The intolerable control factors would still be there. She'd fled back to her parents, who welcomed her with open arms, although accommodation in their apartment in Melbourne in the suburb of Carlton was stretched to the limit, even before Jane's (and Barry's) baby daughter arrived.

In this era, churches and society in general condemned any woman who had a baby out of wedlock and any woman bringing up a child without the support of a husband.

Although technically still married, with a divorce not to be finalised until the following year, Jane had no intention of contacting Barry. When questioned extensively about his whereabouts by hospital authorities, she suspected she was being assessed as a possible candidate to give up her baby for adoption. The government at the time fully supported taking babies from single mothers for adoption, deeming it to be the best thing for everyone concerned. As she'd been working in the local supermarket since she'd moved in with her parents, her entitlement to unemployment benefits of one pound ten shillings a week would not have enabled her to manage without free accommodation and her parents' support.

Girls were often sent away to homes such as Berry Street and St. Joseph's Home for Unwed Mothers (across the road from the Royal Women's Hospital in Grattan Street, Carlton). Single girls without parental support usually stayed in these homes and worked for as long as their condition permitted. Any paltry government benefits they were eligible for were minimal and were paid to the institution that cared for them during their pregnancy.

Jane was appalled to learn that many of the young women worked long hours in the kitchens and laundries of these homes for single mothers without any payment. They were told they were earning their keep and atoning for the sin of getting pregnant. Many of the women were young and vulnerable and made to feel immoral and not capable of taking care of a child. The fathers of illegitimate children seemed to feature very little in the overall picture.

To make the adoption of these babies run smoothly, the birth mothers weren't always directed to counselling services before they signed away their babies. So often they were urged to finalise adoption papers prior to giving birth. They were supposed to be provided with information about financial benefits, their legal right to get financial help from the baby's father, as well as help in finding accommodation both before and after the birth. Information about childcare should have been provided if the mother intended returning to work. The long-term trauma of giving up a baby for adoption wasn't always mentioned; in fact, it may have been deliberately ignored, with the gift of the child to a 'deserving' childless couple often emphasised and applauded. Many parents of single pregnant girls urged their daughters to give up their babies for adoption because the stigma associated with having an illegitimate grandchild was overwhelming for them, especially if they were churchgoing people.

'You will never escape the stigma of having a baby if you remain single.'

'Your illegitimate baby will always be an outcast, growing up without a father.'

'Whatever will people think?'

'My friends at church probably won't have anything to do with me if my daughter wants to bring up her baby alone instead of signing adoption permission.'

Such comments were commonplace and proved to be the norm rather than the exception. At such an emotional time in a potential mother's life, it often proved difficult for them to make rational decisions, taking in all the long-term repercussions. If a girl wanted to keep her baby, she could find her wishes overridden by family, society, and financial obstructions. Her ability to reasonably appraise her options could also be attributed to the hormonal changes rampant in her body as her baby grew.

Jane met up years later with her best friend from school, who told her she'd had a baby while still a teenager. She gave her son up for adoption soon after his birth because she found parental pressure overwhelming. She said she didn't ever stop grieving for him. Twenty years later, she found him in very poor circumstances, a pitiful alcoholic, destitute and living on the streets. Her son wouldn't reconcile with her, blaming her for his current situation because he felt he'd been rejected from birth.

'If you didn't care enough about me as a baby, why do you want to help me now? Feeling guilty, are you? Well, too bad, nothing will make up for being given away and not knowing my birth mother for over twenty years.'

She hadn't been able to convince him she'd been told he'd have a better chance in life if she agreed to his adoption by a childless couple. Giving him up because she loved him and wanted to give him the best possible life made no sense to him at all. Although she offered assistance in various ways, he mostly refused any effort she made to help him. He'd become so entrenched in his lifestyle he seemed thoroughly terrified by the thought of change.

Being suspicious of her motives to find accommodation for him, he would only grudgingly accept food and monetary gifts from time to time. Sadly, Jane's friend never had any other children, and the baby she had given away stayed constantly in her thoughts. In particular, she struggled emotionally every year on her son's birthday.

Jane's pregnancy was textbook until her last trimester, when she began to retain fluid. With her condition being checked weekly, she was admitted to the Royal Women's Hospital for special monitoring and rest.

Her blood pressure skyrocketed, her urine showed protein, and oedema was evident in her face and hands. With a diagnosis of pre-eclampsia—a concerning condition that occurs where the baby could be deprived of adequate nourishment—strict bed rest became mandatory. If untreated, the mother could develop eclampsia and suffer from convulsions. In extreme cases, the condition could be life-threatening for both mother and baby.

Diuretics helped reduce Jane's oedema, and luckily, her baby arrived safely with the aid of obstetric forceps, although a theatre remained available for an emergency caesarean section until after her safe delivery. Rose-Louise was small for her gestational age, perfectly formed but of low birth weight with a gingery tinge to what little hair she had. Jane was over the moon to finally give birth to a beautiful baby girl but was knocked sideways soon afterwards to find herself in the depths of despair. Postnatal depression hadn't been recognised as a crippling condition in the mid sixties.

Soon after she'd delivered her cherished, much-longed-for daughter, Jane rejected her. She didn't want to feed or even hold her. She couldn't understand her feelings and was absolutely terrified she would harm her little girl. In one of her darkest moments, she even considered putting Rose-Louise up for adoption—to protect her!

Rose-Louise was a tiny wrinkly scrap, born to Jane at thirty-five weeks and weighing in at 2,154 grams. This necessitated her remaining in hospital being nursed and carefully monitored in an insulcot for a couple of weeks. Three days after her birth, her skin darkened, and she appeared totally disinterested in feeding. She'd already needed intermittent supplementary tube feedings via nasal gastric tube since birth when she'd tired very quickly when she sucked for any length of time. Nourishment was fed to her via a tube passed through her nose down into her stomach.

Jane learned that Rose-Louise's continued lethargy and bronze colouring were due to her bilirubin levels being elevated. This happened frequently with small slightly premature babies and could be treated successfully by using ultraviolet light to bleach the colour from the baby's skin.

Bilirubin is a waste product of the normal breakdown of red blood cells in the liver. Levels are routinely checked in newborn infants, with a small blood sample taken from the baby's heel. Jaundice occurs when levels are high, and if dangerously high and not treated, brain damage may occur. If bilirubin levels cannot be controlled by lights, an exchange blood transfusion may be necessary.

With all her clothes removed and her eyes shielded, Rose-Louise was treated in a regulated temperature in an insulcot with blue lights placed overhead shining in on her. As she could become dehydrated very easily under this treatment, it was very important to keep a strict eye on her fluid balance. (The name insulcot changed to humidicrib in later years after being modified and improved.)

Humidicribs were continually being updated to provide greater visibility and accessibility. They became easier to clean and the temperature control more reliable. Porthole access was made simpler to negotiate for both nursing staff and parents, who were encouraged to touch their babies regularly. Tiny or sick babies nursed in humidicribs could be observed closely as they required few clothes and no bed covers in the temperature-controlled environments that were closely monitored with alarms.

After being under lights for a day and a half, Rose-Louise's bilirubin levels were acceptable enough for her to be dressed and wrapped up. She was placed in an open cot and moved down to the Special Care Nursery, where she slowly began taking full bottle feeds. Jane also learned that a premature baby's sucking reflexes were not always fully developed before thirty-six weeks' gestation. When Rose-Louise reached 2,260 grams, although big enough to go home, she still needed a lot of encouragement to suck.

Jane was discharged without her baby daughter a week and a half after the birth and was invited to visit Rose-Louise in the premature nursery at any time of the day or night and also to keep in touch with her local doctor. During her time in hospital, when most mothers of premature babies were in the nursery as much as possible following the progress of their babies, nurses soon noticed Jane only visited when specifically instructed to do so. The nursing notes from each shift noted her erratic attendance and recorded her apparent fear of being anywhere near her baby.

At first, it was thought she was suffering from a severe case of baby blues. She knew that around the fourth day after giving birth, hormones in the mother's body begin to sort themselves out, and new mothers frequently suffered teary episodes, fatigue, irritability, moodiness, and being overly sensitive to other people's reactions to them. However, instead of her baby blues diminishing after a few days, she continued to feel terrified of touching or holding her daughter and was desperately afraid of hurting her. She refused to change or bathe her and totally rejected the idea of breastfeeding.

Jane only contributed to Rose-Louise's care by holding an occasional bottle to feed her while she lay in her little cot.

Jane's predicament distressed Olive and Arthur (Jane's parents), so they took turns keeping a watchful eye on their daughter. The nursing staff made sure Jane wasn't left alone with her baby, and they carefully documented her noticeable absences in their nursing reports.

With built-in, ready-made babysitters available, Jane aimed to return to work three months after giving birth. She'd been employed at the local supermarket, where she'd been permitted to work until she'd almost reached term.

'Are you going to contact Barry and tell him about Rose-Louise? He has a right to know he has a daughter, and you are entitled to financial help from him too.'

'No, Mum, he didn't know I was expecting a baby when I left him. I don't want him back in my life. I'll get by if you are willing to keep helping me.'

'Your dad and I will certainly help you as much as we can, but we are not getting any younger, and Rose-Louise will ask questions when she's older. She'll want to know who her father is and maybe want to meet him. She may also want to know why you called her Rose-Louise.'

'I will always see something positive from my life on the farm whenever I look at Rose-Louise. I'd wanted to have a child for such a long time. She is my starting point to the next chapter of my life. When Barry and I moved into the farmhouse with his parents, there were over fifty roses in bloom in the garden, many with amazing perfume. All of them were beautiful. They were planted by Louise—my mother-in-law. She cared about my welfare, often acting as a mediator when I found it hard to cope with Jack's need to control all aspects of our lives. Louise and the roses are both fond memories of my life on the family farm near Clapper's Cove.'

Jane's mother had met Louise on several occasions and had liked her. She felt overjoyed with her granddaughter's name. (She'd actively discouraged the use of her own name, Olive, as she had never been fond of it. If the baby had been a boy, she wouldn't have liked him labelled Arthur, her husband's name, either.) She wholeheartedly supported her daughter's choice.

'It's a name that's suitable for a child as well as for an adult, though you may never see the roses or Louise again.'

Her prophecy proved to be correct, for the rose bushes died off one by one over the years, and Jane and Louise were not united before they both passed away.

CHAPTER 4

Peter was six months older than Barry, and it seemed as though they'd been best friends forever. Growing up with their homes only a mile apart, they'd ridden their bikes the three miles to the main road to catch the bus that took them into school at Wattle Flat, where they'd shared the same classes all through school until the law decreed they were old enough to leave. Their fathers were staunch friends, sharing the same ideas about farming and about not needing to document plans for the future of their farms. Both men failed to see (or didn't want to acknowledge) why so many sons of established farmers were leaving the land to follow other careers.

After marrying his childhood sweetheart from a neighbouring town, Peter had given up on ever taking over his parents' farm and moved away. Like Barry, Peter had been living and working for a promise of one day owning his family's farm. With a wife and two small sons, he wanted to integrate progressive farming methods and to feel secure enough to renovate his parents' old farmhouse. It was galling, especially for his wife, to have all finances controlled by Peter's father. They finally moved north, where Peter worked for wages on his cousin's farm. With both croquet and a golf club in the district, they were able to pursue off-farm interests, and the local progress association soon embraced them as willing fundraisers.

Peter received a small payout after his father sold some recently acquired paddocks, but it was not enough for him to purchase a property of his own. It definitely wasn't anywhere near what he would have earned if he'd been paid a basic wage while working on the home farm. He was grateful to be paying only a peppercorn rent for his cousin's old homestead, as he wanted to save to buy his own property one day. After a while, the memory of working for his father and receiving only pocket money for his labour ceased to leave a nasty taste in his mouth. He wanted to work alongside his two sons if they joined him on the land and not exploit them with a promise.

As Jack's grandfather lived until age forty-two and his father had reached a total of fifty-eight years, both had lived longer than most of their contemporaries. They'd still been working on their farms with the aid of their sons when they passed away. But times had changed. With the advent of vaccinations and better health services and less active involvement in overseas wars, life expectancy for everyone had increased dramatically.

Many farmers were still holding the reins well into their late seventies and eighties, while many of their sons were seeing friends who'd entered employment off-farm planning to retire or change their lifestyle in their early fifties. The future of the farm in previous generations had been clear-cut, but many of the older farmers, including Jack's and Peter's fathers, refused to acknowledge and address the changes. Being too busy to embrace off-farm hobbies or join service clubs had probably contributed to the problem.

From time to time, sons of older farmers could be heard griping about their common problem in the bar of the Wattle Flat Hotel.

'My dad's scornful of people ever wanting to retire, but he doesn't help with the dirty or mundane jobs—just thinks driving the header or tractor or the truck is what farming's all about!'

'Dad said he's going to continue working on the farm until he dies.'

'I am sick of being treated like a boy, an unpaid labourer, and only being dished up pocket money and my keep. I want to be treated as an adult, as an equal. I do most of the work anyway, but I want to bring in some new ideas and utilise the land differently.'

When Felicity married Barry, she had no inkling of how tightly Barry's father controlled all aspects of the farm—and his family. Although they'd moved into town soon after Jane and Barry married, Jack still made all the decisions, and they were final. From the very start she'd struggled against Jack's autocratic control. His stranglehold on all things pertaining to his farm was apparent to the townsfolk, but the family were used to his ways and learned to find ways to make life bearable. They survived with minimal concessions by letting him think that he always instigated any new ideas.

Had Jack and his closest neighbour updated their thinking, shared farm management with their sons, or paid them wages, the future for both Peter and Barry might have been very different.

*   *   *

Louise and Dorothy (Peter's mother) weren't bosom buddies. They were friendly enough but didn't live in each other's pockets. They were both excellent cooks who turned into arch-rivals at the Wattle Flat agricultural show, where they alternately shared cooking and handicraft awards. Having cultivated an excellent garden, Louise often won prizes in the flower and produce sections. The roses she'd exhibited year after year—a mixture of heritage and delicately scented varieties—consistently won recognition from the judges.

Dorothy decided that entering too many sections in the local agricultural show wasn't worth the effort, where the entry fee amounted to only a little less than the prize money. After submitting a few cooking and knitting entries, she happily switched her attention to the literary competition and nearly always walked away with a substantial sum of money after winning the short-story competition.

With more time on her hands after the twins went away to school, Louise finally joined the Wattle Flat golf club and soon turned into a high-ranking committee member (but not with Jack's blessing). Often on a golf day, by some strange coincidence, Jack would urgently require her assistance for some job on the farm—something that couldn't possibly wait another day! While Louise played golf, Dorothy daydreamed and wrote short stories and articles and submitted them to various newspapers. Although Jack didn't totally approve of his wife's defection from total commitment to his needs, he enjoyed being kept up to date with all the town and district happenings consistently relayed through the thriving golfing grapevine!

Dorothy was puppet-like in support of her husband's farming ideas and also couldn't see any need to embrace succession planning. Louise was probably more understanding of Barry's frustration and would stand up for him from time to time until Jack's disapproval and dogmatic attitude proved to be too overpowering—then she'd retreat into her shell. Jack hadn't ever 'walked in anyone else's shoes' and could see no reason for ever doing so.

From an early age, Barry longed to own a pony, but Jack adamantly stated he wouldn't have a horse on his property. He'd toppled from a frisky pony while he was still a young boy and hadn't developed any affection for them since. And while he ruled over everything pertaining to the farm, it seemed that Barry would never get a pony of his own.

'Horses can be very costly, dangerous animals! They require a lot of food and care and maybe vet fees too. We just don't need one! You have your bicycle, or you can ride the farm trike [a motorised three-wheeler]. When you're older, you should be able to buy a cheap motorbike at a clearing sale.'

However, Jack appeared to relent when Barry neared his tenth birthday and began pestering both his parents again about getting him a horse.

'I promise I'll look after a pony all by myself if I can have one of my own. I can house him in the shed down near the cattle yards. It's no longer being used, and I would exercise him every day!'

At the end of his ninth year, he was puzzled one evening to overhear his parents arguing about his birthday present. They appeared to have adopted opposite points of view from those they'd previously held. Louise had been heard to say that it would 'be hurtful', while Jack kept insisting that 'it should satisfy Barry's need for a horse'. It seemed Louise was ignored again, for on his tenth birthday, Barry's present did indeed prove to be hurtful. Jack thought it hilariously funny to give his ten-year-old son a large antique rocking horse he'd bought for a song at a farm clearing sale!

Barry was mortified. He'd hinted to Peter and a few friends at school that it looked like he was finally getting a horse for his birthday. Only Jack enjoyed Barry's birthday that year, while his son disappeared for the day, hiding in the scrub when he saw anyone out looking for him. He finally returned home just before dinner time but refused to join in celebrating his birthday and went straight to bed. He was ravenous and very grateful when Belinda and Rebecca crept into his room after his parents were absorbed watching television. They gave him hugs and brought him some sandwiches and fruit and cake.

Although Peter offered to teach him to ride—he'd had a pony since his eighth birthday—Barry felt sickened each time he thought of his tenth birthday present and vowed he didn't want to have anything to do with horses ever again. He felt no remorse when punished for defacing the rocking horse with the new pocket knife his sisters had given him.

*　　*　　*

Jack and his contemporaries strongly opposed having women working on the farm. Before being sent away to boarding school, Rebecca often cared for orphaned or injured animals or birds and begged Jack to let her join in and help him around the farm.

'Working outside doing men's farm work is no place for girls! You're not strong enough. Your place is in the home, learning about cooking and doing needlework, not driving headers or tractors. I can't imagine what people would think if I let you leave school to work on the farm.'

Jack refused to negotiate any compromise, and although Rebecca tried to change his mind on several occasions, she soon gave in when she saw she only made him angry. He'd become a carbon copy of his father. Jack had also been blind to the fact that if his father had accepted help from the Land Army of willing women workers during the war, he may not have needed to surrender his farm to the bank.

*   *   *

Peter urged Barry to take a stand and move away as well, but Barry knew his father would be very angry if he left the farm, and he was afraid to upset Jack after he'd previously suffered a heart attack following a heated altercation between them. Jack had cautioned him not to leave, intimating that any remuneration from the farm would be minimal. Barry concluded his time to escape his father's tyranny had passed. He'd left it too late. He'd invested too much time and energy to move away and start again. He knew there'd be too much to lose by making the break. But as the years rolled on, he wondered from time to time if he'd made the right decision. Barry loved the farm that had been in his family for generations, and if questioned about his relationship with his father, he would say he loved him too. (In later years, after his first marriage failed, he questioned his judgement and wondered if he'd ever experienced true love.)

Barry had always spoken well of his relationship with his family, and Felicity had been impressed with his passion for his chosen vocation. Farming was all he'd ever wanted to do, but there were times he despaired that he'd never be able to run the family farm the way he wanted.

The twins were given their college education so they could be independent, and it was made clear to them they couldn't expect to receive any payment from the farm even if they remained unmarried. They all knew the farm wasn't big enough or productive enough to support several families. When their parents passed on, Belinda and Rebecca would eventually inherit the house Louise and Jack owned in town.

*   *   *

One persistent question oscillated among the townspeople and district of Wattle Flat. Had Barry contributed in some way to Jack's death?

'Could there still be a sheep somewhere that had actually seen what had happened?'

As each year passed without any date set for Barry to take over the farm ownership, he'd begun to lose heart. He spent longer in town each time he visited, and much of that time was spent in the hotel bar. Recurring despondency plagued him, and he began to argue with his father.

'Dad, when are you going to hand the farm over for me to manage?'

'I've told you before, I'll hand things over to you when I'm good and ready, son, and no amount of badgering from you will change my mind. If you keep on asking, I might just sell the farm instead!'

Barry knew his father could renege on his word at any time. He had known him to break promises within his family circle while presenting a blameless front to people in the town and district. With Gordon, his brother, killed overseas and Arthur running a successful machinery business and his sisters happily married, Jack had complete ownership and control of his farm.

From time to time, he sold off paddocks to replace worn-out machinery, to buy a new car, and on one occasion, to pay for an expensive overseas holiday despite having a tidy sum spirited away in a personal bank account. Barry wondered if the property would remain viable if more land was sold off without implementing some of the new modern ideas on farming he wanted to introduce.

'If you sell off any more of the farm, there won't be enough to support even one family . . . and I might want to marry and have children one day too.'

Such suggestions made Jack angry.

'If you think I want you changing the way the farm is run, you're mistaken, boy. My methods have kept us well-supplied with all our needs up until now. That's good enough for me!'

Barry knew his father wore rose-coloured glasses and still lived in the past. There were fences that needed to be replaced, water connections modified, and new sprays and seed strains on the market bringing increased profits to neighbouring farms. Barry had been so frustrated he'd forgotten his father would always oppose a direct suggestion. (Felicity was astounded when told by some of the townspeople that Jack always made decisions without consulting with anyone and would never be open to suggestions.)

In the end, Jack Clapper was only concerned about himself, his assets, his image, and what people would think. (The fact that he featured very little in other peoples' daily thoughts had never occurred to him.) For years, the townspeople watched as Jack's autocratic control squeezed the youthful zest out of his only son. As each year passed, his treatment of Barry diminished the townspeople's respect for him. Finally, Jack had been living in a bubble of his own importance. Although believing they loved him, the family shed few tears when he died, acknowledging he'd lived his life as he'd chosen to make it.

*　　*　　*

At the end of the season, when all the bills were paid and machinery repaired, any money left over was divided up at Jack's discretion. This meant he kept the major portion. He said he put it aside for new equipment. That wasn't always the case. Barry could only remember three items of equipment bought new over the years—a Horwood Bagshaw header, a 620-bag grain storage bin, and a feisty Massey Ferguson tractor.

Clearing sales had been sourced for the rest of his machinery.

At the end of the first year of their marriage, when monies were handed out after harvest, Jack, Louise, and Barry all received payments, but there was nothing set aside for Felicity.

'What about me?' she asked.

'What do you want money for? Barry can buy whatever you need out of his share!'

Felicity experienced a whole range of emotions, but most of all, she felt incensed.

'I have a right to be treated as a person, not an appendage. I've been available to help around the farm whenever I've been needed, and I have personal and clothing needs that I want to deal with without having to ask for money like a child.'

Jack wasn't impressed with her request.

'You're not a partner in this farm, so you're not entitled to a payment', he replied, 'and what's more, you are never going to be a partner!'

'That suits me. I have no wish to be a partner and be liable for farm debts if seasons fail to bring in good crops, but I am surely entitled to monetary recognition too.'

Felicity finally received a reluctantly surrendered token payment in her own name but had to argue for it to be renewed each year.

Because nobody received a regular wage from the farm, all bills were paid through the farm account from Jack's cheque book. The district had been slow to embrace credit cards, but most farmers kept detailed account books. Once again, Jack stubbornly refused to see any need to change. He paid for everything by cheque and religiously kept his cheque butts in a shoebox. At the end of the financial year, at tax time, he presented them to his accountant to have his income tax return prepared.

Felicity found it galling to have to hand over household accounts for her father-in-law to pay. Prior to marrying Barry, she'd managed her own affairs. After working in various hospitals in management positions, she'd trained as a therapeutic massage therapist and run her business from a room at the local medical centre. She'd successfully prepared her own tax returns as well. Jack frequently chastised her for making interstate phone calls and for using their air conditioner and clothes dryer when she could have been saving electricity by using the wood fire and always drying clothes on the clothes line. He completely ignored the fact that the open fire blew smoke into the room and some items of clothing were often torn by strong winds when hung outside for any length of time.

'Where is the rest of your telephone account? The list of phone numbers you've been calling is missing.'

This was one of Jack's most persistent questions every time Barry collected a new phone bill from their postbox in town.

'You have the total amount. That's all you need to pay the bill.'

'I've always been given the complete list before. Who do you think you are, coming in here and changing things around? I want the rest of the account to keep with my other records.'

'It's actually none of your business who the calls were made to. That's our business, mine and Barry's. You have the total, and that's all you need to make a payment.'

'Look here, girlie, who do you think you're talking to? How about showing respect to your elders?'

'It works both ways. I am not a child, so please don't call me girlie. How about showing respect for me as a woman?'

'I'll give respect where it's due!'

'Thank you, I'd appreciate that.'

Jack felt bemused and was unsure whether he'd lost control of the conversation and wondered why he'd been thanked. Felicity thought afterwards she shouldn't have come on so strongly with her father-in-law but felt proud she had curbed the impulse to call Jack a pompous, controlling dictator!

Barry had told Felicity how Jack had treated his former wife, but Felicity found it hard to believe what she was hearing and questioned whether he might have exaggerated. In all her former relationships, she'd been treated with respect and as an adult. She thought she'd be strong enough to cope. It didn't take long before she found out how tiresome it was as she fought daily to maintain her identity and self-esteem. It became a daily struggle to live on Jack's family farm under his control.

Jack's autocratic rule was slightly tempered when Louise was well and living at home, but even though Louise had excellent negotiating skills, the continual headbutting and constant arguing with Jack exhausted her. She knew much could have been resolved with adult discussion and compromise.

Jack had a problem with Felicity practicing as a massage therapist. He'd suggested to anyone who'd listen to him that his daughter-in-law had trained to work in a questionable occupation, and hinted it probably combined with devious sexual activities. Always concerned about what people would think, he declared that the choice of occupation of Barry's wife cast a dark shadow on his family's respectability.

'Look here, girlie. I don't want my son's wife setting up a massage business. It's not a respectable occupation. Your role is to work around the house and care for my boy!'

'If I choose to continue as a massage therapist, it's my own business. It really has nothing to do with you, and I don't like that you still appear to see both of us as children. We are grown-ups and should be treated as adults. I will work as a massage therapist if and when I choose!'

Felicity felt proud of her hard-earned qualifications, having won the top position in her massage class. She loved helping people who were hurting and providing relief from pain and discomfort. Despite Jack belittling her efforts at every opportunity, she knew she had to preserve her self-esteem at all costs.

Felicity could barely believe exactly how much control Jack held over Barry until many years later. When the adoption of a GST became imminent, they were concerned that Jack would have difficulties keeping detailed accounts of farm records. Some accountants were insisting that all records be kept on computers. Jack had thrust previous years' tax returns at them when they questioned his record-keeping methods and proudly praised his accountant's ability to make sure they didn't have to pay substantial amounts in tax. Even with her limited bookkeeping experience, Felicity saw there were items that had been overlooked that could have been claimed.

She'd challenged Jack once again, and he'd replied angrily.

'Who do you think you are? Why do you think you know better than my accountant? He's been doing my tax for years. You don't know anything about running a farm, girlie! Now that you've married Barry and live in this district, you're meant to fit into the local ways. You're an outsider. What makes you think you know any better ways of doing things? Traditions are what we follow. No one wants some know-all female suggesting we change our methods and accept newfangled ideas. What qualifications do you have, coming from the city, to tell a farmer he needs to upgrade his ideas? Why did you come to keep house for Barry if you don't like the way we do things here?'

'To keep house? I didn't come here as a housekeeper. I married your son because I love him and want to share his life and forge a future together with him. My role as a wife is not as a servant or a commodity. Is that the way you see a wife's role? I envisaged my marriage to Barry to be a partnership where we complement and share all aspects of life together. To keep house? Urgh!'

'Did your father ever suggest it was high time you found someone to keep house for you after Jane left and you were having to fend for yourself as well as working the farm?'

When challenged, Barry returned her gaze sheepishly before looking away. In this way, she suspected she'd received confirmation of her supposition.

CHAPTER 5

Felicity

Felicity grew up in a seaside country town in south eastern Victoria and moved to Melbourne to train as a nurse after completing her schooling, where she'd received excellent grades at the local high school. She consolidated her nursing training for several years by working in varied positions in different hospitals. The death of her parents, killed when their car stalled on a level crossing while travelling to visit her, had left her feeling completely shattered. Her father had been finding city traffic frustrating and difficult to negotiate for several months prior to the fatal accident, and Felicity had wondered how long their monthly trips would continue. Several months later, she accepted a position at Geelong Base Hospital and decided to relocate and move closer to her work.

Her new position working in the hospital theatre involved long hours standing on her feet all day. Mealtimes were irregular, and it was often close to three o'clock before she could find time for a lunch break. Her social life was practically non-existent for many months, but gradually the pain of losing both parents so tragically began to recede. She was thankful they'd survived long enough for her to tell them she'd felt blessed to have them as her parents and tell them how much she loved them. Had they lived, both would have had their active lives seriously curtailed.

The resultant move away from Melbourne proved to be a good idea.

*   *   *

From an early age, Felicity knew she may have trouble having children. A burst appendix culminating in peritonitis had gummed up her fallopian tubes.

Although she'd had treatment to open them up, she knew the procedure held no guarantees of success. Felicity knew she could embrace other ways of becoming a mother, but giving birth was what she wanted, if it could be at all possible. Several partners over the years had indicated they'd be content with life without children but were often laden with immovable baggage or were self-centred, interested only in their own welfare. When she'd met Barry, her longing to have children intensified. He also wanted to have a family, and he seemed to embrace her desire to participate in his farming life.

He and his former wife had been hoping to start a family when the turbulence in their lives settled down. But it never happened. And one day, Barry returned from sorting out cattle to take to market to find a Dear John letter taped to his desktop. Barry had seen signs his marriage to Jane was in trouble but ignored the widening cracks in their relationship, hoping they would go away. After all, when deep cracks developed in the wall in the farm kitchen many years ago, an indoor plant was strategically trained to grow and cover the weakness. He kept hoping the cracks in his marriage would be similarly covered up. The fact his father frequently stirred the pot didn't help.

When the marriage broke down, Barry's relationship with his father was further tainted when Jack stated blatantly, 'She wasn't right for you, boy—just a gold-digger waiting to get her clutches on the farm. You're better off without her.'

After Jane left him, Barry began to frequent the local pub more often. Sometimes he drank very little, although he always took a slab home with him with the option of enjoying a beer in the quiet house of an evening, when he felt his loneliness most acutely.

The pub provided somewhere to go to get away from his father's domination. He grieved as much from the breakdown in the relationship with his father as the ending of his marriage. For a time, Barry had quite a playboy reputation in the district, dating many eligible local girls and staying overnight with others in neighbouring towns wherever he received a welcome.

He started finding more and more reasons to spend extended time away from the farm. He joined the CFS and the voluntary ambulance service and gave blood at the blood bank. He even donated sperm to a friend who wanted to have a child, who'd sworn off marriage after a failed relationship and vowed to remain single forever. He told her honestly his sperm had been classified as containing sluggish swimmers, but she decided to accept his donation anyway. Local church people also welcomed him as a driver taking elderly people to Adelaide for doctors' appointments.

Barry thought he'd adjusted to the fact he may not marry again and never have children, although as he grew older, he would have liked to have a family of his own. He met Felicity at a dance in Newtown—one of Geelong's older suburbs. He'd been to a rural conference with three other farming mates but decided that as the designated driver, he needed some exercise, not alcohol, before the long drive home next day. (His mates were heavier drinkers.)

He was smitten by Felicity's appearance. He watched her for a while before finding the courage to ask for a dance. After only one circuit of the floor together, the music changed and turned into a progressive barn dance where everyone needed to frequently change partners. Before handing her on to her next appreciative partner, they agreed to meet for the following dance. By the end of the evening, they were exchanging telephone numbers and addresses and arranging when to meet up again.

*   *   *

Only a superficial enquiry looked into Jack's death. This brought a finding of death by misadventure coupled with his known heart condition. The local policeman subscribed to a policy of protecting his place and its people, which amounted to keeping paperwork to a minimum and not bringing in outside investigators. (The policeman had gone to school with Barry and considered that he'd probably had a raw deal from Jack.)

Many of the townspeople wondered if Barry and Felicity would sell the farm and move away after Jack's death. If this had happened, it may have reinforced thoughts in the minds of some locals that Felicity had contributed to her father-in-law's death or even that Barry had been the instigator. But Barry had always lived on the farm and worked his whole life looking forward to owning it someday. They decided to stay, even knowing it would be difficult to frequent the area where Jack had met his death.

At first, only Felicity found it uncomfortable when some of Wattle Flat's residents avoided direct eye contact or glanced away when she approached. When she mentioned this to Barry, he said he also sensed some of the locals were giving him strange sideways glances. They agreed that speech often halted when they approached, and they were frequently left to sit alone at public functions. It seemed weird and somewhat distressing to both of them.

Some of the gossip that sped around the small country town could only be described as creative. Many questions were asked. For a while, everyone seemed to have some input as to how Jack had met his untimely death.

'Do you think Felicity pushed him over the cliff?'

'I bet Felicity is glad to be free of the domineering old coot!'

'Do you think they'll have a celebration party?'

'Will Barry feel guilty because he'd been rocking the boat more vigorously in regard to taking over the farm?'

'Did Barry have another argument with Jack, like the one that happened in the bank just before Jack had his heart attack?'

'I bet Barry had something to do with his death. It's a wonder he tolerated Jack for so long, with the way his old man treated him. Fancy still being treated as a child when you've been grown up for years.'

'Do you really think Barry had something to do with his death?'

There were other intermittent murmurings among townspeople as well, which were whispered whenever newcomers arrived in the district. Finally, several months after Jack was laid to rest with Louise in a prime position with a pre-ordered tombstone high on the only hill in Wattle Flat cemetery, the townspeople began to lose interest in Barry and Felicity's affairs. They were soon hungrily looking for new information to send whizzing round the district. Mating and dating proved to be indiscreet at times but always proved to be a source of juicy speculation among the most avid gossipers.

For a time, when Barry and Felicity were comforting each other, their relationship thrived. They worked together mending fences, rounding up cattle, and checking the condition of the small flock of sheep they'd kept for meat and as lawnmowers. They trimmed trees and prepared the ground near the salt lake, ready to plant saltbush and trees native in the area.

They selected Old Man saltbush to fill up the lake surroundings in an effort to leach the salt out of the ground. They'd applied for and been given a grant to fence the area to keep the cattle away from the newly planted seedlings. They planned to set sheep loose among the bushes after they'd grown to maturity to strip the leaves when other feed became scarce. Apart from the saltbush adding a grey-green foliage to the landscape, previously sparsely clad with samphire ground cover, the meat from sheep who'd eaten the saltbush had a pleasing sought-after salty taste.

One particular variety of samphire ended up being popular in many upmarket restaurants, but the local variety proved to be too small to be utilised in this way. For a nominal joining fee, Trees for Life provided native seedlings specially selected to suit the local climatic conditions. The seeds were nurtured in controlled conditions in Adelaide by volunteers until they were big enough to be transplanted. Planting out small trees proved a time-consuming but rewarding occupation and something Felicity could do on her own when Barry worked on the tractor. (Sitting jammed with Barry inside the tractor designed to carry only one person had soon lost all its attraction.)

Barry helped by mechanically ripping trenches for the small trees, and in the hotter months, before they were fully established, he carefully watered them using water from their mobile fire-fighting unit. Although the salt-lake area was only a short distance from the homestead, Felicity usually rode there on the trike, bringing everything she needed to plant out more trees. After using a planting machine for a limited time supplied by the local landcare group, she reverted to planting several thousand trees by hand. Using the mechanical planter hadn't saved her a lot of effort, as many of the plants weren't firmly positioned in the ground, and she'd needed to check each one and often replant them.

Surprisingly, although the fences weren't rabbit-proof, the rabbits concentrated their efforts on the native trees she'd planted close to the house. Casseroled rabbit was a tasty dish that soon appeared regularly on their dinner table. Felicity had a favourite recipe handed down from her grandmother. Baked rabbit tended to be dry, but cooked in a casserole with bacon and herbs, it retained texture and moisture as well as taste. Barry baulked at the idea of eating rabbit at first, referring to it as poor man's mutton, but after Felicity learnt to skin and clean them, he agreed they were a welcome change from the meat obtained from their sheep.

However, she relied on Barry to remove them from the humane mesh rabbit traps and swiftly kill them for her to skin and gut. Felicity enjoyed the treat of being able to access their own meat from the farm, with both lamb and beef readily available. Without a cool room on the farm, it soon proved easier to take animals destined for the table to a local butcher to be killed and cut up. Traditionally, the cut-up meat returned in bulk packages. After Felicity found turning the time-consuming packages into usable portions tedious (traditionally destined to be her job), she insisted they pay a little extra to have meal-sized portions packed by the butcher.

Felicity enjoyed riding the trike, but because it only had three wheels, it didn't travel well on uneven ground. (Trikes were manufactured between 1967 and 1987, when they were replaced by quad bikes with four wheels, but many survived on farms well beyond 1987.)

Agricultural carriers had been fitted front and back, made from a disused plastic box once used to carry milk bottles. These crates were useful for carrying anything, from rocks and bags of weeds to refreshments or even a farm dog. She particularly enjoyed helping burn the paddocks prior to seeding when Barry needed her to make up the required numbers for the procedure to be legal. Riding on the trike and setting the grass alight always gave her a buzz, especially as she felt useful.

*   *   *

Jack's crossbreed kelpie, Kimba, spent many weeks returning to the place where they'd found Jack until finally shifting his allegiance to Barry and Felicity. He spent many hours riding on the trike in the back carrier, whenever it left the confines of the locked shed. In recent times, it became necessary to lock up equipment after several farms in the district had been targeted by thieves. Fuel and tools had mostly been pilfered, but unlocked vehicles had also been stolen. Some were later found intact, while the owners of other cars or utes were not so lucky when vehicles were found crashed or burnt out.

Felicity felt astonished to overhear a certain conversation while she queued for refreshments at the local agricultural show one day, soon after she'd moved on to the farm.

'It's easy to catch a sheep and knock it off for free meat. Most of the farmers don't know how many sheep they own, and anyway they can always claim a loss on their insurance!'

She didn't know the scruffy speaker talking to a couple of equally scruffy mates. She didn't recognise them as locals, and by the time she'd found Barry to see if he could identify them, they were nowhere to be found. The thieves chose to ignore or were ignorant of the fact that sheep could not be insured against theft.

The spate of thefts had been an unwelcome wake-up call for the farmers in the district. Until then, there'd been no need to lock up homes or vehicles, and farm equipment frequently remained where it was last used—sometimes with the key in the ignition, under a seat, or tucked into a slot behind the sun visor.

Although fierce rivalry existed between farmers to produce the best crops or livestock, they respected the effort put in by their fellow farmers to do this and would never steal from one another—although some were renowned for borrowing items and forgetting to return them.

Barry continued to miss his mother's wise counsel and acknowledged the mediation she'd often instigated between father and son over the years. Despite their differences, Barry was also deeply saddened by the loss of his father and the mixed response of people's reactions as to how he died. It came as an enormous shock to lose both parents within two years of each other when it appeared both of them were healthy and should have lived for much longer.

It took several months before Barry adjusted to being his own boss and to the unfamiliar role of decision maker. He didn't find the transition easy, and there were many times he would have liked to consult with his father about important farm issues. Although Barry had always looked forward to taking over the farm, he hadn't received any encouragement or assistance from his father before being propelled into the managerial position following Jack's sudden death.

Jack had done Barry a great deal of harm in continuing to treat him as a juvenile, even after Barry had proved his capability to carry out all men's duties on the farm. Self-esteem for Barry didn't increase overnight, and he often made instant decisions without thinking about the consequences. He also began to refuse to take on board anybody else's suggestions or accept or ask for help from anyone either. This had been one of his father's most noticeable traits, along with his controlling attitude. Felicity noticed disturbing changes in Barry during this period and was both puzzled and alarmed by them. It made her question whether attitudes were learned or inherited and whether either or both could be modified or eliminated.

Felicity wondered, *Is Barry unconsciously taking on his father's characteristics?*

CHAPTER 6

From the time he could walk, Barry idolised his dad and followed him around the house and farm. Jack felt out of his depth with the birth of his son. He frequently got annoyed at having him constantly underfoot as a toddler trying to attract his attention. A flicker of interest surfaced when Jack started teaching Barry simple things, noting how quickly he learned and eager to add to his repertoire. Jack would tell anyone who would listen, 'I'm so proud of Barry. My boy is amazing. He learns things so quickly.'

But he didn't convey those feelings to his son. Barry was small for his age, perhaps because he was conceived and grew up in an era when many households included heavy smokers. It was commonplace in the early fifties. In his early years, he tended to be sickly and slightly underweight. He suffered from asthma and from allergies to many pollens. This wasn't a recipe for being a successful farmer in Jack's books.

However, Barry grew up to be a happy little boy full of vitality and energy. He was gentle with his tabby kitten and revelled in playing ball with the farm dog, a feisty crossbred kelpie, at the end of each day. Climbing trees and bird-nesting were his favourite pastimes.

He tolerated school, and when he put his mind to it, he could always achieve a place near the top of his class.

Holidays were spent either visiting cousins or having them come and stay on the farm. Barry's memories of those times were of busy activities loaded with laughter. There were a few near misses, but somehow he'd managed to escape serious injury or broken bones. Skinned knees were his most usual childhood affliction, although he'd also had chicken pox and measles, along with most of the children in his class. He'd been grateful he was mostly sick during school time and not during the holidays.

Polio had felled a sister of one of Barry's classmates while he was in first grade. She was struck down suddenly and flown to the Adelaide Children's Hospital by the Royal Flying Doctor Service, where she spent several weeks in an iron lung. She'd felt off colour for a few days before losing all control of her limbs and having difficulty breathing. The iron lung encased her small body and cleared her lungs of mucus, helped her breathe, and enabled her to be fed through a tube. After many weeks, when she could manage to breathe outside the lung, she was moved to a device called a rocking bed. This tilted her up and down so that gravity would help force air in and out of her weakened lungs.

Many polio victims required braces and crutches when they recovered, but they were expensive, heavy, and often painful to use. Wheelchairs were clumsy and difficult to manoeuvre, and access ramps were mostly non-existent. Many young people ended up crippled—with misshapen spines, hunched backs, and shrivelled limbs.

Those were scary times because the cause of the disease was unknown and affected people from all walks of life. Fortunately, not all cases resulted in paralysis. During the same period, there were influenza and tuberculosis epidemics, but a complete recovery could be made from these, even though in the case of TB, it might take up to twelve months of treatment. However, they all claimed many lives at the time. Approval of the Salk vaccine occurred in 1952, and the Sabin oral treatment against polio was approved three years later. (The author Alan Marshall contracted polio in 1908 at six years of age, and his book *I Can Jump Puddles*, published in 1955, tells of his struggle to cope with the disease and the impact it had on his life. It turned out being a popular addition to many school libraries).

*   *   *

Barry's father often made fun of him in front of other family members, shearers, or casual farm workers who were employed on the farm from time to time. Barry secretly worked hard at strengthening his skinny body. He was rewarded by being able to do most jobs around the farm at an early age. By the time he turned sixteen, he'd become a slim, strong 184-centimetre-tall young man—and still growing.

Although taller than his dad by several centimetres, Jack still belittled him. Barry didn't mind at first, feeling an added closeness to his dad despite or maybe even because of the put-downs. As he grew older and taller, he considered he deserved the respect he had for his father to be returned in kind. But Jack didn't let up, so Barry learned to cope and ignore being constantly belittled.

He'd only attended school because the law decreed he must do so. The sound of the sea and the beckoning of the beach frequently found him failing to connect with the school bus. Sometimes he spent the day alone. At other times, he met up with Peter, and they spent the day together. The rode their bikes, checked rabbit traps they'd hidden in the scrub, or tobogganed down the sandhills on sleds fashioned from discarded cardboard cartons they found in the illegal rubbish dump that was hidden back from the roadway.

He had a light-bulb moment that he might be heading into dangerous territory, when he repeatedly topped the class in year six. Murmurings surfaced about him pursuing a professional career away from the farm. Louise wanted him to stay at school longer to make sure he had some qualifications if unable to pursue his farming dream due to allergy issues. With talks of alternate occupations surfacing more frequently, Barry decided to rebel. He'd tried talking to his dad, but true to form, Jack wouldn't listen to him. Barry decided to make some changes. His grades soon dropped alarmingly—only halting in their downward spiral when it looked possible he would repeat a year in the same class if his marks remained low.

Barry missed the day that would have been his last at school. He'd been looking forward all year to leaving and not having to catch the school bus at the end of the dirt road each day. The last few months had been lonely as Peter had left school twelve weeks earlier. Barry couldn't sleep the night before, and after breakfast, he kept vomiting with excitement. He'd brought his belongings home previously, so attending on his last day would only have been a formality. His sisters said he rated a mention at the morning assembly, where the headmaster praised him for being a cooperative student, and everyone hoped he would enjoy being a farmer.

In Barry's first year on the farm, he picked a lot of rocks and pulled out heaps of weeds. Hand-picking rocks from paddocks proved to be a tedious, never-ending job, as limestone rocks of all sizes frequently worked their way through the topsoil and damaged machinery if they weren't collected and removed. An allergy to dust and pollen plagued Barry for about ten years, and although he wasn't comfortable carting hay or driving the header at harvest time, he persevered. Although still slight of build when he left school and too young to have a driver's licence, he revelled in being allowed to drive all types of vehicles, from tractors to trucks, across the paddocks as long as he didn't venture on to the road.

Most vehicles were registered so they could move equipment between the away and home farm blocks.

Barry also used a smaller, lighter boxthorn puller Jack had bought at a clearing sale and could frequently be found pulling out new boxthorn plants from underneath native trees, where birds indiscriminately spread the seeds, or along the roadways where many were missed when the district council workers sprayed noxious roadside weeds.

Barry wasn't a prolific reader, and novels didn't come on to his radar at all, although he'd occasionally read an autobiography. He'd found the life story of Douglas Bader amazing when he read it at school, when he'd had the option to stop learning Latin and read library books instead. In later life, the story of Fred Hollows, the eye surgeon, fascinated him, as he hadn't been aware he'd not only helped indigenous Australians regain full sight but had worked in twenty-five countries. Had he lived to old age, Barry would most certainly have become a loyal supporter of the Fred Hollows Foundation, helping people avoid blindness worldwide.

Jack used to read *The Advertiser*, a daily paper printed in Adelaide, which he kept to share with Barry, but Barry showed more interest in making things than spending all his leisure time reading. He usually read *The Rural Times* and learnt about new farming practices from *The Stock Journal*. He read about innovative advancements in farming techniques and stored them in his memory for future reference. Jack remained adamant that he wouldn't embrace change and often loudly underlined his one-sided view.

'We don't need any newfangled ideas on this farm!'

Barry was often frustrated his dad hadn't wanted to be more open to new developments. He'd been stuck in a rut of his own making and wouldn't look sideways or forwards. Barry joined Rural Youth and the local Agricultural Bureau and felt embarrassed when he heard his father's farming methods had long ago been discarded by most of his contemporaries, and his dogmatic attitude to new ideas made him an object of ridicule.

His mother insisted Barry find some off-farm interests and take part in activities with other lads his age farming in the district. He felt immensely grateful for this wise advice. Barry and his family were keen followers of their local football club and rarely missed a match. SANFL matches were followed on television, with occasional visits to Adelaide for the finals, and Barry became a loyal supporter of the West Adelaide football club.

Louise wisely observed that as Jack had no other interests off-farm (except for watching football with his family, usually sitting in his car parked near the boundary fence), he remained rigidly caught in a time warp.

Every month, they attended the local church as a family, more for the social aspect than having a fervent wish to worship or to have their souls saved from the ravages of hell. Both Barry and his sisters attended Sunday school, although their teachers wondered if attending only once a month would make any great impact on their lives.

*   *   *

Felicity's connections with the church had been very different. She'd grown up in a country town proudly displaying three Protestant churches in the main street and another in a prime position at the better end of town, while the Catholics, in their building with the highest steeple, lorded over all from the clifftop overlooking the bathing beach. It was a magnificent bluestone church where Catholics worshipped regularly for decades. The stone doorsteps were hollowed out at all the entrances from constant foot traffic, causing dust to be a constant challenge brought in by the ever-present wind.

The convent stood slightly further down the hill, with all its lower windows painted out so daydreaming students couldn't soak up the magnificent view across the fishing harbour instead of attending to their lessons.

The church Felicity attended had been positioned in the centre of the main street. Over the years, its extensive front garden had been reverently manicured, and generations of children gathered acorns from under the huge oak tree near the entrance. When falling attendance numbers deemed it necessary for the Methodists and Presbyterians to unite, they rebelled and kept both their buildings and only changed the name to United on the main street church.

Felicity's parents weren't regular churchgoers. Her dad opted for the teachings of Christian Science, which he credited for giving him strength during the four long years he served in the army. Her mother had attended church and Sunday school so often as a young girl she rejoiced at being able to choose which direction to follow as an adult. Felicity's Christian education had been zealously guided by a next-door neighbour, who saw it as her duty to escort Felicity to church and Sunday school each week. During the first half of the service, the children were included, with the minister giving them a special address. During the second half, the children filed out of the church to spend the rest of the time in Sunday school classes.

Each year, from the time she turned eight, she enjoyed going to CSSM (Children's Special Service Mission) beach meetings.

They were held on the sand of the main swimming beach not far from the kiosk, where every afternoon, for ten days, a large sand pulpit was built by the CSSM team members.

In the mornings, the children were divided into age groups and taught Christian values and Bible stories. There were picnics and hiking expeditions for the older children, while others joined in with craft classes, where they made plastic string bags and cane baskets. The younger children were supplied with brightly coloured pencils and colouring books. There were evening activities such as a sausage sizzle, a lantern parade, and on the last night, a final concert put together by the team leaders. Those ten days each year were the highlight of Felicity's summer school holidays. As she had a birthday on the day the CSSM usually arrived, she felt she was celebrating her birthday for the whole ten days.

A special friendship developed between Felicity and the minister's daughter, a classmate for all her primary school years. They attended Girls Club and Christian Endeavour and went with their Sunday school teacher, complete with a fold-up portable organ, to sing hymns to elderly parishioners who, for various reasons, were unable to attend church.

The Girls Club performed in an annual concert for parents and friends. One year, their leaders wanted to put on a production of Snow White and the Seven Dwarfs, but most of the girls complained that they were too old to act out a fairy story. When Felicity accepted the challenge to organise one of her favourite Enid Blyton stories into a play, they acted out 'Where's My Skipping Rope?' instead—adapted from a *Sunny Stories* magazine.

(Years later, she tried to find the original story by searching through catalogues, antique stores, and on the Internet, but her search was unsuccessful.)

She remembered marching with her Sunday school class in Anzac processions and the excitement of climbing up the tiered seats erected on scaffolds in the church for Sunday school anniversaries. These celebrations were always special occasions, and their very best, and often new, clothing and shoes would be proudly worn for the first time. (For the next year, for as long as they fitted, these clothes were kept for best.)

Tea meetings followed the Sunday school anniversaries a week later, rewarding the efforts of everyone who'd practiced diligently for many weeks to present a program of choruses for parents and friends.

Tea meetings were fiercely competitive, and it didn't matter which denomination you belonged to (or whether you spent your Sundays somewhere elsewhere other than church)—you were always welcomed. Although it had the smallest congregation in town, the Baptist tea meeting was usually voted the best, with their cooks producing vast quantities of children's favourite party foods for the occasion.

On reflection, over the years, Felicity felt immense pride to have been given the opportunity as a sixteen-year-old to play the piano accompaniment for that year's Sunday school anniversary. She didn't remember making mistakes with her playing but often blushed as she recalled that long-ago anniversary day when the minister asked her to include a selection of music while the offering was being collected. She played the only other piece she knew at the time and was later asked by the minister (with a twinkle in his eye), 'Were you aware you played a lullaby before my sermon?'

Felicity gratefully acknowledged how her parents had scrimped and saved to enable her to have piano lessons from respected teachers. On thinking back over her growing-up years, she thought she probably sailed through puberty because she was able to play the piano. When angry, sad, or frustrated, she could be heard playing quiet, thoughtful music. Happy times were often linked with loud, triumphant pieces. As she grew into a young woman, songs from musicals became popular, but hymns with their variety of tunes always remained firm favourites.

She'd been taught by three music teachers over the years. Miss Vera Mack, her first teacher, was the eldest of three spinster sisters who all lived frugally on Vera's music teaching earnings and the small amount the younger women earned from cleaning the town hall and council offices. Miss Mack mostly wore short sleeves, gathered skirts, and no stockings, while her sisters rugged up in heavy cardigans and leggings, and both of them often wore scarves. Vera Mack's figure was well-padded—a complete opposite to her sisters' tiny frames. They'd rented their old cottage from the council for as long as most townspeople could remember.

The path to the music room at the back of the main house meandered in a circuitous route bordered by overgrown shrubs on both sides, casting deep shadows and harbouring all manner of creepy-crawlies. An overhead canopy dripped water for ages after a shower of rain. Spooky shadows often made Felicity feel quite scared.

Miss Mack prepared her students each year to perform in an end-of-year concert on the town hall stage.

This meant many fingers were practicing all year to be proficient in front of family and friends. Their reward at the end of the evening was always a sumptuous feed of creamy delicacies they enjoyed backstage like celebrities.

Eventually, when Miss Mack was too old to teach, she and her two frail sisters moved in as the first residents of the newly completed retirement home. (Felicity often wondered what happened to the wooden knitting needle Miss Mack used intermittently to rap her on her knuckles when she made mistakes.)

Her second teacher didn't bother about concerts. Her main concern seemed to be earning Brownie points for having candidates achieve high grades in examinations. Spending most of her time practicing the same four monotonous compositions for a whole year didn't enthuse Felicity at all. She lasted with Miss Walker for only one year.

Although most of the nuns who taught music at the convent were interested in having students who achieved academic results or wanted to pursue music for a living, Mother Seraphina thought differently. She happily helped Felicity become a competent accompanist and showed considerable pride when Felicity played for her Sunday school anniversary service. However, she viewed Felicity as a heathen because she was a Protestant, and each lesson would begin with the preface 'In our church, we do [this and this and this]!'

Fed up one day, Felicity countered with 'In our church, we do *[this and this and this and this]!'*

From then on, their discussions during lesson time were only about music. Felicity grew very fond of Mother Seraphina. Her lessons were held in a music cell—a soundproof room in a cluster of similar rooms in a building away from the main convent. A very Spartan building, it contained only a piano and stool, a chair for the teaching nun, and the requisite blacked-out windows.

Mother Seraphina always walked her to the door after her lesson. When a distant relative passed away and left money to buy Felicity a bicycle, Mother Seraphina shared her excitement and joy and looked longingly after her as she rode away.

Felicity often wondered from the interest she'd shown in her home life and activities whether Mother Seraphina regretted becoming a nun, shutting herself away from the everyday world.

Felicity felt privileged to receive piano lessons because her parents wouldn't have been able to afford them if her father, a part-time piano tuner, hadn't been charged reduced fees by the convent because he tuned and repaired their pianos whenever necessary.

Barry's introduction to music began at school at an early age, playing the recorder and later as a drummer in the school band. He wasn't passionate about either, so he didn't continue with them after he left school. Secretly he loved singing but refused to join the choir. He'd overheard several of his mates talking.

'Singing is such a sissy thing to do.'

'You wouldn't catch me in a choir or joining the drama club either!'

But it didn't stop him from singing songs made popular by Slim Dusty and Jim Reeves when he spent time on his own. His voice deepened as he grew older, and it had a unique tone. It was a pity he hadn't brought it out in the open. With the right promotion, he could have become famous.

CHAPTER 7

arry studied woodworking and welding at night classes after he left school. Both subjects were useful when he began building extra sheds or repairing machinery. (He'd been glad to stop learning Latin and reading English literature—subjects that held no relevance whatsoever for someone who wanted to be a farmer.) As a young boy, he'd loved construction toys, especially when permitted to make things with a well-preserved Meccano set belonging to his father.

He was also adept at pulling clocks apart and reassembling them. As he grew older, he explored the construction of all types of motors and how they worked. He saved many a piece of aging machinery with his innovative adaptations or by being able to repair them.

Snails were often problematic on their farm at harvest time. In some years, large areas of crops were completely wiped out. Baiting early in the growth season helped, but small conical snails were hard to eradicate. When the time came for the grain to be harvested, there could still be challenges getting it to market without too many snails in each load. The quotas for weeds and snails and small stones and contamination with animal waste were set and rigidly enforced at the storage silos.

Their Horwood-Bagshaw header was no longer new, but it did have the advantage of being able to save screenings (small grains and weed seeds), which could be used to add to stock feed. So while it was still serviceable, Jack had no intention of trading it in or purchasing another model, even second-hand at a clearing sale. On a particularly bad year for snails, one of their carriers had been turned around at the silo and sent home to have a truckload of wheat cleaned. This proved to be embarrassing, costly, and time-consuming. After a great deal of thought and experimentation, Barry devised a method of dislodging most of the snails before they joined the bulk of the grain in the header.

It was a simple device. He secured two rows of strong fencing wire covered by Polypipe a foot apart and fixed three feet in front of the comb on the header. The idea was to slightly flatten the crop and at the same time knock off most of the snails. They were dropped back on to the ground without damaging the grain. Although some grain was dislodged, it was minimal and not wasted, as it added nourishment for cattle that fed on the stubble after the harvest. Barry happily shared the idea with his mates. He wasn't interested in spending a great deal of time and money getting his idea patented. He'd seen the toll it had taken on an uncle years previously when he'd tried to register an original, innovative idea for manufacturing a dual flush toilet to conserve the use of water.

Jack ridiculed Barry's invention when presented with Barry's ideas of how to deal with the menace of snails in the harvested crop.

'It won't work, boy! What makes you think you can find a solution to get rid of snails? They've been bugging us for years! Stop wasting your time and get on with real farm jobs!'

He grudgingly had to eat his words when he saw the device being successful and saving both time and money. His pride in his son's ingenuity became evident when he told Louise, but he didn't see any reason to tell Barry how he felt.

'Why don't you praise him occasionally?' Louise asked.

'Don't be silly, woman! I don't want him getting a swelled head or becoming too big for his boots!'

Barry showed considerable scepticism when Louise told him his father had praised his invention.

'Oh yeah? That'll be the day. Why doesn't he tell me himself?'

This saddened Louise as she watched her husband's need to control and to always be in control prevent him from developing an adult relationship with his son. She could understand her husband's insecure feelings. For all Jack's bluster about being prosperous and making a good living, she knew the farm would be hard-pressed to support more people if Barry eventually married and had a family. (After his father had lost the farm to the bank during the Second World War, Jack had invested too much of his life in getting it back to want to face losing it again.) She wished Jack would get his head out of the sand.

For the first three or four years after he left school, Barry seemed to be content to pursue blokeish activities. He bought a second-hand motor bike with money he earned helping out in a neighbour's shearing shed. He enjoyed working on cars and cared for their motors better than most of his contemporaries, who screamed around in their utes or did circle work in designated paddocks. A nearby neighbour who had a graveyard of broken-down equipment told Barry he could take anything he wanted. From a pile of household white goods, discarded vehicles, and worn-out farm equipment, Barry made go-karts, cubby houses, and unbolted useful bits and pieces to make something later on. He was always happiest when he made something useful, even from discarded junk.

Because Barry was quietly spoken and well mannered, and because of his good looks and height, he became a popular choice as a regular partner at debutante balls. While attending the compulsory dancing lessons, he found he thoroughly enjoyed the experience and started going to local dances regularly. He developed proficiency in modern and old-time dance as well as a wide range of rock 'n' roll moves. He felt saddened when line dancing started being fashionable, but he could see the benefits available to many singles, especially women, who wouldn't otherwise venture out of their homes.

It was acceptable for men to go dancing without a partner, but the character of the woman and her reasons were often questioned if she went alone. Two women together also raised eyebrows, although several entering a dance hall together wasn't frowned upon. A lone woman had no guarantee of being asked to dance and could remain seated on her own on the sidelines. Mostly at the dances Barry attended, it was usual for a male to ask a young lady to dance with him, and ladies' choices were rare occurrences.

Dancing soon turned out to be a binding force in Felicity and Barry's marriage, an activity in which they were both proficient. Their bodies melded together, and misunderstandings or hurts were momentarily forgotten.

Felicity's dream of working with Barry each day on the farm soon became clouded, an area of upheaval and conflict. While Jack lived, Barry tried hard to please him and longed to be appreciated. After Jack was found dead in a tidal inlet tangled in a roll of barbed wire, Barry appeared to be driven to do everything on the farm by himself. It seemed as though he felt he had something to prove.

Felicity noticed the subtle change in their relationship and challenged him.

'We're drifting apart. You're spending so much time doing farm stuff on your own we're not doing anything together any more. I could help more often. There's no need to do everything. You only ask for me to work with you when you're desperate and all the neighbours are busy. You don't seem to want my company any more!'

'Don't be silly!' Barry replied, then suddenly he realised he had started sounding like his father. He added her name just before he called her 'woman,' as he'd heard his dad often address his mother.

When Barry and Felicity were first married, they'd walked along the beach often and climbed the sand hills together. The native plants along the walking track were abundant, and they frequently discovered plants they hadn't seen previously. They'd swum together and spent time watching dolphins cavorting around the end of the jetty. But after Jack's death, everything changed, and Barry seemed to have lost interest in anything that wasn't connected with the farm and making it more profitable.

Felicity's feelings for Barry hadn't changed. She still loved him but felt frustrated that he'd become so focussed on the farm. They even struggled to find intimate times together. At the end of a day's work, Barry would slump down in front of the television flipping channels with the remote control or fall asleep in his chair. When he finally went to bed, he retired with nothing on his mind except sleeping. Barry insisted his feelings hadn't changed. Felicity wasn't so sure about that. His priorities appeared to have shifted radically. She was often lonely, and it seemed as though she shared a house with a stranger. Feeling very isolated, she ultimately faced the fact she'd become very depressed.

*　　*　　*

Some of Barry's mates from wealthy families had invested in flying lessons, and one had even bought his own plane on his fortieth birthday. Barry managed to tear himself away from the farm on two occasions to accept flights over the district, supposedly to check his crops. Andrew Brown loved impressing his friends with his flying ability, and some of his mates had taken fantastic photos and videos of activities and the changing landscape. (Little did they know that many years later, beautiful clear photos would be taken from drones that were remotely controlled by an operator on the ground.) Although Felicity asked Barry to tell Andrew she would love to see the farm from the air, he didn't ever offer to take her up in his plane.

At the time she suffered from frequent feelings of sadness and of always being tired, there was a lot of publicity about how to deal with depression. She tried to tell Barry about her frustrations, but he mostly brushed off her feelings as being trivial and deflected the conversation towards the happenings about the farm. She suspected he didn't know how to deal with his thoughts on this matter, let alone know how to help with her disturbing feelings.

'Go and see a doctor. They deal with depressed people all the time,' he called back to her on one occasion as he went out the back door, heading for the machinery shed.

'I don't want to be put on antidepressants. Rightly or wrongly, I feel they are just a prop and won't cure my problem. They may treat the symptoms temporarily, but they don't get to the source of the problem. And besides, I don't feel very comfortable seeing a doctor where two relatives of yours are sharing receptionist duties. I'm sure they'd have a field day.'

'Employees in the medical centre are not allowed to divulge or discuss the contents of anyone's medical consultations. Not everyone in this town is a gossip!'

Felicity nearly choked on her cup of tea but decided she'd be whipping a dead horse trying to have him see that their lack of communication was part of the problem. She would have bet all her bank balance that if she consulted a doctor, she wouldn't be asked the questions that were most likely contributing to her depression.

These were questions such as 'Do you and your husband share quality time together?' and 'Is your sex life satisfying for both of you?' Or even the questions 'Are you lonely?' and 'How is your self-esteem?'

Advice she'd read in a *Reader's Digest* suggested she talk to the person closest to her or chat to someone at Lifeline. However, each time she mentioned to Barry that she felt depressed, he looked uncomfortable. She wondered if friends and relatives had the skills to deal with such a revelation. Did emotional involvement with the sufferer tend to cloud the issue? Do close relatives somehow wonder if depression is catching? Did they feel threatened or ashamed to be associated with someone who suffered from depression?

Ignorant advice such as 'Just pull yourself together' could be very damaging, but it was frequently given as an option by a relative seeking well-meaning ways to assist.

An attempt to bring up the subject of depression with friends or acquaintances frequently found conversation deflected or quickly terminated. When Felicity finally went to a professional in another town for advice, she clearly remembers being cautioned not to ask 'why' questions, as they were too confronting!

On thinking it over, she realised the answers to many 'why' questions were what she needed to help get her out of her predicament.

There were questions like:

'Why won't you listen to me?'

'Why do you let people refer to you and treat you as *the boy*?'

'Why can't you try and walk in my shoes occasionally?'

'Why do your parents see us as children and expect us to give a daily detailed report of all our activities to them?'

It was suggested she join clubs and go and meet more people, but in her despairing state of mind, this didn't work for her. If she joined in and presented any new ideas, she was considered to be pushy; and if she remained in the background, she was labelled as standoffish. Coming from the city (despite spending her early years in the country), she was labelled as being different.

She found the effort of getting ready to go out more than a little overwhelming. Frequently, after she drove away from the farmhouse, she would become unsure of her directions and give up and return home. Even if she managed to reach her destination, she often felt alone, although surrounded by people. From time to time, she imagined everyone either avoided or talked about her.

Felicity read somewhere that many depression sufferers benefited by volunteering and helping others. She already had a steady stream of clients who occupied two days a week wanting therapeutic massages. She was fortunate to be able to use a vacant room at the local medical centre for consultations. Assistance was also given with bookings and occasional referrals.

She considered the option of joining the local ambulance volunteers. However, on thinking it over, she decided that her sense of direction (or lack of it) would be a disadvantage, as most of the local roads weren't signposted.

The fact that she would have a fifteen-minute drive to the ambulance station after being called out may also have been a handicap.

After obtaining a copy of their teaching manual, she knew for sure she wasn't ready to embrace the advanced emergency procedures that had never been her forte. Felicity knew she could be a good gofer but not a good first responder. She knew it wouldn't be right to take on a challenge that could add more stress to her life.

She lost her way one evening while returning to the farm from Wattle Flat soon after she and Barry were married. She took the wrong turning and became disorientated.

No problem, she thought, then she felt apprehensive as she noticed she was low on petrol and her phone showed only one bar. She rang Barry for directions.

'Where are you?'

'I'm at the end of a road where there's a pier out into the ocean.'

'We don't have any piers, only jetties in this district. See if you can find a signpost somewhere, then call me back.'

Felicity didn't ever forget that incident. It conjured up feelings of shame and frustration. Her phone contact dropped out, so she decided to go back to the T-junction and finally found her way back to Wattle Flat. Carefully setting out again, she stayed alert, watched the distance, and didn't turn on to the wrong side road. She felt triumphant when she finally drove up the winding driveway to the farm. Luckily bulk fuel was always kept on hand, so all she had to do was to make it home without running out of petrol. She knew Barry would fill her car for her next morning.

Ambulances in rural South Australia are mostly manned by everyday people who are proud to be volunteers. Felicity thought differently. As the volunteers worked to a roster, they could be called from their workplace or from their beds at a moment's notice and often attended to farm or road accidents involving friends and neighbours. It was a position of immense responsibility, and Felicity was appalled there was no remuneration or concessions of some sort for volunteers to reward their willingness to be of service.

'If ambulance officers can be paid in the city, why aren't they paid in the country?' she could often be heard asking.

'It's not fair that such a responsible position receives no financial recognition. The training is extensive. It must be extremely difficult having to attend the unexpected injury or death of a relative or close friend. It's particularly traumatic if several children or families are involved. As volunteers living in the area, they are frequently assisting locals—people they grew up with and friends who went to school together. This has to be harder than the job of city ambulance personnel dealing with strangers!'

Felicity accepted the roles of volunteers in situations such as delivering Meals on Wheels or Community Transport and the many school and club activities done by willing helpers, but she considered it to be exploitation and a totally different situation to have ambulances manned by volunteers. However, if she voiced her indignation, she frequently met with opposition.

'This is the way we have always done things here. We are proud to be volunteers. You're a newcomer—you wouldn't understand how we feel!'

After a while she gave up and stopped rocking the boat.

Another suggestion to deal with depression she'd gleaned from the internet was to choose something she really wanted to do, something she could become passionate about. But that was easier said than done. Finally, after nearly a year, she found a way to come out of her dark tunnel of despair—and it happened gradually.

Felicity began writing prize-winning rhyming poetry. She wrote about how she felt, her life on the farm, and her love of books. In fact, she wrote about anything that came to mind. And she loved it. She entered her poems in competitions and won many of them. A whole new world opened up for her, and Barry appeared proud of her achievements. And although the state of their relationship hadn't altered, it didn't seem like the end of the world any more.

Seasons muddled on with Barry and Felicity existing side by side with little communication but without any great upheavals either. They took no precautions to prevent a pregnancy but were not rewarded. August, the month suspected to be notorious for an increase in cases of depression, passed without notice. In their own way, they were comfortable together, but their passion for each other had paled. As each month passed, the possibility of Felicity becoming pregnant seemed more and more remote.

CHAPTER 8

Olive and Arthur often felt overwhelmed when helping care for a baby as tiny as Rose-Louise. Their own daughter, Jane, had weighed in at nine pounds five ounces at birth in 1941 and been breastfed until she started taking solids. They found all the kerfuffle of sterilising bottles and making up milk mixtures for Rose-Louise very time-consuming and the responsibility more than a little scary. They felt privileged but also enormously challenged to care for a grandchild—a far greater responsibility than looking after a child of their own.

But the frightening way Jane acted caused them to be very concerned. She didn't want to have anything to do with her baby—said she was terrified she'd harm her. Although she didn't want to reverse her decision to not tell Barry about their daughter, deep down she felt a sense of guilt that compounded her day-to-day feelings of despair and inadequacy.

Finally, after a phone call from Olive to Jane's GP, a day before Jane's scheduled six-week check-up, positive moves for a solution to her baby rejection problem were put in place. Dr Jones secured a live-in placement for her in the Berry Street Babies' Home in

East Melbourne. It was a training school for mothercraft nurses and provided help and instruction for young mothers who needed extra assistance after giving birth.

She booked in with Rose-Louise for a month to bond with her baby and learn how to look after her. She began taking an antidepressant drug prescribed for her that was beginning to be used successfully for postnatal depression patients. The staff were asked to observe and monitor Jane closely, as they could see she appeared reluctant to handle her baby daughter.

Jane's parents relaxed for the first time since the birth. All was well until Arthur discovered a lump in his right groin and was diagnosed with an inguinal hernia. He accepted the offer of an immediate operation instead of wearing a brace or supportive belt. He'd been told if his hernia strangulated, he could be a very sick man. They'd agonised over what would be the best way to deal with the situation and found that, if necessary, Jane and Rose-Louise could delay their homecoming by another two weeks, enabling Arthur to maximise the time he could take it easy.

Luckily, Olive enjoyed driving and willingly agreed to be his chauffeur for as long as needed. Many of her friends allowed their husbands to take over all the driving after they both retired and soon became nervous and unsure of their capabilities after not driving for a while. Olive was glad she'd insisted on continuing to drive regularly and was happy that their little grey Austin A40 was easy to manoeuvre, able to turn in a small circle, and could be parked easily.

Jane's time at Berry Street ended up being a mixed blessing. Under the diligent supervision of helpful mothercraft nurses, she learnt to care for her baby and was helped to get much needed rest so she could enjoy her baby more.

Women of all ages and from vastly different backgrounds had been referred to Berry Street so they could gain the confidence to take their babies home and cope on their own. Berry Street Babies' Home organised adoptions, but there were also single girls staying there who wanted to keep their babies despite opposition from their families or having limited financial support. There were older first-time mothers with menopause babies who hadn't any experience with children—those who'd married later in life, having spent years looking after elderly parents or had consuming careers—and young women whose own mothers had passed away. These women were often lacking confidence and a support system. If requested, in the 1970s, local councils supplied home-help assistance at an affordable cost for six weeks after the birth of a baby if no other help was available. (When the home-help service proved very popular in later years, it could only be offered to mothers of multiple births.)

Jane was encouraged to do everything for Rose-Louise. The only thing she didn't have to do was wash out her baby's cloth nappies. When babies were born in hospital in the 1970s, new mothers received a baby bundle containing vouchers and samples of many of the products they would find useful when caring for their newborns.

A nappy wash voucher was in Jane's bundle, but she knew that after taking up the introductory offer, she wouldn't be able to afford to continue with the service once she returned home.

She appreciated having her baby's nappies washed for her during her stay at Berry Street. (It would be many years before disposable nappies were readily available and widely used.) If birth announcements were inserted in a newspaper, the new parents were often inundated with advertising material and free samples ranging from baby products to insurance opportunities.

Although Jane resided in Berry Street for a prolonged stay, she found it difficult to make friends even though her erratic behaviour remained controlled to a certain extent by medication. When she confided in several young mothers that she was afraid of harming Rose-Louise, they chose to keep their distance.

However, her friendship with another mother, who later suffered from depression, was to have a profound effect on her life.

*　　*　　*

Rose-Louise often thought about her early years. She recalled going to preschool at the kindergarten, where her grandparents were cleaners after everyone went home at night. She'd helped them with her small broom and toy vacuum cleaner. She proudly wiped down tables and tidied the tiny farm animal toys in the sandbox. William and Linda had been her best friends there, and at first, she'd visited their homes to play and went to their birthday parties. But after Jane had been observed acting strangely the first time, William's and Linda's mothers hadn't asked her to visit any more.

Her grandparents were especially kind to her when Jane was feeling unwell. On her first day at school when she was five, it was her grandmother who escorted her there and who waited at the gate at the end of the day. The times spent sitting on the couch looking at picture books together or being read stories about people who did wondrous things and visited astonishing places were fond memories for Rose-Louise.

For her very first fancy-dress party, she remembered her gran making her a fairy costume. It made her feel like she could really do magic to make people happy. She often went shopping with her granddad too, and he always bought her a Chupa Chups (a round long-lasting lolly on a stick) to suck on the way home. And he spent hours with her as she learnt to master her first bicycle until it was time to finally remove the training wheels.

When Jane was out of sorts, she would often be asleep when school ended for the day, and Rose-Louise's teacher would need to call to remind her to collect her daughter.

Rose-Louise always felt very ashamed sitting in the main office waiting for her mother to come and take her home. Jane would promise her she'd attend school functions, but would often let her down at the last minute. Rose-Louise learnt at an early age to deal with many disappointments. Even though only aged seven at the time, Rose-Louise remembered when Jane had a huge fight with her parents. This milestone was the day she left with Rose-Louise in her old Ford Falcon sedan to live in a battered caravan in a country town on the banks of the Murray River.

'Can't you see what's happening to you?' Olive challenged. 'You are not being fair to Rose-Louise. She deserves a better start in life, and your dad and I will be very happy to look after her while you sort yourself out!'

'I'm not handing her over to you! Rose-Louise is the most positive addition in my life. We'll go to the country away from all my contacts and make a new start.'

Rose-Louise often wondered if she'd done something wrong to make her mother quarrel with her grandparents and then move so far away. They left while her grandparents were shopping, but she couldn't take her bicycle, her dolls' house, or many of her toys because they wouldn't fit in the car after the rest of their luggage was loaded up.

'We'll come back soon and collect the rest of our things,' Jane said, but they didn't return, as Jane had 'borrowed' a large sum of money she'd found in a secret drawer she'd discovered in her father's desk. She knew her dad would be very disappointed in her for stealing from him to have enough money to live the way she had chosen.

Her resolve to clean up her life was good, but she hadn't factored in her dependence or how easy it would be for dealers to find her and identify her need wherever she went.

Rose-Louise grew up mostly in Mildura. She knew her mother and grandparents had argued before she was bundled into Jane's car and settled between blankets and pillows for the long drive north. Jane, with the help of antidepressant pills, had recovered well from the crippling postnatal depression that had necessitated her staying at the Berry Street home for six weeks. Her father's hernia had been successfully repaired, and he was fully recovered when she returned home.

At the time, he'd been glad Jane was able to extend her stay for the extra two weeks they'd requested. However, those last two weeks when Jane met up with Kelly, a single mother who lived close to the preschool, would change her life forever. Arthur would have regretted requesting Jane's longer stay at Berry Street if he'd known how Kelly's influence would affect his daughter. Against all reason, he would have blamed himself if he'd learnt Kelly was the instigator of the out-of-control situations that were to so radically alter his daughter's life.

After the argument with her parents and bundling their possessions and Rose-Louise into her car, Jane drove through the night. She had no definite plan in mind except that she needed to get as far away from Melbourne as she could in order to change her life. A couple of times she nearly dozed off, and the huge interstate haulage trucks scared her as they roared past, making the car shudder. Mercifully, Rose-Louise slept most of the way, oblivious to the many kangaroos that frequently challenged night-time drivers.

It had been an impulsive, spur-of-the-moment decision to leave the haven of her parents' home. With very little money of her own, no definite plans, and a small child dependent on her, the reality of her plight was evident when she began enquiring about accommodation when she arrived in Mildura. Motels were prolific, competitive, and pricey. Finally, she found a caravan park advertising on-site vans available for rent.

The caravan allocated to her in Riverview Caravan Park was old, small, had two single bunks, and smelt very musty. The caravan park wasn't far from a primary school, which meant Rose-Louise could walk there and back each day.

With very few options available to her, Jane agreed to rent the dilapidated caravan for a month while she looked for somewhere permanent for them to live. In fact, they stayed living there in the caravan park until Jane passed away.

Despite being taunted by some of her schoolmates for being a caravan kid, Rose-Louise thrived in the park. There was a children's playground and always someone to play with. (Four decades later, when she visited Mildura, she found the caravan park had been converted into a retirement village, with 200 modest two-bedroomed transportable homes on the old site.) In later years, if someone ever indicated she was disadvantaged by living in a caravan in a park, she would become irate and admonish them.

'Some of the most honest, down-to-earth people I ever met used to live in that park. They didn't put on airs and graces.

They were good people, and family loyalty was paramount. Some people lived there choosing to have a home without the overheads of ownership, some were very poor, and others enjoyed the feeling of being part of a family without family tensions. If you've never lived in a caravan park, you have no idea what you're talking about!'

Kevin, the son of the park's owner, befriended Rose-Louise. He was only a few months older but much taller. They walked to and from school together, and afterwards Rose-Louise helped him feed his pets. When an old lady who rented an on-site van on the other side of the park moved into full-time care, Kevin adopted her two tabby cats rather than have them put down. He also looked after two red hens, three rabbits, and a lazy black-and-white border collie, whose energy was mostly expended in keeping out of people's way.

The hens were fairly consistent in providing an egg a day, but sometimes they shunned the laying boxes and distributed their bounty under bushes in the park. As they had favourite bushes, the eggs weren't very hard to locate. Occasionally Kevin would give one of his eggs to Rose-Louise for her breakfast or to have a hard-boiled egg with curry in a sandwich for her school lunch. A sheep he'd raised since birth trailed after Kevin like a faithful companion from the minute he came out of school.

Apart from her parents and their immediate neighbours, Jane's impulsive departure from their Carlton flat barely caused a ripple among the people she'd lived alongside for nearly eight years.

Some of her supermarket customers asked after her, but mostly they quickly forgot her. A couple of Rosie's school friends missed her when they played games at lunch time but were soon enjoying the company of the new little girl who sat in Rosie's place at her table.

Because of her coping difficulties and struggling with all the challenges of being a single mother, Jane had made very few friends in Carlton. Kelly was the exception.

'It's very important for me to contact Jane,' Kelly told Arthur and Olive. 'Why did she leave without saying goodbye? I thought we'd become good friends. Can you give me her address please?'

'We don't know where she went. We had a terrible argument. She'd been acting very erratically recently—moody, not sleeping, and at times, she'd been very aggressive.

She had times when she managed to be so disorganised she forgot to collect Rose-Louise from school. She seemed to resent us helping care for our granddaughter, but sometimes she would have sent her to school without food for lunch if we hadn't intervened. We suspected something odd was happening to Jane. From time to time, it felt as though she was a complete stranger or a creature from another planet.

She recovered from the depression she'd suffered after Rose-Louise was born with the help of medication, then a few months ago, things seemed to go terribly wrong for her. We questioned whether she was taking some sort of recreational drug and told her we'd be supportive and mind Rose-Louise while she sorted herself out. That's when she packed up and left.'

After several persistent phone calls, Arthur asked Kelly not to call again. He obtained Kelly's phone number and said he would pass it on to Jane when they found out where she was staying. That way, Jane could call Kelly if she wanted to keep in contact. Olive didn't like Kelly but couldn't convince Arthur she may have been a bad influence on their daughter.

'Kelly's very secretive and sly. Her eyes are often bloodshot, and she perspires a great deal. We know very little about her, except that she lost her little boy when he was only a couple of months old. He was said to be a cot death victim. Jane got very angry when we dared to suggest she may be taking drugs of some sort. If Kelly was supplying drugs to Jane, it could explain the changes in her, since she really appeared to be her only close friend. When we find out where Jane is living, it might not be a good idea to pass on Kelly's new telephone number.'

'Oh, I think our Jane is much too smart to dabble in drugs, and wherever she is, she might be in need of a friend,' replied Arthur, blinded by his love for his daughter and ignoring the fact that many smart people thought they could try drugs once or twice and not get hooked. (Luckily, he would never learn the truth.)

'Some people appear to be friends when they often have hidden agendas,' Olive replied sagely. Olive hadn't been fond of Kelly and had been unaware that Arthur had eventually passed Kelly's telephone number on to their daughter. Jane had debated with herself whether it would be wise for her to call Kelly, as she didn't want to slip back to using drugs as a crutch.

However, after wondering what to do for several days, she had chosen to ring from the park phone box and apologise for not saying goodbye. She decided not to give out her address or the phone number of the park.

By the time Jane rang Kelly, an unidentified female had been delivered dead on arrival to the Royal Melbourne Hospital casualty department, and Kelly's phone continued to ring out each time Jane called.

Drugs were becoming commonplace. Many young people accepted them as 'something everyone tried these days!' What often started with occasional marijuana use could lead to heroin and speed and, in later years, to the scourge called ice. Jane was lonely, and although Kelly only supplied friendship at first, her praise of marijuana and heroin and how she used them to give herself a 'lift' soon made Jane curious. She felt so ashamed when her parents guessed the cause of her erratic behaviour, and she knew she had to move away from temptation and start afresh. It hurt her to walk out on her parents, but her determination motivated her to make a life for herself and her daughter in new surroundings.

She rang her parents one afternoon from the phone booth in the caravan park soon after she'd settled in Mildura just to let them know she and Rose-Louise were safe and well. She didn't tell Arthur where they were living or even the name of the town. Olive had gone out shopping, while Arthur decided to spend time searching, trying to remember where he had hidden several large bank notes he'd secreted somewhere in the house.

He'd planned to take Olive on a cruise for her birthday. He suffered greatly from frustration by the fact he seemed to be getting more forgetful every day. He also forgot that Olive didn't want Jane given Kelly's telephone number.

Jane felt guilty she'd 'borrowed' a large sum of money that belonged to her father, but she didn't mention it to him.

'I'm having more and more trouble remembering things, and I thought I'd put some money away for Olive's birthday present in a safe place, but I must have been mistaken,' Arthur told her. Jane hoped he wouldn't link her to the loss of the money when he couldn't locate it, as she fully intended to return it as soon as she could. She'd used some of it to buy grocery essentials and the rest to pay in advance on their rented caravan.

When challenged by her parents, she'd denied having a drug problem. Until they'd confronted her, she hadn't acknowledged the truth to herself. Her hasty departure from Melbourne was a spur-of-the-moment decision, but she wasn't stupid. She felt overcome by the enormity of her decision because she now understood she would be on her own, without her parents in the background to compensate for the times she wasn't coping.

She knew addressing bouts of depression with recreational drugs wasn't the way to deal with her life. Her foremost focus needed to be the welfare and happiness of her small daughter.

Rose-Louise had been excited to be going for a long drive in their car. The ramifications revealed themselves to her slowly over the next few days.

'Will Granny and Granddad still be able to read me a bedtime story? Where are we going to live? Will they come and visit soon and bring my doll's house and my new bike? Where will I go to school? Can I have a pet in our caravan home?'

'No', 'I don't know', and 'Perhaps' were the only truthful answers Jane could supply to her inquisitive daughter. Luckily, although far from being flash, Rose-Louise regarded the caravan as a holiday adventure. She began to make up travelling stories and telling them to her favourite teddy bear. (Jane could have hugged that little bear for giving her some breathing space.)

Their neighbours in the park were accepting without asking questions. Bertha was a permanent resident who lived in a converted garage next to their caravan. She was a cheerful well-rounded lady who looked after her ten-year-old daughter who had suffered a brain injury after a runaway car mounted a footpath and crushed her stroller against a shopfront. Cheryl had been only three years old at the time, and what should have been a happy shopping outing with her parents turned to tragedy.

Cheryl was confined to a wheelchair, and the park kids often took turns taking her for walks and to school and did wheelies with her in her chair. She would beg for more when they stopped, and sometimes a small child would perch on her lap to share the whole experience. Her father blamed himself for not being quick enough when he tried to push Cheryl's stroller out of the path of the car. No amount of reassurance could convince him he couldn't have changed the course of events, and several months after the accident, an elderly couple walking their identical poodles along the bike path found him hanging from the rafters in a derelict boat shed down on the riverbank.

James, who occupied an almost identical caravan on the other side of them, had a toffy English accent and told them he used to be a butler at Buckingham Palace during Queen Elizabeth's early childhood! The children in the park would often strut some distance behind him, mimicking his mannerisms. Being good-natured, he would sometimes exaggerate his walk if he saw them following him.

No one knew exactly how he filled his days, but occasionally, a well-informed article, written by him, appeared in a magazine or newspaper. In fact, very few people knew he was a very successful writer of children's spine-chilling adventure stories.

The residents of Riverview Park soon developed into an extended family for Jane and Rose-Louise. Their first few weeks were harrowing as Jane's withdrawal symptoms made themselves felt. Jane struggled with having a dry mouth and suffering from nausea. Extreme tiredness plagued her, and she was unable to sleep for long periods. Depression threatened to engulf her again. The prescription for the antidepressant drug prescribed for her after Rose-Louise birth hadn't all been used. It had expired long ago, and the thought of going to a doctor frightened her. She couldn't risk having a perceptive GP deduce she'd previously been using drugs. She wanted to start her new life in Mildura with a clean slate. As it turned out, it wouldn't have made any difference in the long run.

While Rose-Louise attended school during the day, Jane continued struggling with her body sweating and shaking. The constant feelings of anxiety began to eat away at her resolve to stay off drugs for the sake of her daughter and her own health. With her savings running out and her 'borrowed' money spent, she knew she would soon have to get a job. The government support pension didn't cover all expenses, and she hoped to find alternate accommodation and move out of the caravan park. There were casual and part-time seasonal jobs available picking grapes, citrus, and stone fruit around Mildura. After proving herself to be a willing worker, Jane rarely had weekdays without work—at first.

Backpackers came to Mildura from all round the world, so the mix of nationalities was diverse, and many stayed at Riverview, where, by now, Jane and Rose-Louise were semi-permanent residents.

Having excellent references from working in the supermarket in Carlton, Jane was keen to pick up more than relieving work in local stores. She wanted a permanent job, but more often than not, long-time Mildura residents seemed to get the advertised positions. She guessed her caravan park address probably played a part in discriminating against her. Although she kept looking for other accommodation, she found nothing available outside the park she could afford until she secured a full-time job. She felt like she was riding on a merry-go-round. Although it looked as though it could be workable, in theory, working part-time or casual jobs proved to be

Jane's downfall. Perceptive people soon began to notice Jane's erratic behaviour and unreliable attendance record.

Soon the worms came out of the woodwork, and she was offered drugs—just a taste to tide her over until she managed to cope.

'Bullshit!' she said to herself. 'It doesn't work like that. If I give in again when I'm almost free from this rotten scourge, I could be lost forever.'

The huge ever-present struggle relentlessly defined her days. Coupling her cravings with a lack of money and the enormity of being totally responsible for feeding, housing, and caring for her small daughter, Jane often despaired. Bertha could see Jane's struggle slowly eating into her resolve. She had lived at the caravan park long enough to recognise the signs for what they were. All types of people came and went in the park, and to survive, it became necessary to be accepting without being judgemental.

Many things seen and heard were rarely spoken about. Life wasn't a piece of cake for Bertha, but she'd learned to be thankful for any blessings that came her way. For Bertha, Rose-Louise emerged as one of those blessings. Each day, the little girl would skip up the gravel pathway to visit Bertha and Cheryl. They did jigsaws and explored books and puzzles together. Bertha always had a tasty treat for Rose-Louise when she visited.

'I love your hedgehog slice best of all,' she often told Bertha. 'But if you don't have any slice left, can I please have a piece of fruitcake or some of your yummy shortbread?'

Although Jane tried very hard to remain clean, a predator living in the park recognised Jane's struggle. He'd been watching her ever since she'd arrived, and when he finally approached with friendly overtures and a sample of what he could supply, she made a fatal mistake. She accepted the sample, telling herself she had no intention of ever using it. At first, she felt stronger knowing its whereabouts high up in the back of a cupboard. Proudly she resisted the urge to use it. Finally, she faced the fact she could succumb to temptation at any time if she knew where to find the offending package of powder, so she threw it out. She put it in the plastic bag with her household rubbish and into the bin outside the communal laundry.

What if someone finds it in the rubbish and recognises what it is? she wondered.

Jane panicked, and after dark, she retrieved her bag of rubbish and extracted the bag containing the package of powder. She hid it again behind things in a high cupboard, ignoring the fact she could have safely flushed it down the toilet and it would have been gone for good.

Meanwhile, the predator watched and waited.

CHAPTER 9

Rose-Louise felt ecstatic. After a lot of badgering, Jane had signed all the forms for her to join Little Athletics held every Saturday morning at the sports oval adjacent to the primary school. Jane had read all about Little Athletics—the idea that although children competed against each other in races in their own age group, improving their personal best times was more important than winning. Little Athletics proved to be popular as well for children who didn't have special sporting ability. Even the least talented child, with help, encouragement, and practice, could improve personal best times and soon be earning a collection of ribbons and medals.

Jane talked to other mothers to discover more information about Little Aths.

'Both boys and girls have the opportunity to learn new skills, like throwing a discus and competing in the long jump as well as participating in track events.'

'It's good for children to make friends apart from those they mix with in school.'

'You are very welcome, Jane, to join other parents who voluntarily set out the oval to be ready for events each week. As anyone who's been involved in running any sort of event will know, volunteers are the backbone of non-profit organisations.'

Jane watched her daughter participate in a variety of events, excelling in all sprint distances and blossoming in the competitive atmosphere. Spending time with other parents was also a plus, as Jane's social life had been practically non-existent since arriving in Mildura. Bertha had minded Rose-Louise on a couple of occasions to allow Jane to join members of Parents Without Partners at a meeting and a bus trip. However, she didn't feel especially comfortable in the group, as many members were in the early stages of separation from their partners and were more intent on running them down than forging new positive relationships.

A couple of the men who appeared to be interested in forming a friendship with her soon lost interest when she told them she lived in a rented caravan in a caravan park. One even told her blatantly, 'I let my wife have our house because most of the ladies I meet also have houses, so I don't need to own one as well!'

Jane also dabbled in answering advertisements in *Single Life* magazine, where people entered their particulars, hoping someone would meet them with a view to forming a friendship or meaningful relationship. This didn't prove to be a particularly successful venture as most of the advertisers seemed to be based in Melbourne.

But she did meet a couple of men who lived locally. The man who'd not been married seemed to be looking for someone to care for him in his old age, which may have been nearer than he'd stated in his advertisement. The other suitor, on their first date, introduced Jane to his three daughters and straight away indicated he wanted her to stay the night at his place, in his bed. Not wanting to be a carer for a geriatric or an instant substitute mother and wife, she gave up on answering advertisements and settled for borrowing more books from the library.

Several of the little girls in the caravan park joined the Brownies (a precursor to Girl Guides for girls aged eight to eleven), and Rose-Louise wanted to join up and go along with them. For several weeks, she attended to see if she enjoyed the activities before she needed to wear a uniform. They were usually very expensive, but Jane found everything her daughter needed, even the distinctive leather pouch and belt, in good condition in a second-hand shop.

Rose-Louise particularly enjoyed activities related to nature and the environment. On one occasion, when instructed to attend out of uniform and wear old clothes, she came home very excited.

'Mum, we went and explored the grounds of the old house called Rio Vista, where some of Mildura's early settlers used to live. They were the Chaffeys. We had super fun. We crawled and wriggled along the ground around the house and found all sorts of tiny plants and insects. We were told about being safe around water after we saw an empty fountain, like the one where one of the little Chaffey boys drowned many years ago. They don't put water in it any more.'

Jane smiled. She couldn't remember doing anything like that as she grew up. On another occasion, Rose-Louise came home chattering about what she'd learnt about rabbits.

'Mum, did you know that rabbits have so many baby rabbits that farmers don't like them at all? The farmers don't like having too many kangaroos either. If there are lots of them, they eat all the grass, then on really windy days, all the good dirt gets blown away. The rabbits and too many kangaroos help make our horrid dust storms.'

Jane intensely disliked the Mildura dust storms. They invaded every crack and cranny. Sometimes they lasted for up to three days, with the red dust swirling around in an orange cloud, coating everything with a layer of topsoil rich in nutrients taken from unprotected grazing land further inland. People living in Mildura were always encouraged to keep vehicles away from trees and to secure anything that could be blown away. However, there were often accidents during wind storms, many caused by corrugated iron sheets being blown off roofs. Power lines were frequently brought down, causing inconvenient power blackouts.

At times, the thick dust in the air made it hard to see, even indoors. The red dust irritated eyes, noses, and throats and often made breathing difficult, especially for those who needed to venture outdoors. The Mildura weather station had recorded a peak gust of 42.8 miles per hour in one storm with more gusts of up to 41.6 miles per hour occurring as a thick cloud enveloped the town and surrounding district.

Visibility became very poor as the eerie orange-coloured sky filled with dust. An average of five severe dust storms a year occurred in the first few years Jane and Rose-Louise lived in Mildura—until understanding trickled through to landowners that planting banks of trees could slow down the erosion. It took many years before farmers accepted they needed to maintain a grass cover and not overstock their land to guard against the ravages of the wind eating away at their rich topsoil.

It was extremely difficult to see very far ahead in a frightening windstorm. Visibility reduced alarmingly and could be as little as ten or twenty feet during a severe storm. The dust could be blown to as far away as Sydney or Melbourne, casting a gloomy pall over those cities. Jane found it hard to comprehend that fence lines and even buildings could be buried by drifting soil and that parts of railway lines could be covered up.

Even after being warned and trying hard to cover up all cracks and crevices in the old van, the brick-red dust would find its way inside and coat every surface. Mildura residents braced themselves whenever the Bureau of Meteorology issued severe weather warnings and forecast damaging winds.

They knew the temperature could drop alarmingly—perhaps five degrees at first before plunging down a further seven degrees minutes later. Although some of the rich soil would fall on other farming land, much would be blown to the coast and end up falling into the sea. Each destructive storm meant great hardship for the farmers who lost their topsoil, distress to people caught out in the bad weather, and extensive damage to many buildings.

During a major clean-up after a lengthy windstorm, Jane rediscovered the sample powder covered in dust in the high cupboard. At that particular time, she was feeling distressed and strapped for cash, as the starter motor and water pump on her car needed to be replaced. When she found the white powder where it had lain undisturbed for months, she wasn't thinking clearly and momentarily saw it as a welcome temporary relief from her stress.

Finding the packet very nearly seared through her resolve to stay clean. She struggled with her decision. But despite thoughts like *Nobody will notice if I use it* and *I won't buy any more*, she knew if she finally gave in to temptation, it would be downhill all the way.

*   *   *

For over a year, Jane had managed her finances reasonably well, picking up casual work to supplement her supporting mother's benefit. Her withdrawal from the drugs Kelly sold her had been the most harrowing period of her life, but being free of them was liberating. She enjoyed living in Mildura, where over 60 per cent of daylight hours were sunny. Bertha loaned her an old 28 inch Malvern Star bicycle with a basket and luggage carrier attached. This helped Jane financially by enabling her to cycle to most places she needed to go.

Bertha chuckled as she'd extracted the bike from a tangle of creepers that threatened to strangle her converted garage home.

'I don't expect to be riding a bicycle again in the near future. I'm much too heavy now to be comfortable on that flimsy seat!'

They borrowed a bike for Rose-Louise as well until they could bring her own from Melbourne. Jane and Rose-Louise frequently rode together on the bike paths along the river or to children's playgrounds. They would ride past the milk bar on the way home and sometimes stop for a rest and an ice cream cone. They enjoyed watching the water birds too, especially the stately pelicans.

'We learnt about pelicans at Brownies, Mum. Those big white waterbirds have a huge wingspan, and their pink bill is the biggest on a bird in the whole wide world. They eat fish as well as scraps and sometimes other small birds. They manage to fly because their bones aren't very heavy.'

Jane was impressed by her daughter's interest in birds and made a note to look for one of her favourite books, *What Bird Is That?* When she returned to collect the rest of her belongings from Melbourne. She knew her mother collected bird cards from packets of Tuckfield's Ty-nee Tips tea every time she bought a packet. Olive pasted them into special albums ready to give to Rose-Louise when she reached an age when she would enjoy them. She would have been quite chuffed to know Rose-Louise shared her interest.

*   *   *

Arthur gave up looking for the money he thought he'd hidden in a safe place. Instead, he banked any spare cash he managed to save and soon had enough to treat Olive for her birthday. Olive's face lit up with excitement and wonder when she heard what he'd planned for her.

She bubbled with excitement to be finally going on a one-way cruise and fly home package holiday.

'I've always dreamed of one day going on a cruise ship and not have to cook or clean for the whole time. I've heard the meal choices are absolutely amazing, and there will be so much to do on board, as well as exciting trips on shore. It's something I'll always cherish. I'll keep a diary so I can share my memories with Jane and Rose-Louise one day.'

They enjoyed their trip on the Mediterranean immensely, but Olive didn't get a chance to share memories with anyone. On the flight home, their plane crashed into the Indian Ocean, and there were no survivors. The crash made headline news in newspapers all round Australia for many days.

Jane felt gutted. It wasn't meant to happen like this. Her parents should still have years of happy retirement ahead of them. Jane had been planning to visit them as soon as she managed to cope well and be confident she could stay free of drugs. Now she would never have a chance to explain why she made the sudden decision to leave Melbourne or tell them how much she appreciated the help they'd given her when she arrived on their doorstop, pregnant and with very little money. It was a blessing that Arthur's erratic memory loss hadn't developed into Alzheimer's—she could still remember him as a loving, vital, supportive parent.

She knew she'd have to return to Melbourne and struggled with how she would explain to Rose-Louise that her beloved grandparents were dead and she would never see them again. Jane's grief and the ache in her heart almost engulfed her.

The flat in Carlton her parents had rented needed to be emptied out. Out of respect for them, the landlord gave Jane two weeks' grace and waived the rent for that period. Jane was stunned. She had no idea they didn't own the little unit. She needed to face the question of what to do with her parents' furniture and belongings. She felt uncomfortable being in her parent's home with them gone and thought Rose-Louise would have been unsettled also.

The landlord came to her rescue.

'I've found a replacement tenant who is also willing to pay a fair price for your parents' furniture and could move in as soon as the unit is vacated and cleaned.'

Jane tried to contact Kelly, longing to talk to a friend, someone who could give her comfort. When Jane finally called to see her, she was horrified to hear from a neighbour how Kelly had died.

'Kelly had been depressed for some time. Her best friend moved away without saying goodbye, and she felt abandoned when her family declared they didn't ever want to see her again if she didn't stop taking drugs. Drugs had too great a hold on her, and the police found her late one night collapsed on the footpath. Although rushed to the Royal Melbourne Hospital, she was pronounced dead on arrival. Such a sad waste, because she had the whole of her life ahead of her—if only she could have given up the drugs. It was heroin that killed her. It breaks up families, and because it's so costly, many folk sell their possessions and homes to pay for their addiction. Children go hungry, and addicts become emaciated, malnourished, and covered in weeping sores. Drugs have infiltrated every town and are in many of the schools, and they're being used by rich and poor people alike. These days, your next-door neighbour might be a dealer or an addict.'

Jane knew Kelly first dabbled in drugs after the cot death of her baby son before he'd lived six months. At first, Kelly thought taking drugs would only be a passing phase to numb her grief until she recovered from the shock of finding Bradley cold and blue early one morning. At that stage, there hadn't been a lot of information readily available about the effects of taking recreational drugs and the hold they could have on a person, even after using them only once or twice.

Olive had been more perceptive, noticing changes in Kelly's behaviour when she visited from time to time. Jane didn't, or wouldn't, acknowledge anything untoward had begun happening to Kelly at first. When Olive discussed the issue with Arthur, he couldn't be convinced a problem existed.

'We need to mind our own business, Olive! Jane has been so busy caring for her small daughter and working rostered hours at the supermarket, we should be pleased that she's found a friend in Kelly. Jane is much too smart to take drugs. Stop being an alarmist.'

Arthur could never see Jane as being anything but perfect. He wore blinkers in regard to any questionable activity when she was young, and as she grew older, he didn't ever change his views.

Following the death of her parents, Jane had given considerable thought about taking Rose-Louise with her back to Melbourne as company on the long drive. Afterwards, she'd been glad Bertha offered to have her stay until Jane returned. Rose-Louise always helped by assisting with Cheryl's care, exhibiting empathy and compassion, and Bertha came to love and respect the little girl with the big heart. She helped lift and change Cheryl and wasn't put out at all helping with her personal care. (Without Bertha and Cheryl, Rose-Louise's life would have been very different, and who knows whether she would have succumbed to society's pressures to sample drugs herself as she grew older.)

*　　*　　*

The two weeks Jane spent packing and sorting her parents' belongings were emotionally traumatic. At first, she tried sleeping in her own bed, in the room she'd shared with Rose-Louise for seven years. But she missed her daughter's presence so much she moved into the larger, sunnier room where Olive and Arthur had shared a double bed. Sleep still evaded her with ghosts of times past bringing both good memories and bad and often greatly upsetting her. After spending days feeling numb and achieving very little packing progress, she decided to seek help from a local doctor.

Fortunately, Jane found stability in that one area of her life—being able to consult with Dr Jones, the same GP who'd cared for her when she'd returned to Melbourne to stay with her parents after she'd left Barry for good. The doctor knew of her previous history of postnatal depression and that she had dabbled with marijuana and finally progressed, with help from Kelly's suppliers, to having an addiction to heroin. She proudly told him she was now clean but was having trouble sleeping due to the shock of her parents' deaths.

'I suggest you take a couple of Panadol tablets at night prior to going to bed for a couple of nights, then come back and see me in a few days' time. If you need more help, I will consider prescribing a mild sleeping pill or another course of antidepressants.' Having been able to confide her innermost feelings to someone who knew her history immediately made a difference to how she coped.

*   *   *

The elderly Ford Falcon seemed packed to bursting point when Jane returned to Mildura and her caravan park 'family'. Rose-Louise's grief for her grandparents was tempered slightly by her mother's return, bringing back her bicycle and other favourite toys. Jane had been living in a haze since the dreadful reality of her parents' death hit the headlines. She wasn't always thinking clearly at all. The enormity of emptying their home and tidying up tax and legal matters had left her emotionally drained. She returned to see Dr Jones before she left the Carlton flat for good, and he gave her a prescription for a mild antidepressant.

National and local newspapers continued to report and speculate on the ill-fated flight that should have brought her mother and father home from their holiday of a lifetime. There were sightings of debris floating at sea, and some was found distributed on isolated island shores. But for months, none of it could be linked conclusively to the missing plane, and no personal items were retrieved. Jane's relationship with two of the victims of that ill-fated flight was soon revealed to the local community, who offered friendship and support.

When Jane ran away from drug contacts in the city, she didn't expect to be located by drug traffickers when she lived hundreds of miles away in the country. A few days after he had originally approached Jane, the predator began watching her more closely. He watched, waiting for her to need her next hit. He wondered why she didn't seek him out after giving her a sample of what he could supply. He didn't know his packet of powder remained hidden high up in her caravan cupboard.

The predator approached Jane again when she was most vulnerable—soon after her parents had been reported missing. However, her determination to stay clean gave her the courage to send him away. She knew she had to be strong and stay in control. Her quality of life and that of her daughter depended on her.

'I don't want anything to do with drugs. Go away! If you keep pestering me, I'll report you to the police.'

She knew if she went to the police, they would probably find out about her history of drug-taking, and then they mightn't believe her. She would be on shaky ground. But the reappearance of the predator jogged her memory, and she searched the top cupboard in the caravan and found the packet she'd put up there almost a year ago. This time when she looked at it, she felt contempt for what she knew might have happened if she'd used it. Feeling disgusted that it had been sitting in the caravan for so long, she took it to the community toilet block and flushed the contents of the packet down a toilet. She thought she would feel relief, but instead fear invaded every part of her body.

The predator, who hadn't been seen near the caravan park for many months, started appearing frequently in the park. (In fact, he'd spent some time in gaol after getting caught manufacturing and selling drugs to schoolboys attending the local high school.) He'd seen newspaper reports of the plane crash, and some reports had printed her name and photo with those of her parents.

The predator tried approaching her again. This time he hoped he would get repeated requests for his packages. Two days later, Rose-Louise came rushing into the caravan after school and very importantly unpacked a small packet of powder from her school bag and handed it carefully to her mother. Jane felt the contents of her stomach churning, making her want to vomit up its contents.

'What is that, and where did you get it?' she demanded.

'The nice man who spoke to you the other day said you asked him to give me this packet to deliver to you. He made sure he was giving it to the right little girl. He knew your name and my name and that we lived in a caravan in Riverview Park next to Bertha. I told him I would give it to you as soon as I got home from school. Aren't you pleased with me, Mummy?'

Jane was aghast at the predator's cunning. How horribly sick it was to use her daughter as a courier for his filthy drugs! *What could she tell Rose-Louise without frightening her?*

Jane wondered how best to deal with the situation. If she moved from the caravan park, she knew the predator would manage to find her. Jane decided to allow Rose-Louise to start riding her bicycle to school each day, and she would meet up with her to ride back home at the end of the school day.

Two days later, the predator saw Rose-Louise playing near the school-ground fence at lunchtime and beckoned to her.

'Mummy said she doesn't need any of your packages, and I'm not to speak to you any more,' she called to him.

'I wasn't going to ask you to deliver anything more, but tell her I need to be paid this time—and soon!' he replied as he walked away.

The new packet of powder resided high up in the caravan cupboard. Jane wanted to flush it down the toilet too but knew she'd still have the predator breathing down her neck wanting payment. On some days, she carried it with her to give back to him if he approached her. She knew she could be in trouble if drugs were found on her person. Slowly, insidiously, she was being drawn into his web.

After her parents died, Jane struggled daily with feelings of loss and loneliness. Learning what had become of Kelly had added more feelings of guilt to her overloaded depressed emotions, and Bertha felt alarmed at the depth of her friend's despair. Even Bertha's welcome proximity and support wasn't enough to prevent what happened next.

It took only two weeks before Jane succumbed, and from then on, though she tried several times to break free, she didn't succeed. She soon used up most of the money from the sale of her parents' furniture and slipped behind in her caravan rent. She borrowed from Bertha and sold everything she could to feed her habit. When caught stealing, she received a caution the first time, but she was sentenced to time in gaol for subsequent thefts and for being in possession of drugs of addiction. To her shame, she even resorted to selling to schoolchildren.

Without Bertha stepping in and looking after Rose-Louise while Jane was incarcerated, her daughter would have been taken from her and put into care.

CHAPTER 10

Anna and Derek

Anna and Derek were married three months before Luke was born, and Derek became the only father Luke ever knew. His birth certificate stated his father's identity and whereabouts as unknown, and his biological father died without knowing he'd fathered any children.

Derek's love for Anna was strong and unwavering, even though he knew she'd been pregnant with another man's child when they married. He loved Luke unconditionally too, despite all the challenges their son presented. He looked a lot like Derek. A good-looking lad with dark curly hair, his dark brown eyes were framed by long lashes, and his skin always remained flawless. Anna and Derek felt blessed to have Luke, as they were told they would be unable to have children together after Derek contracted mumps two years after their marriage.

They had known each other since grade three. However, they'd gone their separate ways after leaving school. Derek trained to sell real estate and only dated intermittently after his long-time girlfriend succumbed to cervical cancer. Anna had qualified as a preschool teacher. They'd never previously considered being more than good friends. Anna dated a local policeman for several years, but when she intimated she longed to settle down and have children, he applied and accepted a transfer interstate before telling her he didn't want to have a serious relationship with her any more.

After that bombshell announcement, Anna went a little wild one evening, leaving a dance with an acquaintance from a nearby town. They ended up sleeping together in her little unit above the bread shop in Port Vincent.

Such an action was uncharacteristic of Anna, and her guilt was profound. Next morning, they went their separate ways and didn't meet again, although they'd exchanged addresses and phone numbers. Over the years, she had often wondered why she kept his details tucked inside the Bible she rarely opened. Their encounter had occurred four months after she'd been with her policeman boyfriend, so with confirmation of her pregnancy, she had no doubt who had fathered her baby.

When she was six weeks pregnant, she bumped into Derek buying some bread rolls from the bakery. She was returning to her unit after picking up some groceries and visiting her local doctor, where the pregnancy had been confirmed. Anna's GP had known her for many years. They'd first met in his surgery while she was a young teenager still in school. She'd been on the receiving end of a very hard pitch while practicing as a catcher on the softball team in her first year of secondary school. He'd treated her for a dislocated thumb after reassuring her she hadn't broken any bones.

Pregnancy testing wasn't done routinely in the middle sixties. The only tests available involved a live mouse or rabbit being injected with the woman's urine and then killed to examine the ovaries for changes. However, her GP authorised the test for Anna, as she'd presented as a visibly distressed single girl whom he'd known for years. She'd waited several days for the result, and when Derek met up with her, he could tell she was distraught.

'Hello, Anna, are you OK?'

'Yes, I'll be all right as soon as I get inside and have a cuppa.'

'Here, let me help you,' he replied as he reached for her groceries.

Derek helped her up the stairs and, once inside, flipped on the kettle and looked at her closely. His concern was too much for her in her fragile state. She burst into tears. As he comforted her, she explained the reason for her distress punctuated by deep, heaving sobs. Her normally flawless facial features soon became marred by blotchy puffiness. She hadn't meant to tell anyone, at least not until she had sorted out her feelings and how she would deal with the situation. This set of circumstances was way beyond anything she had envisaged for her future. She felt totally drained, even before she'd explored how her unplanned pregnancy would have a flow-on effect on her family and friends.

Somehow, she knew she could trust Derek as he stepped forward to support her and held her close to his body. She'd desperately needed to talk to someone. Derek convinced her he would respect her wishes and not discuss the content of their conversation with anyone. At that moment, she knew he was indeed a special friend, and their friendship and respect for each other had been there for most of their lives. She felt comfortable and safe with him. He was sympathetic and non-judgemental, and he held her until all her sobs were spent.

Getting rid of her baby had never been considered an option. This had been true, right from the very first day she learned of her pregnancy. Her doctor told her of places she could go to await the arrival of her baby if she chose to give her child up for adoption. Anna loved children, hence her choice to train as a preschool teacher, and the thought of carrying a baby in her womb for nine months then giving it away—even to a childless couple who desperately wanted a family—filled her with horror. No, even if she was going to remain single, she was determined to keep her precious child.

Anna and Derek made a handsome couple. Their families were happy when they started going out together—until it looked as though they were seriously contemplating marriage. Then it appeared as though religious differences would cause friction. Derek had been raised a Catholic, while Anna had been brought up Protestant and had attended church and Sunday school regularly as a child.

In this era, Protestants still crossed the street rather than walk close to a Catholic church, and children of both denominations shouted insulting slogans at each other. One commonly chanted by Protestants was 'Catholic dogs, sitting on logs, eating maggots out of frogs.'

Mixed marriages were condemned by both churches and were often doomed to fail due to family or church interference.

'Our religious differences are nobody else's business! If we are sure of our feelings for each other, we'll work together to overcome obstacles as they come along,' said Anna while it was still early days in their relationship.

As it turned out, the controversy about which church they'd attended as children proved to be only a small challenge compared with what tested them in the future. When Anna's pregnancy became obvious, they decided against any more discussions and wisely kept the baby's parentage to themselves. At least, their families were eventually united in support of their marriage to avoid the stigma of illegitimacy.

Derek wasn't a practising Catholic, and Anna had become disillusioned with organised religion, so they decided to go with the flow and leave further decisions about churches for the future. It didn't seem a big issue for either of them. Eventually, Anna took a course of instruction in Catholicism, and they agreed to bring up their child and subsequent children in the Catholic faith.

Working in the local kindergarten proved to be an ideal job for Anna, as she met many mothers of young children who were also expecting babies at the same time as her baby was due. She attended antenatal and exercise classes and had the usual check-ups and tests requested by her doctor. After her initial emotional upheaval of finding she was expecting, Anna embraced her pregnancy as a blessing, as it had also brought Derek back into her life and a healthy glow to her appearance.

She took prescribed vitamins with added folate and made sure she ate healthy food and exercised regularly, determined to do everything within her power to give her baby the best chance of a healthy start in life. Two weeks before their marriage, Anna and Derek received some news that left them feeling shocked and upset. Anna had gone confidently for a routine ultrasound and found out she was carrying a boy. The ultrasound also revealed her baby boy had a neural tube defect. She was informed that her baby would be born with spina bifida.

They were told—and they subsequently verified the information at the local library—that spina bifida occurred when some of the spinal vertebrae didn't form properly around part of the baby's spinal cord. The condition varies in severity according to the size and location of the malformation, whether it is covered, and which spinal nerves are involved. All nerves located below the malformation could be affected to some degree.

Derek felt inadequate as he held a sobbing Anna close to his chest.

'You can't marry me now, Derek.'

'What are you talking about? I am marrying you, for better or for worse. Let's not make rash decisions without thinking and talking things through. I've always cared for you, but now I am sure my feelings are much stronger. I want to spend the rest of my life with you . . . and this baby boy. I have no qualms about not being the biological father. I already feel as though this baby is part of me.'

'But what about him having spina bifida? Although it looks as though his impairment is only minimal, we have to face the fact he may have muscle weakness of the legs or even paralysis. He may even have to wear braces on his legs or need a wheelchair. He could have bowel or bladder problems as well.'

'OK, remember I've read the literature too, but hopefully because the lesion is low down on his spine and not uncovered, he won't have seizures or require a shunt. Even if he's born with deformed feet, uneven hips, or a curved spine, we can cope if we work together.'

'But you have a choice. We didn't make this baby together. There is still time for you to opt out. You could meet someone else and have a healthy baby one day.'

'I don't want to meet someone else, and I'm looking forward to the arrival of our son. Didn't we agree to acknowledge him as my biological son even before he is born? So our son is going to have a disability. What sort of a father would I be if I packed up and left whenever an obstacle presented itself? I chose to marry you because I'm sure I love you and I realise I've always cared deeply for you.'

'But it's all happened so quickly because I'm pregnant. I hope we're not rushing into marriage for the wrong reasons. Sometimes I wonder if we would be contemplating marriage at all if I wasn't having this baby.'

'I think we would have gotten around to it eventually. It's not as though we were total strangers, and we've both been involved in relationships with other partners. I love you, Anna. I know this is sudden, but it feels so right . . . and our son's health challenges may give us an opportunity to both bond with him and for us to truly work together. It's not being dropped on us at the time he's born. We have time to read and learn as much as we can to plan for our future as a family together. Let's face it, those other conditions we read about—depression, skin problems, or gastrointestinal conditions that could afflict him when he's older—they can occur in other children or adults too, even without having spina bifida.'

'I love you too, Derek. I'm so glad you came back into my life. It's great that we can talk things out. I feel so much at ease with you, and I won't let you down.'

'Perhaps, now that we know we're going to be parents of a special baby boy, we should start thinking about finding a name for him.'

*   *   *

Anna didn't discriminate between any of the children in her care at the kindergarten. Some were of Chinese origin, some Indian, as well as some from Sri Lanka, Syria, and Australia. There was a girl with Down syndrome and a boy on the cusp of the autism spectrum. She loved them all and knew she would love, with all her heart, the little person growing inside her. She knew that although there would be some tough times, he would bring them many blessings too.

As potential parents of a child with spina bifida, Anna and Derek were determined to leave no stone unturned to provide their son with every opportunity to reach his full potential. They read extensively and consulted knowledgeable health professionals and the Spina Bifida Association. They discussed how parents cared for the worst affected in contrast with spina bifida children who were hardly affected at all. They hoped their son would be one of the lucky ones.

They learned there were four different types of spina bifida and the actual cause hadn't been conclusively isolated, although heredity or a lack of folate in the mother's diet during pregnancy were considered possible contributing causes, along with environmental and nutritional factors.

'I included folate in the multivitamins specially designed for pregnancy I've been taking since I knew I was going to have a baby, and I haven't heard of anyone in my family with spina bifida,' Anna said after they'd read about folate requirements for a healthy pregnancy.

Anna couldn't see any point in delving into the medical history of the father's family as it would only be distressing to too many people and would achieve nothing positive in the immediate future. There would be a time and a place for that later on if it became necessary.

'There's no point doing any further investigations now. What's done is done.'

Anna hadn't told Derek who'd fathered their child. He didn't want to know and hadn't asked. Anna agreed nothing would be gained if disclosures were made, and after a while, their son's parentage held no importance to them. They were determined that caring for their small son would be their top priority.

Anna opted to have a caesarean section, although expert advice had decreed she could safely give birth vaginally without endangering the baby or complicating his condition. She knew that with Derek's help, she could cope with the aftermath of a surgical intervention as well as caring for their newborn son.

As far as could be determined, Luke—as he would be called (his name meaning 'light giving')—was a category three spina bifida.

This meant he would be born with a meningocele—a condition where spinal fluid is covered by the membranes which surround the spinal cord and protrude out through an abnormal vertebral opening. This malformation wouldn't have a nerve supply and might not be covered by a skin layer. They learned he may have few or no symptoms or could have complete paralysis with bladder and bowel dysfunction. They would have to wait for some time to be sure of the outcome. Meanwhile, they were determined to celebrate every milestone Luke achieved along the way.

They shared their wedding with family and former school friends in St Michael's Catholic Church. Anna wore a simple full-length gown made of delicate cream brocade with a high waistline, short cap sleeves, and a slightly scooped neckline. When she'd started looking for her wedding dress, she'd been horrified to find bridal wear was tagged with what seemed to be excessively high prices. With the loss of her wage as her pregnancy advanced and all other expenses associated with their marriage, she opted for an elegant evening gown that could be shortened and reused in the future. Derek invested in a new suit of a deep-grey wool-mix fabric he would later use for work.

St Michaels' Catholic Church was where Derek had taken his first communion, and just by chance, the elderly priest who had presided over the congregation all those years ago was back in a relieving capacity for twelve months—that included Anna and Derek's wedding day. They opted not to have attendants, and the ceremony went off without a hitch to the accompaniment of music played on the elderly pipe organ by an equally elderly organist. A finger-food reception was held in the parish hall before the happy couple sped off in their car, which was liberally decorated with wedding slogans.

Anna's pregnancy hadn't been widely publicised, but she was sure many friends and family members had added two and two together as their courtship had been very brief. As Derek had been living at home, it proved convenient to move into Anna's tiny flat. Straight after their honeymoon spent in the quaint town of Hahndorf, they began searching for roomier accommodation more suitable for a couple with a new baby.

They were given tenancy of a friend's townhouse, free of charge in Hahndorf in the Adelaide hills, for their honeymoon. Hahndorf was settled by nineteenth-century Lutheran migrants and was renowned for its original German-style architecture and artisanal food.

Numerous wineries in the nearby Adelaide Hills tempted them with tours and tastings, but they were mostly happy to explore the quaint local shops and sample the many types of different foods.

Working at the preschool proved challenging as her pregnancy became more obvious. Sitting on any of the small children's chairs soon turned out to be impossible, and the packing away of heavy equipment was undertaken by other staff members or willing work-experience helpers. Many of the mothers of her preschoolers were also pregnant and often shared their experiences and advice with her, while they were rostered for milk and fruit or playground duty. When Sylvia, the mother of a little blond boy, learnt that Anna had chosen to have a caesarean section, she shared her experience.

'I have a small pelvis, so I had no option but to have an elective caesarean. I coped well because I'd been cautioned not to refuse pain relief in the first couple of days. If I'd let it get on top of me, I wouldn't have managed. My husband was a great help to me too after I came home from hospital,' Sylvia volunteered.

It was an exciting time for Anna and Derek, and they didn't dwell on the fact their son would be born with a malformation that would require surgery soon after his birth. Everyone rejoiced for them as Anna's pregnancy visibly progressed.

Two weeks before Anna's due date, Luke arrived quickly and safely in the middle of the night in mid September. He was delivered vaginally and entered the world without any undue drama. The birth notice announced:

'To Anna and Derek, a boy, six pounds, twelve ounces. Mother and baby doing well.'

CHAPTER 11

Luke

Anna and Derek became alarmed when it was suggested Luke could be baptised before he was taken to theatre to have his meningocele surgically repaired. She and Derek had been told he would be having a straightforward procedure, even though it wouldn't be apparent for some time whether his initial condition would affect his quality of life. After being reassured, they agreed to the simple baptism ceremony, which comforted them while Luke was in the operating theatre. While Anna and Derek sat waiting for him to return to the ward, they made a pledge to each other.

'There must be many young people born with spina bifida who could use some extra assistance in some way. No matter what the outcome is with Luke, let's put some time and money each year into making someone else's life with spina bifida a little easier.'

*   *   *

Luke was considered to be average, or just slightly above average, when growth and progress milestones were assessed. He sat up at six months, crawled at thirteen months, and walked at a year and a half.

Taking his first steps brought great relief and rejoicing for Anna and Derek—the parents of the little boy whose condition at birth could have sentenced him to life in a wheelchair. However, they had an anxious waiting period, prior to him attending kindergarten, as he was slow to become potty-trained.

During the operation soon after his birth, the surgeon found Luke's neural defect to be more extensive than expected, and they were advised he would have some level of disability.

Was Luke's congenital neural defect going to affect his bowel or bladder control?

This question always lurked at the back of his parents' minds as each year passed. They felt lucky Luke showed very little outward indication of his birth condition, although his legs tired after prolonged activity. They hoped Luke's disability would still be minimal. As they watched him grow, Anna and Derek felt blessed to see him becoming a happy, healthy boy and ultimately a strong, well-adjusted young man.

Derek felt particularly grateful Luke had come into his life as he'd had a severe case of mumps two years after he and Anna were married, which he learned could render him sterile. It coincided with when they began trying to have another baby to complete their family.

Luke didn't totally escape his spina bifida condition—his bowels were not always cooperative. However, by drinking lots of water, using an aperient, enjoying packets of liquorice, and doing exercises to strengthen his legs and abdominal muscles, he managed to keep reasonably regular. He also had access to small enema sachets whenever necessary. On two occasions as a toddler, before his personal management regime was worked out, he required admission to hospital to ease his pain and evacuate his bowels.

Luke's bladder ended up being slightly more troublesome, as he needed to use a catheter tube at regular intervals to empty it properly so he would remain dry. Until this routine was established, he suffered from repeated urinary infections. By the time he turned five, he could proudly insert his own catheter regularly, four times a day.

Luke took his bladder and bowel care in his stride. After all, he didn't know what he would have experienced if the nerves had not been damaged. (Anna had been assured that Luke being born vaginally and not waiting for his scheduled caesarean section had not adversely affected his condition.)

Derek and Anna were supportive in every way but didn't coddle him. He was encouraged to participate in sports and excelled on his trampoline, in swimming, and in rollerblading. He'd received a mountain bike when he was eight years old and did amazing manoeuvres over all types of terrain. Only his teachers, his Cub leaders, a close neighbour, and family were told of his disability. Anna and Derek couldn't see anything to be gained by telling his schoolmates. Luke didn't see it as a topic for discussion either.

School camps and sleepovers at his friends' homes were probably the only activities Luke missed out on in his early years. He became quite creative with reasons why he couldn't attend. However, he was encouraged to have friends stay over at his home, where he could continue with his usual catheter routine without questions being asked.

In primary school, an aide collected him from class at the same time each morning to supervise his catheter care. A special room with an adjacent toilet was made available for his use with a cupboard for his equipment. As two classmates were called out regularly at different times for supervised administration of medications, Luke's regular exits were never questioned.

Scouting formed a large part of Luke's life. Apart from his body's everyday challenges, he revelled in the opportunities to test his capabilities in other areas. He joined the Cubs as soon as he turned eight and, in his second year, became a sixer. He worked hard to obtain different badges and particularly enjoyed earning the ones for gardening and swimming. These interests were to become a lifelong passion. As the Scouting movement relied heavily on its volunteer leaders, Derek happily took part as a group leader, and Anna joined as a volunteer. One of their proudest moments was when Luke became a Queen's Scout.

Anna and Derek were immensely gratified by all he could achieve despite his disabilities. They hadn't forgotten their pledge to help others who found themselves in situations similar to their own. They also honoured their commitment to be involved with the Spina Bifida Association.

Anna returned to working in the kindergarten when an opportunity arose soon after Luke started school. However, she began to suffer from excessive tiredness, which ultimately led to a totally unexpected diagnosis of a wholeheartedly welcomed pregnancy! Derek's ecstatic reaction affected everyone around him. Knowing he could father a child after all was wonderful news.

Anna's second pregnancy was uneventful, and nothing untoward was detected during her routine medical consultations. They called their perfectly healthy daughter Sally (which meant princess). She grew to be a petite image of her mother with the same flawless skin and curly blond hair. Anna and Derek were both over the moon to have a daughter and very grateful to see her free of any disability. Not surprisingly, Luke excelled as a very caring brother for little Sally. His loving, unselfish parents were great role models.

Sally accepted Luke's condition as normal and amused Anna when, at four years old, Sally had asked innocently, 'When will I start using catheters, Mummy?'

She had noticed a bundle of catheters stored in the bathroom cupboard and been told they were for Luke (Anna uttered a grateful prayer of thanks that her daughter wouldn't need them).

Derek progressed well with his real estate business, and they soon moved into a well-appointed four-bedroom brick home high on the clifftop at Port Vincent, with unparalleled views across the water. They'd bought a large block enabling them to install an in-ground swimming pool surrounded by a large rambling garden. (Although Port Vincent had a dedicated swimming area at the beach, the tides governed when the water was deep enough for swimming.) Fruit trees were slotted in among shrubs and flowers, and vegetables appeared randomly wherever there was a suitable space. When the children were small, they spent hours swinging on a tandem swing, sharing fun, and competing in the pool. It proved to be a very popular meeting place for neighbourhood children.

Both children did well in school, and Sally excelled in swimming and netball, becoming a coach and mentor in her early teens. The Girl Guide movement played a large part in her growing years, and like Luke, she enjoyed the challenges of gaining different badges, which she carefully sewed on her uniform. While Luke turned his hobby of gardening into a rewarding landscaping career, Sally (possibly influenced by the family involvement with the Spina Bifida Association) wanted to become a prosthetist/orthotist. However, because she also wanted to return to the country after she graduated, she decided there would be more opportunities for employment if she trained to be a physiotherapist. With her parents' help, she was soon able to buy a two-bedroomed unit in North Adelaide. Whenever Anna and Derek visited, they had somewhere to stay overnight.

After graduation, she obtained a position at the Royal Adelaide Hospital to gain as much experience as possible before applying for various positions in South Australia and other states.

Luke attended technical school and lived at home at first. As his vision and expertise at redesigning landscapes gained popularity, he was in demand all around Yorke Peninsula. He soon chose to live in a transportable home on a large block on the outskirts of Wattle Flat, large enough to include a swimming pool. He set up his property as a showplace for his business.

On the whole, Luke kept fit and healthy, apart from occasional urinary infections and bouts of constipation. He maintained contact with the Spina Bifida Association, as did the rest of his family.

The name of Luke's biological father had never been mentioned. Derek hadn't ever questioned Anna, as he'd loved both children equally from the moment they were born. He felt very blessed to have them and Anna in his life, but there was always the niggling question of whether they would someday need to give Luke information about his origins.

They trusted they would know when the time was right, little knowing how things would develop in the future.

Derek and Anna lived fulfilling lives. Their love for one another strengthened with each passing year. Even though there had been some medical challenges with Luke, they worked through them together, acknowledging they were lucky to be able to do this. By being involved with other people with various degrees of spina bifida, they learned they were fortunate he had only minor complications from long-term intermittent catheterisation compared to other males about his age who were following similar regimes. Some suffered from urethral/scrotal situations that included bleeding, urethritis, stricture, and epididymitis—especially those who were confined to wheelchairs.

Luke's bladder-related crises were relatively minor. They consisted of urinary tract infections with occasional bleeding but no bladder stones. With specialist guidance, Luke was introduced very early to a variety of catheters and lubricants to find out what suited him best. He'd learnt he needed to take care to always attend to his catheters in scrupulously clean surroundings. He took vitamin C and cranberry juice as prophylactics against infections. This seemed to be successful most of the time.

Luke had known from an early age that Derek wasn't his biological father. At first, he had no idea what that meant, as Derek had always been his dad. People often remarked how alike they looked, with the same brown eyes and dark-brown curly hair and even the way they walked. Later on, Luke questioned Anna occasionally, and at one time, when she rediscovered the name and address inside the cover of her Bible, she debated with Derek whether to tell Luke the name of his biological father.

Anna finally decided. 'The only real need to tell him would be to check out any medical history in the family. But if he insists, he has a right to know.

It was an uncharacteristic fling for me when his father and I had overindulged with alcohol. He didn't know about my pregnancy, and I can't see any good reason to bring about soul-searching or heartache for any of us now.'

So the matter wasn't pursued. As a teenager, part of Luke's sex education had been to point out that one-night stands could result in unwanted pregnancies, which often resulted in abortion or babies being given up for adoption. Luke knew he was fortunate to have both his parents, and the identity of his biological father was of no interest to him, although he knew Anna would tell him if he asked sometime in the future.

Finally, it was too late.

CHAPTER 12

The Crash

The accident on a major highway in South Australia made headlines nationally, and television coverage was swamped with images taken from every possible angle.

Semi-trailer Laden with Sheep Capsizes at Notorious Intersection

Lone Occupant of Subaru Brumby Ute Killed when a Transport Carrying Sheep Capsized near Port Wakefield. Frightened and Injured Sheep Caused Traffic Hazard

Male Occupant in Subaru Utility Killed Instantly When Sheep Transport Capsized at Controversial Intersection

Scattered Sheep Difficult to Find after Semi Capsized after Colliding with Red Subaru Brumby, Killing the Ute Driver Instantly

Yorke Peninsula Farmer Died at the Accident Scene and a Large Number of Injured Sheep were Destroyed after Semi-Trailer

Loaded with Sheep Overturned at Intersection on Main Highway to Adelaide near Port Wakefield

The early reports said the identity of the occupant of the red Subaru Brumby wouldn't be made public until relatives were notified.

Felicity was home alone watching the news while she ate her lunch. The pictures showing on her television set were extremely graphic.

Injured and dying sheep were all round the overturned vehicle. Thankfully pictures of the Subaru driver or the extent of his injuries weren't shown, while the semi-trailer driver was seen to be in shock and extremely distressed.

Anyone could see the ute was a write-off. The right-hand side was totally crushed, and despite the driver not being identified, the number plate could be clearly seen for a brief moment. Felicity heard that the occupant of the utility was reported to have died at the accident scene while waiting for the Jaws of Life to arrive.

Unsure what she had seen and not wanting to believe what had flashed on her screen, Felicity began surfing all the TV channels. She started to shake, and things around her drifted in and out of focus. She struggled to stay in control and kept searching for the elusive frame that identified the red Subaru. She knew there weren't many vehicles of that colour and make in the district. Her gut told her the unidentified driver had been Barry. She considered the unlikely idea that someone other than Barry was driving his ute, but she knew the odds were against it.

He'd told her where he'd be driving that morning, and she knew where he would have been about the time of the accident. Realisation hit her.

Her husband was dead.

She couldn't recall how long she stood frozen in front of her television, hoping desperately to bring back the news report of the accident. She watched more local news, followed by parliamentary and reports from overseas wars, but information about the highway catastrophe wasn't repeated. It seemed like no time at all before the telephone rang and the doorbell chimed together. Soon there were people everywhere offering support and sympathy and bringing casseroles and plates of sandwiches. (How she wished she and Barry had received this sort of support after Jack died, instead of the feelings of suspicion and unease that lingered even now, many years later.)

Felicity's life drifted around her for many weeks. There were all sorts of formalities to deal with, and nothing seemed real. It seemed as though she was sitting outside a bubble of her life looking in. The horrible pictures of the accident were imprinted on her mind, and she'd wake up in the night bathed in perspiration, desperately hoping it was all a dream.

It felt surreal to have that accident happen that day. The evening before had been a rare but special occasion. They'd gone to bed early and talked for ages about all manner of things.

They'd made love, and with both their needs sated, they'd slept curled up together. They'd hugged, and Barry had kissed her gently before he'd driven off down the driveway. After working through some rocky times over the years, Felicity cherished the fact they had parted in a happy state of mind and knew she'd treasure those moments forever.

The local gossips' comments didn't take long to start circulating.

'How will Felicity cope with losing Barry? She's not one of us. I bet she'll pack up and leave the district. Did he have any life or funeral insurance? She could end up being our very own Merry Widow, 'cos I've wondered if everything was love and laughter in their marriage, even after Jack died. Pity Barry didn't have longer to enjoy running his own farm.'

'Who do you think will be asked to cater for the funeral, the CWA or the Uniting Church? I wonder if she has access to ready cash? Barry was following a lot of his old man's traditions, and Jack always controlled the cheque book.'

'Will she try and work the farm on her own, or do you think she'll move back interstate? She isn't a local. She wasn't born here, and she's never really fitted in. She keeps suggesting things she thinks should be changed or upgraded. She'll soon find out how hard it is to change things that have been in place for years. Good luck to her! Do you think she will sell up or lease the farm?'

Although they'd had relationship difficulties during their marriage, Felicity felt glad the extent of their troubles hadn't been common knowledge in the wider community. They always managed to appear in tune when mixing with friends or attending public functions. They'd often walked hand in hand, and to some observers, this translated as having a close relationship. (Barry and Felicity knew they were less likely to stumble on uneven footpaths if they were connected to each other).

From time to time over the following weeks the spare refrigerator on her veranda was stocked up with food, and practical help was offered from the menfolk in the district. They were pleased to be appreciated when they offered to look after the maintenance of her vehicles and assist Felicity with the heavy jobs around the farm. It felt strange because they didn't welcome outsiders readily, but now one of their own had died so tragically they were finally being supportive and even protective in anticipating her needs.

Many of the wives began to be suspicious of the time their menfolk spent with her.

After all, she was a very attractive woman in her early forties and bound to be lonely! She sensed occasional hostile sideways glances when she shopped in the local supermarket. Occasionally, one of the wives would visit while her husband did some maintenance on machinery for her—almost as though she didn't trust either of them!

She found the thought of being interested in one particular husband hilarious—a big hairy, heavily tattooed brute whose permanently black fingernails frequently scratched the crease in his ample backside. Even in her darkest moments, the idea of 'tangling' with him made her feel like bringing up her breakfast.

Felicity's frozen-in-time sensations and the unfairness of the situation constantly tumbled through her thoughts. Somehow she managed to arrange the funeral, although after the accident, she lived in a fog of disbelief for several months. Although she wasn't unduly concerned about outside appearances, Felicity honoured Barry's memory with a simple respectful ceremony and hoped he would have been proud of how the story of his life was presented. The townspeople and farming community turned out in force.

*   *   *

There were mutterings at the cemetery when a tall auburn-haired woman attached herself to the line of mourners and paid her respects at the graveside after accepting an ear of wheat to place on the coffin.

'Haven't seen her around here before. Wonder if she's one of the nieces. I think both Belinda and Rebecca had at least one daughter. She looks a lot like Barry.'

'Apart from that stunning redhead, there are other family groups and several people I don't know. There's a young man who looks like a younger version of Barry too. Maybe they are distant relatives—second or third cousins, maybe?'

'It must be over twenty years since his first wife walked out on him. Someone said Jane died, so she won't be here. I believe she had a troubled life, and it was cut short too soon. It can be a bit uncomfortable if former spouses turn up to funerals pretending to be heartbroken.'

'I heard a few interstate friends have returned for the funeral, and that Johnstone woman who left here about twenty years ago is here too. She went to school with Barry.'

The town gossips, curious about Rose-Louise's identity, were disappointed that day. The golf club had won the right to cater for the afternoon tea following the brief ceremony at the graveside, but Rose-Louise opted not to go back to the clubhouse for refreshments. Instead, she drove down the coast to where she'd booked a three-day 'stay for two nights and get the third one free' deal in a complex of cabins overlooking the ocean. In fact, the whole story regarding the identity of the auburn-haired stranger with dark-brown eyes didn't whizz around the town until much later. It seemed she'd disappeared when she left Wattle Flat after the graveside service.

The locals had a field day. Theories which seemed plausible at first were soon embellished, and people who couldn't wait to hear the correct or slightly adjusted version managed to make something up that sounded believable. Despite the fact many of them knew Barry and Jane tried unsuccessfully for many years to have children, none of them hit the jackpot by guessing Rose-Louise's parentage.

*   *   *

Felicity struggled to cope on the farm on her own after Barry's death. Although there'd been times in their marriage she'd longed to choose how she spent her days and nights, the reality thrust upon her now wasn't always appealing. From the time Jack died, Barry protected his right to run his farm. Felicity found it hard to deal with Barry's compulsion to be a one-man band, doing everything alone when she longed to be helpful. She tried to tell him he had nothing to prove to anyone. She wanted to move on from the past and work on their life together. But it didn't happen.

During their marriage, she'd often felt alone, and although she'd tried to fit in by joining many local groups, she would rather have spent quality time with her husband.

After Barry's tragic death, the people of Wattle Flat rallied round and helped Felicity until the wheat crop was reaped and taken to the silos at Port Giles. After reaping, they mostly left her to fend as best she could on her own. How she hated the fact Barry neglected to teach her about farming techniques or about managing their finances either. She'd wanted to work closely with him, but after pleading her case on many occasions, she'd given up and found other activities to fill her time.

Ownership of the farm wasn't in dispute. When they'd married, Barry and Felicity updated their wills and directed all assets to each other. Felicity's dilemma was how to manage the farm now that it all belonged to her.

When she consulted her solicitor, he replied,

'If you don't feel able to work the farm on your own, you need to examine all your options. You might find the local farmers aren't very helpful after a while. You could employ workers, but this may not be a viable proposition. Other options include share farming, leasing, or selling the farm. Both your neighbours may be interested in leasing now or buying at a later date. If you want to stay in the farmhouse but sell the land, you'll need to see a surveyor to set this up. Another thought would be to use some of Barry's life insurance and superannuation and value-add to the farm if you can think of some way to use the property to bring in extra income.'

*　　*　　*

After the people of Wattle Flat and surrounding districts helped with the harvest, Felicity set a three-year lease in position with Peter, whose farm adjoined her property. Peter, the same Peter who had been Barry's best friend at school, had moved back from interstate to manage his father's farm when his dad was cruelly felled by Parkinson's disease soon after his mother (Dorothy) had passed away. When his dad died in Melaleuca Aged Care facility two years later, Peter took over as the owner of the farm he'd grown up on.

He'd left the farm near Clapper's Cove as a young man with a growing family and worked hard to finally be able to buy a property interstate considered to be one of the best in that district. However, he was grateful only one of his sons showed interest in farming, as his small farm would not have been able to fully support more than one family. His other son showed great aptitude for words and worked as a journalist and had aspirations to write travel books. He'd taken after Dorothy, his grandmother, who'd also enjoyed writing.

When Peter returned to the family farm, he found it was run-down, and fences and tanks needed replacing. He'd agonised over whether to move back interstate and try to resurrect his family farm. In its present condition, the sale price would be very low.

Cropping had been discontinued several years earlier when his father's header had caught fire and couldn't be replaced because his equipment insurance hadn't been renewed that year. Only a few paddocks were fenced securely enough to contain the small flock of sheep, a prize Brangus bull, and a small herd of twenty cattle. At least the large hay shed could accommodate many bales of hay.

With the opportunity to lease the Clapper farm and equipment, it meant Peter had a chance of putting in crops on both properties. On the downside, his wife wasn't keen to trade her modern home for an old farmhouse requiring considerable maintenance. Their marriage had become shaky over the past years, so they'd decided if they lived apart for twelve months, they would either get back together or separate for good and get divorced. He knew he could leave his interstate farm in the care of his older son, who would eventually inherit it anyway.

Felicity had really wanted to 'share farm', but she knew she wouldn't be much of an asset until she learnt more about how things worked. After sorting out the details of the farm leasing agreement and being assured Peter was willing to allow her to help from time to time, Felicity decided to take a holiday and sort out her priorities.

Although feeling devastated from time to time, Felicity knew she had to make some difficult decisions. Barry had only managed the farm for a short time before his untimely death. As they hadn't been able to have any children, Felicity wanted to do something with her inheritance in his memory. With Barry's insurance, his superannuation, and income in some form from the farm, she was very grateful to be financially secure.

Finally, her life was to pan out very differently from how she thought it would when she first moved on to the Clapper's Cove farm.

CHAPTER 13

Rose-Louise

Jane passed away three weeks before Barry's fatal accident. Alcohol had been added to the crippling drug-taking that had ruled her life for the previous ten years, and after being admitted to hospital in a semi-comatose state, her ravaged body finally stopped functioning. In the ten years since losing her parents when their plane disappeared, Jane's life had slowly spiralled out of control. Despite several periods when she seemed to be conquering her addiction, it didn't take long before she was arrested for theft or drug-related offences again.

Jane and Rose-Louise remained living in the rented caravan in Riverview Caravan Park even though they were often behind in the rent. Kevin, the son of the park owner who'd always acted like a big brother to Rose-Louise, persuaded his father to allow Jane to build up credit by doing odd jobs in the park—anything from cleaning toilets to gardening or painting. Although life wasn't great, they managed to cope after a fashion. Bertha helped care for Rose-Louise and encouraged her to stay at school until she obtained work in the restaurant of a nearby motel, with an opportunity to train in all aspects of the hospitality industry.

Rose-Louise read through the solicitor's letter many times. It told her the identity of her biological father and had finally confirmed why her mother had visits from policemen periodically over the years and why Jane had asked Bertha to care for her daughter from time to time when she went away for a month or two.

'Please take me with you,' pleaded Rose-Louise on more than one occasion when she was left in Bertha's care. 'I love Bertha and Cheryl, but I'd rather be with you.'

Rose-Louise felt immense sadness when she saw the news reporting the accident and heard the identity of the occupant in the Subaru that collided with the truckload of sheep. She had been so close to fulfilling her dream to finally meet up with her father, only to have it snatched away at the last minute. Now she would never be able to meet him. She decided to attend his funeral to get some final closure, despite the fact she wouldn't know anyone else there. It would be as close as she would ever get to Barry, and she would be able to see where he was buried.

So many people had died suddenly and tragically. It was almost beyond belief it could all happen in such a small time frame. As soon as she learned her father's identity, Rose-Louise decided to go and find him. It took over two and a half weeks to organise time off from work, and she'd just arrived in Ardrossan when she heard the report of Barry's death on her car radio. She felt cheated. First, her grandparents died in the plane crash, then her mother passed away, and now, on the way to meet up with Barry, she learned of his tragic accident not many miles from his farm. All the deaths had happened far too soon.

Jane's death, long before she reached her three score years and ten, had been difficult for Rose-Louise to deal with, although at the same time, it proved to be almost a relief. How she hated the drugs that had crept into Jane's life again after her grandparents died. Rose-Louise never knew why she and her mother suddenly left Melbourne many months before that tragic plane crash, or why they'd not gone back for a visit. She had turned eight soon after they moved to Mildura, and although Jane gave her a book she said came from her grandparents, she guessed her mother had bought it for her. Her grandparents had always been there for all her other birthdays, and that year they missed Jane's birthday too. It wasn't until she received the letter from her solicitor when Jane died that many puzzling things were clarified.

Although Rose-Louise had no siblings or cousins, she enjoyed life growing up in Riverview Caravan Park. With the arrival of her bicycle, when Jane returned after two weeks away in Melbourne following her grandparents' death, she was able to ride her own bike to school. Kevin usually kept her company, acting like an older brother, while Rose-Louise looked on Cheryl as her slightly older sister. Mildura was a wonderful place to ride a bicycle. The landscape was flat, and the roads were wide, set out in a grid planned way back by the forward-thinking Chaffey brothers, early pioneers in the district who migrated from Canada to set up an irrigation system on the Murray River. Rose-Louise remembered the times she and Jane rode alongside the river and how they'd often stopped for a rest and an ice cream cone on the way home.

The letter from her mother was sent to Rose-Louise by Jane's solicitor several days after her death. Finding out the identity of her father felt weird to Rose-Louise, but weird or unconventional were things she had coped with all her life. How she longed to know what living normally actually felt like. In the distant past, she remembered living with her mother and her grandparents in their modest apartment in Melbourne. It was adjacent to the preschool she attended and convenient for the elderly couple, as they were employed to clean the building after the littlies went home each day.

Things were hazy for many years after that. After reading Jane's letter, she learned about the many periods Jane had spent in detention centres. Rose-Louise remembered happy times with her grandparents and sad times when her mother 'had to go away for a while'. Many years later, she learned her mother had been convicted of shoplifting multiple times and of having drugs in her possession to use and to sell.

Five days after Barry's funeral, Rose-Louise arrived back home in Mildura. She'd planned to be away much longer and take time to meet her family. She'd found it hard to cope with her grief, coupled with the questioning looks and whispered conversations around her as she paid her respects at the open grave of the father she'd never known. She stayed three days in the rented cabin trying to sort out her feelings.

Her father was dead. She would never be able to meet him now.

She wanted to know more about him, to meet his friends and his wife, but her courage deserted her. She wondered how the population of Wattle Flat and district would have reacted if she had gone to the golf club after the funeral and let people know who she was—introducing herself as Barry's daughter!

Would Barry's widow believe I am his daughter? Will I be labelled a gold digger?' she wondered. 'How will Felicity react if I approach her and tell her who I am? Is it too soon after the funeral to make myself known? When will it be the right time to appear out of the blue and make my connection to Barry known? Will I be welcomed, or will his widow feel threatened?

These were some of the questions Rose-Louise mulled over.

Should I write and tell her I was on my way to meet Barry when I heard the account of the accident on my car radio? Will she believe me when I tell her I only found out details about my father and his divorce from my mother from an envelope given to me by Jane's solicitor after her death? If someone told me a tale like that, I would be very sceptical. It would seem a pretty unlikely story.

I want to go back soon and visit, but I wonder if I should ring or write to his widow first or just drop in unannounced? Is my father's widow technically my stepmother? Will I be able to convince anybody that all I want is to learn more about the family I never knew?

So many questions bombarded her brain. Rose-Louise desperately wanted to contact and meet Felicity and learn about her father, but she sincerely wanted to avoid distressing her in any way. The photos with captions on them shown during the funeral service were the sum total of her knowledge of her father.

Would my life be different if I'd known the identity of my father and information about my mother's marriage and divorce before my mother's death? she'd wondered.

Life didn't return to normal when Rose-Louise arrived back home in Mildura. Each day her mind filled up with questions about her origins. There were times she wished she'd not chickened out and skipped attending the gathering of family and friends after Barry's funeral. She'd felt strongly it wasn't the time or place to make her revelation, but this didn't stop her wishing she'd been braver. Now she faced the how and when to approach Felicity.

Rose-Louise knew she'd probably glimpsed photos of close family and other relatives in the slide show during the funeral service, but not all the pictures had been captioned. She guessed an elderly lady with hair the same colour as her own would probably be an aunt or grandmother. The recurrent questions burned inside her like an infection, until she finally felt compelled to seek some answers.

Writing to Felicity wasn't easy. She began by opening her letter with her sincere condolences. Then came the challenges of how to introduce herself and being sure her motives for making contact weren't misconstrued. Always mindful of other people's feelings, she spent days pondering what to say. Finally, she visualised her favourite schoolteacher admonishing her, as she had on more than one occasion, 'Believe in yourself and be guided by your intuition. You're a good person.'

Deep inside, Rose-Louise knew she needed to stop procrastinating, to stop trying to find answers for all the what-ifs that buzzed around in her head, and just do it! After deliberating for ages about what to say in the letter, Rose-Louse finally sat down and poured out what was in her heart, then folded her letter, found a stamp, and posted it before she could make any alterations. Then came the hard part, waiting for a reply.

It was almost unbelievable what happened next.

*   *   *

After all the events that followed Barry's death, Felicity felt completely devoid of energy and emotion. With the funeral over and after organising to lease the farm land for the next three years after the crops were reaped, she decided to go on holiday and use up some of the timeshare holiday credits she'd accumulated over the years. Not wanting to leave the farmhouse empty in her absence and needing someone to care for her animals, she contacted a nursing friend living in Melbourne who was thrilled to be asked to house-sit and tend the chickens and other animals while also providing company for Jack's elderly kelpie for fourteen days.

Margo was very conscientious and grateful to have a free holiday in the country with very few responsibilities. She kept a notebook by the phone where she recorded messages, and twice a week, she drove into Wattle Flat to empty Felicity's post office box. One of the letters she collected was the one to Felicity from Rose-Louise, introducing herself and asking if she could visit. Margo would have been deeply distressed if she'd known the letter remained in the plastic bag she'd used to carry the mail into the house. That plastic bag, still with Rose-Louise's letter inside, remained undiscovered in a kitchen drawer in the farmhouse until several months later.

Rose-Louise waited apprehensively for a reply from Felicity, oscillating between wanting to hear from her and being afraid she wouldn't want to make contact. Most days, she felt sure she would hear from her, but when days stretched to weeks, she decided to stop stressing and get on with her life.

What did you hope to achieve by contacting Felicity anyway? she asked herself. *She probably thinks it's safer not to reply at all, in case I want to rock the boat in some way.*

*   *   *

Felicity had noticed the tall auburn-haired young woman at her husband's graveside. She was one of many people Felicity didn't recognise. There were groups of people who'd come to pay their respects and several others who appeared to be on their own. One young man sporting a ginger beard and moustache looked uncannily like Barry. Felicity hadn't seen Rose-Louise inside the church, but it wasn't surprising as she'd been ushered into a front pew after all the straggling latecomers had been seated.

She didn't know the identity of the auburn-headed young woman she noticed at the cemetery and made a mental note to catch up with her or ask someone about her identity when refreshments were served to the townspeople, family, and friends back at the golf clubhouse. She was startled by the tall young lady's remarkable likeness to her late husband and wondered if she could be a distant relative.

CHAPTER 14

Jenny and Ken

Ken had always known he was conceived differently from his peers. IVF was in its infancy, and the first sperm bank in Australia wouldn't be set up in Adelaide until 1972. But Jenny had decided several years previously she wanted to be a mother. She'd met Jason, the love of her life, while still at high school, and they moved in together when they'd left school to continue their studies at the University of Adelaide.

They worked whenever they could, but money was tight even though they each had regular part-time jobs. They intended to get married soon after they both graduated. Unfortunately for Jenny, her life changed dramatically after they decided to save money by taking a boarder into their spare bedroom.

Sarah fitted in well. She shared the cooking and housework as well as helping out financially. But when she had the opportunity to share a house with three other girls who were also doing arts degrees, she decided to join them. She'd only boarded with Jenny and Jason for four weeks. Robert stayed for a few months, then he was followed by Eric for several weeks and Gavin, who remained with them for nearly a year.

With each boarder, Jenny could see her relationship with Jason deteriorating bit by bit, but her parents reassured her by saying this happened to many people as they grew older. They rarely seemed to spend time together and were mostly too exhausted to make love. She believed, and she thought Jason agreed, they would always be together. When Jason made his announcement, confusion and distress overwhelmed her. She couldn't believe what she was hearing.

'I know this will hurt you, but I need to tell you our relationship is over.'

'Why? I thought we'd be together forever. What's gone wrong? What have I done for you to make this decision?'

'Jenny, you will always be special to me, but I have come to understand I am more attracted to men than women, and Gavin and I have formed a relationship. What I am trying to say is, I'm gay, and now that I've acknowledged that, it would be wrong to marry you for the sake of appearing normal in the eyes of other people.'

Being dumbfounded didn't come even close to describing Jenny's feelings, and even after Jason's announcement, she knew she would always care deeply for him. She was heartbroken, totally shattered, and would take a long time to adjust to her sudden single state. She knew Jason wouldn't be happy continuing to deceive her and that hurting her caused him considerable pain and anguish. She wasn't prejudiced against gay relationships. Some of the nicest people she'd ever met were gay. In a matter of weeks, she'd accepted a teaching job in Ardrossan and moved back to live with her parents in Wattle Flat until she found other suitable accommodation. She vowed she would never marry, but her longing for a child would lead her on a pioneering path.

She was attending a social evening at the Wattle Flat football club one Friday evening with a group of young people her own age when she met up with Barry Clapper again. They'd started school together and continued in the same class until Barry left school to work on the family farm. (As a small child, Jenny had been very impressed that Clapper's Cove had been named after Barry's pioneer relative who'd settled in the district.)

It was in that club where the seed of an idea was sown. Feeling very strongly she wanted to have a child but not wanting a physical relationship, she knew she would need to find someone willing to donate sperm. She'd always liked Barry, but no one had ever previously measured up to Jason in her eyes.

When she finally found the courage several weeks later to approach Barry with her idea, he found it hard to comprehend what she was wanting him to do. It had been a vulnerable time for him. He and Jane had been trying for a baby for almost twelve months, and three weeks previously, she'd left him. He could partly blame his father. The way he'd treated Jane was unforgiveable, and Barry had been torn between being supportive of his wife and being loyal to his father and farming traditions.

Barry suggested Jenny may do better trying to find someone younger and more virile. He explained that his sperm had been found to be somewhat lazy, at least prior to having hormone injections to spark them up.

'I'm probably not the best candidate for the job, but I'm willing to donate some of my *'wrigglers'* for you you if that's what you have your heart set on.'

Jenny knew very little of Barry's family history, but it seemed to her he was fit and healthy. He didn't drink excessively and had never smoked. She liked his rugged, well-proportioned appearance with his dark-brown eyes, neatly trimmed beard, and curly ginger hair. He was intelligent and caring. He seemed to be the perfect answer to her quest to find a sperm donor. It was soon after Jane had left and just prior to a whirlwind frenzy of one-night stands that blotted out his loneliness for a while but left him feeling less than proud of himself.

'Maybe if I give Jenny a sperm donation or two, it will help to take my pain away,' he reasoned to himself.

He told her, 'I'm ambivalent about whether any resulting child knows of my identity. I can help you with regular support payments if you conceive and get into financial difficulties, but I don't need any recognition in any form. Don't even feel obliged to tell me whether you manage to have a child.'

'Thank you. This means the world to me. I've always wanted to have a child, but I loathe to become entangled in a relationship where I could be let down again. I'll be able to manage for a couple of years with money from my savings, and then I plan to resume teaching. I will tell any child that results from your sperm donation how he or she was conceived, but will only divulge your name when the child turns twenty-one and can make an adult choice about whether to contact you.'

They agreed that such an arrangement was acceptable for both of them. Barry didn't want to know any more about the ins and outs of syringing his donation high up into Jenny's vagina. (She intended to sleep on her back with her buttocks elevated to give Barry's 'swimmers' every chance to succeed in their search for a suitable place to lodge.) He knew he wouldn't have any difficulty abstaining from having sex for at least three days before collecting his sperm.

Although moving back home with her parents after Jason's momentous announcement seemed right at the time, Jenny felt embarrassed by what had happened to her relationship with him.

She felt uncomfortable with the Wattle Flat townspeople knowing her history and regarding her with pity. When a short-tenure teaching appointment became available in Marree, she jumped at the chance to apply for it. While teaching there, she learned she'd become pregnant, and the enormous unconventional decision she'd made threatened to overwhelm her. She'd knowingly chosen to bring a child into the world into a one-parent situation!

Knowing she would need some support but unwilling to return to her parents and the gossiping townspeople of their small country town, she chose to accept a short-term teaching position in Horsham. Her favourite aunt lived in Pimpinio, several miles west of there. Margaret was her father's sister, and she remained living on the farm after her husband, Jim, died instantly in a freak farming accident when his tractor rolled over, trapping him beneath it. Auntie Margaret didn't have any children of her own, but she and Jim had fostered infants for many years. She welcomed Jenny with open arms and immediately started knitting for the expected baby.

'I still have baby furniture, clothing, and toys from when Jim and I fostered babies from time to time. I couldn't bear to get rid of anything. Although difficult at times, caring for babies and young children even for short periods was the happiest time of our lives. I've kept anything that might be of value to someone someday, so please use whatever you want.'

With her living arrangements fully catered for, Jenny settled down to enjoy her pregnancy and the birth of her baby. She had made a momentous decision, way ahead of her time for what in the future would be a scientifically managed procedure used to help women who had no other means of conceiving to deliver healthy babies.

(Kenneth James Johnson conveniently arrived, yelling robustly, in the middle of a Saturday morning in July after a three-hour labour.)

*　　*　　*

Margaret chose to share-farm after her husband's death, as she enjoyed living on the land, and the old farmhouse held many great memories for her. Jenny felt very privileged to receive her aunt's generous offer to consider the farm her home, and she knew she'd made the right decision not to return to South Australia.

The main crop grown on the Pimpinio farm was wheat, which mostly brought in good yearly returns unless cruelly decimated by frost or drought. Jenny found some of the farming terms were different from those used in South Australia.

Sowing and *harvesting* were terms used in Victoria, differing from the South Australian terminology of *seeding* and *reaping*.

Kenny grew up a cheeky, mischievous boy, always getting into scrapes. He thrived on the farm and benefited from starting his education in a one-teacher country school. The share-farmer, with his wife and three children, lived within sight of the main homestead and were friendly and supportive of the two women who doted on the small boy growing up in their care. Kenny was precocious and spoiled but not overly indulged. From the time he went to school, he spoke to Margaret and his mother using their Christian names. Jenny didn't mind and saw no need to correct him, although his classmates and visitors sometimes thought it strange.

'If it makes him important, I can't see any harm in it,' Jenny replied to anyone who voiced an objection and said he was disrespectful.

Kenny loved everything about the farm and seemed mostly attracted by anything to do with tractors. He learnt from an early age to see them as great machines but also to be aware that many farm accidents involved them. He'd grown up knowing the story of how his great-uncle had been killed by a tractor rollover. Ken went on to high school in Horsham and chose to study subjects related to farming and the environment. With changes happening on the land at a great rate, he became determined to keep up with advances in techniques and methods of conservation.

During his school years, after he'd told some of his mates how his birth had come about, Ken was occasionally the subject of good-natured ribbing when his mates dreamt up outlandish characters who might possibly be his sperm donor father.

'Maybe your dad was Superman or Darth Vader. Or maybe Prince Charles. He spent some time in school in Australia.'

'No, it's more likely he was an alien from outer space.'

He was also subject to abuse from ill-informed people who concluded Jenny and Margaret were in a gay relationship.

'It isn't true. Margaret is Jenny's aunt, and Jenny is my mother,' Ken usually answered if he bothered to reply. 'Anyway, what would it matter if they were gay? It's none of your bloody business!'

'I bet. Who are you kidding? Why don't you call Jenny Mum then if she is your mother?'

'That must be why you were born from a sperm donation, because your mother is gay. Who is your father anyway? Why doesn't he want to know you?'

'Oh, get lost! Go and find something useful to do!'

It used to worry him at first, and sometimes he became thoroughly upset by their constant harassment. But he soon understood he was only being tormented by ignorant newcomers to the town, people who'd never known Margaret's husband. Ken had been brought up to honour people of all colours and beliefs and found it hard to understand how some people could be so prejudiced against others. Jenny heard the rumours too and wasn't amused by them. She hated to see them causing Ken distress.

The share-farmer who farmed with Margaret had a son called Ewen, who was the same age as Ken, and they soon bonded as great mates. They went to school together then on to different agricultural colleges. Ken won a partial scholarship to Dookie, where he lived on campus. Dookie Agricultural College was set up in 1886—the first agricultural college in Victoria and the second in Australia. (Australia's first agricultural college was founded at Roseworthy, fifty kilometres north of Adelaide in 1883.) Dookie was established on rolling hills between Shepparton and Benalla, and in 1972, it opened its doors to female students for the first time.

Ewen attended Longerenong Agricultural College, situated near enough to Horsham for him to live at home. He used their old Holden farm ute to commute so he could still help his dad at busy times on both their own and Margaret's farm. Longerenong was the second agricultural college to be established in Victoria. Founded in 1889, it was forced to close from 1897 until 1905 because of several severe droughts and a lack of students and cash flow.

When age crept up on Margaret and it became obvious Ken had a passion for farming, she gladly subsidised his scholarship to Dookie Agricultural College. It pleased her that he wanted to further his education rather than follow the pattern of many farmer's sons— leaving school as soon as they were able, often as young as fourteen.

It thrilled her to have her gift well-received and subsequently spoke to him about eventually taking over the farm without the aid of a share-farmer.

He respected the fact he was extremely lucky to be given such an opportunity while so young. It meant he could begin to integrate his passion for new farming technology.

He loved working with his laptop, preferring to use an Apple computer, but he was frustrated when he needed to embrace Windows technology while at school and subsequently run a farm accounting program until he devised a similar program of his own on his Mac. Although often fired up about new ideas and technology, he'd become astute enough to link them with the tried-and-true methods of farming that had been the foundation of his great-aunt's farm for years.

As they didn't keep livestock, many of the old wooden fences were removed, and paddocks were enlarged to cater for bigger machinery equipped with computer technology. Ken occasionally had voluntary assistance from local high school students who were learning about climate and conservation. They planted banks of trees in strategic positions to minimise the effect of the wind that could whip topsoil from his paddocks and blow it away in a few short hours. This nutrient-rich topsoil contained costly fertiliser, and if blown away, it would leave the poorer subsoil needing to be nourished all over again, adding extra expense.

Margaret passed away at the age of eighty in Horsham Hospital after struggling with dementia for several years. She died happy in the knowledge she'd made a difference to two people who'd come into her life soon after the death of her husband. She knew the farm would be in good hands, and maybe Ken would one day marry and raise another farmer on the property.

Margaret fully supported Jenny's decision to have a child outside a relationship and to never marry. Jenny's parents were more judgemental and governed by what other people thought. Consequently, although they kept in touch and enjoyed receiving updated reports of Kenny's progress, they mostly visited her in

Pimpinio, and Jenny and Ken rarely visited them in their home in South Australia. When they'd occasionally visited Wattle Flat, they hadn't crossed paths with Barry, and Jenny didn't see any reason to seek him out.

Initially, no one except Jenny knew the identity of Ken's biological father. As Barry hadn't heard from Jenny after she left the district, he assumed her attempt to become pregnant using his sperm had failed. After a while, his donation failed to be of importance to him. It was part of his past and soon disappeared from his thoughts.

When Ken started asking questions about his origins, sperm donation was explained as simply as possible.

He grew comfortable with the knowledge his biological father didn't know of his existence and even ambivalent about making contact after he turned twenty-one. Jenny assured him he came from healthy stock with no known debilitating conditions. Growing up in a loving household with the share-farmer and his family always available for support, the only times he experienced a niggling loss was on Father's Day or at times when schoolmates had their fathers turn up at sporting events. During these periods, he felt a little angry Jenny had knowingly deprived him of a father by using a donor and never marrying or entering into a relationship with anyone he could adopt as a father figure. But these negative feelings were usually short-lived, and he acknowledged he wouldn't exist at all without her decision to have a baby the way she had.

Ken preferred exploring technological possibilities rather than sporting challenges. He was considered to be quite a whiz kid with his computer, and many farmers who struggled to keep accurate farm records with the introduction of the GST willingly paid him to sort out their BAS statements each quarter. Most people coped with their basic accounts until it came to keeping correct records for different vehicles and farm equipment and the complicated grain marketing statements. Many farmers found the use of computer programs difficult to master, especially those who had not kept account books and their only records were their yearly collection of cheque butts in shoeboxes!

Jenny returned to teaching after Ken started school, choosing to work at a Catholic school rather than the one attended by both Ken and Ewen. Although lonely at times, her resolution not to marry and to keep out of a relationship never faltered. During Kenny's early years, she had wonderful support from her aunt Margaret in many facets of her life.

There were plenty of things to do. Jenny joined a craft group, and soon every bedroom in the farmhouse sported new patchwork quilts. She served as a valued member of the Horsham CWA, where Margaret had been awarded life membership, and helped when money needed to be raised for community projects. She worked on the hospital auxiliary and played in the number one position for Pimpinio's A-grade tennis team.

*   *   *

When Jenny glimpsed the account of the horrific road accident on television, it shook her to her very core. She could hardly breathe as she learned the identity and fate of the Subaru driver. Barry had been her age, although the pictures in the paper must have been taken many years ago, even as early as his late teens before he grew his beard and moustache.

He'd been far too young to have his life terminated—and in such a brutal fashion. As she watched the account of the accident, Jenny experienced a kaleidoscope of emotions. She suddenly realised she had no legal record of Ken's paternity, as his father was listed as unknown on his birth certificate.

The biological father of her son was dead.

Ken would never get to meet him now, even if he wanted to do so. Jenny wondered if Ken's startling resemblance to his father would be noticed if he attended Barry's funeral, now that he had opted to stop shaving and to nurture a ginger beard instead. Would it be upsetting for his widow to discover Barry had fathered a son with a sperm donation?

What should I tell Ken now? Jenny wondered. *Would attending the funeral be the only way for Ken to make contact with his relatives, and would this be a good thing to do? Would Barry's widow be distressed if we went to Barry's funeral?*

After a sleepless night and much soul-searching, Jenny finally told Ken about the disturbing news item and purchased several newspapers that gave an account of it. She also told him a little of Barry's life history and gave him the option of whether or not to attend Barry's funeral.

'It shouldn't be distressing for Felicity to meet you, as Barry's gift had been given to me after Jane left him and some time before he married Felicity,' Jenny explained. 'Would you like to make contact with your father's widow?'

'I guess going to his funeral could give me some connection to my biological father, and I'm never going to have an opportunity to meet him now. I'd almost decided to contact him when I turned twenty-one.'

With their decision made, they were lucky enough to secure the last cabin available for a couple of nights at the Wattle Flat Caravan Park. They hoped they'd have an opportunity to meet Barry's widow and maybe some of his relatives after the funeral service.

It was Ken's startling resemblance to Barry that prompted Felicity to approach him and Jenny at the golf club rooms after her husband's graveside service. Felicity was amazed but not phased at all by their story, as the resemblance to Barry would be obvious to anyone who'd known him. With many people waiting to offer their condolences, she quickly made arrangements to contact him after he returned home to Pimpinio.

Ken and Jenny left the golf club soon after they'd each had a cup of coffee and a piece of strawberry cream cake. They decided not to return home for a couple of days, as Ewen was feeding their dog and cat and chickens for them. Ken felt overwhelmed by his mixed emotions. Receiving so much incredible information in such a short time had left him feeling gutted.

Jenny recognised some of the town's notorious gossips viewing them with interest and could imagine the juicy pieces of information they'd be processing. As Ken's startling resemblance to Barry was duly noted and commented on, the small town of Wattle Flat soon buzzed with new theories. But like their surmising about Rose-Louise, the inventiveness of even the most creative of the local gossips had no idea and would never have thought of how Ken was conceived.

'Isn't that Jenny Johnstone with Barry's lookalike?'

'You mean the girl who used to go with Jason what's-his-name until he developed a relationship with one of their male boarders and ditched her?'

'Yeah, that's the one. I think it happened about twenty years ago. She came back to live here for a while before going teaching in the Outback somewhere.'

'Do you think she had an affair with Barry?'

'Who knows? The lad looks about twenty and is the spitting image of Barry, so the timing could be right.'

'I thought Barry couldn't have kids. He had to have special injections to wake up his sperm when he was married to Jane. I recently heard from a friend of mine who lives in the Mallee that drugs and booze finally caught up with her. I think my friend said Jane died a few weeks ago.'

'It's a pity Barry and Jane didn't manage to have kids. It might have cemented their marriage, and Jack, the old tyrant, might even have mellowed if he'd had grandchildren.'

CHAPTER 15

Felicity had bought a timeshare at Yarrawonga soon after the holiday complex opened. This meant she could enjoy a holiday in luxury surroundings for a week each year for the cost of an annual maintenance fee, and she had the choice of different places, not just in Victoria. (There were a couple of timeshares in South Australia, but most were in New South Wales and Queensland.) After Barry's death and all the legal paraphernalia were tidied up and the farm leased, Felicity decided to use up some of her timeshare credits (accrued during the years she hadn't gone away) and holiday in Northern Victoria. She also wanted to accept Ken and Jenny's invitation to visit the farm at Pimpinio and get to know them.

Was Ken technically her stepson? Would he allow her to be part of his life? Would Jenny feel threatened by her wanting to know more about the young man who looked so much like her deceased husband, and who'd been a precursor to a pioneering procedure that would ultimately result in many childless couples being able to have children?

Felicity had always wanted children, although she'd known from an early age that her fallopian tubes were gummed up after she'd had a burst appendix removed as a child. She'd been told she may never be able to conceive. Nevertheless, her hunger for a family never went away, and now, with Jenny's permission, it looked like she would be welcomed to share Ken's life. She stayed in the timeshare in Yarrawonga for a week, relaxing in the pool and generally unwinding before driving on to Horsham.

Ken felt proud to show Felicity his property and tell how he came to own it. They shared the differences between their two farms. Both were growing wheat, but Ken often faced frosts, which rarely occurred on Yorke Peninsula. While Ken's paddocks were large and often unfenced, Felicity's were much smaller, and because she kept some livestock, her fences where better maintained.

Of Barry's offspring who attended his funeral, only Ken's identity was immediately revealed to Felicity. Rose-Louise decided to contact Felicity at a later date. Although she first responded by writing to Felicity, she wanted to wait for a reply before she visited again. She grew despondent waiting to hear from her, not knowing her letter sat unopened in one of Felicity's kitchen drawers.

Rose-Louise had lived in Mildura since aged seven, and for all her time there, she'd resided in the same rented caravan in Riverview Caravan Park. Now, with her mother gone, she decided it would be a good idea to relocate. Because of her mother's track record of drugs and alcohol, Rose-Louise always found it difficult to make friends. At school, her peers weren't encouraged to befriend her, in case the insidious drug menace had caught up with Rose-Louise as well. Bertha, Cheryl, and Kevin were probably the only people who weren't wary or afraid to maintain a friendship with her.

As they entered their teenage years, Kevin tried to deepen his relationship with Rose-Louise on several occasions. He attended special events with her, but she always introduced him as her surrogate brother.

'I love you dearly, Kevin, and I don't know how I would have survived over the years if you hadn't been there for me. Please don't be offended, but I am not looking for a relationship with you or anyone else at the moment. You've always been like a brother to me, and I hope we'll always be close, but not together as a couple.'

Rose-Louise obtained work in a management capacity at a busy upmarket motel with a restaurant in Horsham connected to the same motel chain where she'd been employed in Mildura. It took just three weeks before she could transfer, and she was grateful she didn't have to look for somewhere to live, as the motel had reserved a unit for her.

It wasn't easy for her to say goodbye to her friends and her life at Riverview. She'd spent most of her life there, where she'd experienced so much loss. She knew Mildura, despite the dust storms, would always have a special place in her heart. Kevin was particularly sad to see her go.

'Things won't be the same without you living in the park. Please send me an email from time to time to let me know you're OK.'

'I'll email or write every now and then. Make sure you have some fun, and find a nice girlfriend soon.'

Bertha and Cheryl also said they would miss her but acknowledged she was doing the right thing making a new start in a different town now that her mother had passed on.

Rose-Louise revelled in her new position, adapted well, and excelled in her job. She quickly gained the respect of her co-workers and patrons, who began to eat in the restaurant regularly. Jenny and Ken ate there once a month and took Felicity with them on her first week staying on the farm. They were escorted to their table by a tall young lady with beautiful auburn hair, who appeared to be in charge of the restaurant. They were intrigued when they realised where they had seen her previously—at Barry's funeral. It was mutual recognition, and at the end of their meal, when the restaurant had nearly emptied out, Rose-Louise approached their table to talk to them, wondering what had brought them to her motel, so far away from Wattle Flat.

Rose-Louise had hesitated at first, wondering whether she should approach Felicity and the young man who looked so like her father in the pictures on the slide show at his funeral service. After all, she hadn't received a reply to the letter she'd sent Felicity several weeks ago, and she'd conjured up multiple reasons (none of them correct) as to why Felicity hadn't written back. She wondered if she would be able to get an explanation now.

Taking the initiative, Rose-Louise introduced herself to Felicity.

'Hello, Mrs Clapper. We haven't met officially, but I'm Rose-Louise. I recognise you from attending your husband's funeral recently. Please accept my condolences.'

Rose-Louise paused momentarily, wondering how to make her announcement. She continued talking in a rush, hoping to make a welcome connection with Felicity.

'How have you been? It's a difficult time. I know how it feels because I lost my mother recently as well, but not suddenly in an accident. The writing had been on the wall for her for some time. It must have been a terrible shock to see all those graphic pictures of the accident in the newspapers and on the telly.'

'Thank you. Please call me Felicity. I noticed you at the cemetery. Did you go back to the golf club rooms? I looked for you but didn't see you there. Do you know how much you look like my husband? Are you one of the family's second cousins?'

'I know this will probably sound unbelievable, but I was on my way to meet Barry when I heard an account of his terrible accident on the radio as I turned into Ardrossan. Did you get my letter? I explained everything in it and hoped you would be willing to let me visit you. I continued on to Wattle Flat so I could go to his funeral— the closest I would ever come to being near my father now. I only found out the identity of my father in a letter left to me from my mother when she passed away. I didn't stay for refreshments at the golf club rooms. I just needed time for myself for a while and couldn't face being gossip fodder for the locals at that stage. I've heard what small towns can be like. My full name is Rose-Louise Winter. I have my mother's maiden surname. She used to be Jane Clapper, your husband's previous wife.'

Felicity was dumbfounded.

'What a whammy! It seems my husband may have fathered a daughter he knew nothing about. My understanding was that Barry had low fertility and he'd had treatment to boost his sperm motility when he and Jane were trying to have a family. We wanted a family too, but my fallopian tubes were all gummed up after having a mucky appendix removed. I've had treatment to try and clear them but without success. My being nearly forty probably didn't help either.'

'Yes, Mum told me about Barry's low sperm count in the letter she left me. Said she didn't know she was pregnant when she left Barry. She decided not to go back or tell him but to live with her parents in Melbourne instead. We stayed with my grandparents until I was seven. Apparently, Jane had issues with Jack, Barry's father, who must have been very controlling because he'd made life pretty difficult for her. It didn't help their marriage either.'

'I know all about Jack and his need to control everything. We weren't on the best of terms very often either. I gather you learned at Barry's funeral that Jack had passed on too. But please let me introduce my companions to you. They were at the funeral as well. Rose-Louise, let me introduce you to my Barry's lookalike, Ken, and his mother, Jenny.'

'Wow! Ken, you're the spitting image of Barry, from the photos I saw on the slide show at the funeral service. Pleased to meet you both. Are you close relatives?'

'I know this is going to sound incredible, but when Jenny saw the account of Barry's accident on the television, she decided to tell me the identity of my biological father. I knew I could find out when I was twenty-one, but as circumstances changed, she thought I might want to go to my father's funeral.'

'Are you telling me Barry fathered you too? He had both a son and a daughter he didn't know existed? This is bizarre. You're telling me we were both fathered by someone whose sperm had poor motility and a low count! This will take some digesting.'

'I'm as amazed at the turn of events as you are. When I saw you for the first time, I noticed the resemblance to Barry straight away. I wondered if you could be one of the nieces or a cousin perhaps, never dreaming I was seeing my half-sister for the first time. The weird thing is that I haven't always had a beard and moustache. I've only grown them since the beginning of the year. Eight of my mates are also nurturing facial hair for a whole year as a fundraiser to buy a new ambulance in our district.'

Felicity watched as Rose-Louise's expressions changed at each revelation, knowing the most astounding piece of information was yet to be shared.

'My mum was still married to Barry when I was conceived,' Rose-Louise mused. 'My birthday's in March, and I'm twenty. If what you say is true, the answers to how, when, and where may prove to be interesting! I'm not doubting you're Barry's son, Ken—the resemblance is too strong—but what else can you tell me?'

'I think Jenny—I've always called my mother by her Christian name—can give you a more detailed account of my origins than I can. Over to you, Jenny!'

Rose-Louise looked around and registered that all the other diners had left the restaurant.

'There are a few things I need to tidy up so my staff can finish for the night. If it's OK with you all, I'll get coffee sent out while I lock up the restaurant. Please stay, and we'll open a bottle of port together. I can't wait to hear the next episode of this saga!'

When Rose-Louise went to organise coffee, she wondered what Jenny was going to tell her.

Is Ken older or younger than I am? Did Barry, our father, have an affair while married to my mother, or did he have a fling with Jenny or a relationship with her after Jane left him?

What Jenny was about to reveal didn't enter her thoughts as a possibility. And if it had, she would have dismissed it as being too way out.

*   *   *

Jenny pondered over where to start to explain how her pregnancy came about. Finally, she realised the whole story, right back from when she'd been to school with Barry and her relationship and the subsequent outcome of her time with Jason, needed to be included. Jason's part of the story explained why she'd chosen to have a baby alone and to shun marriage or future relationships. With coffees cooling, they waited while Rose-Louise set out four port glasses and poured generous amounts into each.

'Now, Jenny, please tell me how Ken is my half-brother. It seems we all agree Barry fathered both of us. This will be a great story to tell my grandchildren if I ever have any!'

Jenny began.

'Nowadays, assistance for couples who are having difficulty becoming pregnant is available using IVF, in vitro fertilisation. It has become very popular and is now being used by couples, people in gay relationships, and even single girls. Twenty years ago, when

Ken was born, the technique was in its infancy and only available for childless married couples. Perhaps I was being selfish, but I desperately wanted to have a child. I knew I could provide a good home and afford to educate a child on my teacher's salary. After being in a relationship where we had promised to be together forever and then being dumped for a male partner, I vowed to stay single forever!

I'd done everything I could to make that relationship work. As you can imagine, I felt humiliated. My self-esteem plummeted. I went back to Wattle Flat for a while, where it occurred to me I could have a child on my own. This wasn't a decision I made lightly. I thought about it for some time before progressing to asking myself who I could approach to father my child. I needed to get a donation of sperm from a healthy, good-living guy who came from sound stock without any known health problems.

Remember, in this era, single girls who gave birth were frowned upon if they didn't do what authorities considered acceptable—give their child up for adoption. And I was deliberately deciding to have a baby on my own! I felt entirely certain this was what I wanted to do.

Many couples who marry progress to having children without giving much thought about their responsibilities or how they will rearrange their finances to encompass rearing a baby. Finally, when I'd examined the idea from every angle, I became convinced that what I hoped to do would be of benefit to me and any resulting child.'

'Jenny probably won't tell you how often criticism was directed towards her because of her decision,' Ken said. 'Some people can be really cruel without knowing all the facts. Because we shared her widowed aunt's home, she frequently heard whispers she must be gay, otherwise she wouldn't have needed someone to donate sperm, and how terrible it was to choose to rear a child with only one parent! These comments reared their ugly heads periodically over the years.'

Rose-Louise wanted to hear more of Jenny's story at this point and in particular how she approached Barry. But she let it go. Her patience was rewarded when Jenny took up the story again.

'I'd often seen Barry in town at the football club and when he collected his mail each Thursday. I knew Jane had left him a few months previously, and when I bumped into him one day at the post office, we chatted for a while, and I told him I had something important to ask him. We wandered over to the park. I told him I wanted to do something considered unconventional, and I hoped he would help me achieve my goal. He was intrigued at first, then when I mentioned I would like him to donate sperm, I guess I wasn't really surprised by his reaction.'

'You're kidding me, aren't you? You want me to shoot sperm into a sterile container so you can syringe it into your body close to your womb, hoping you will get pregnant? Are you sure you don't want to try out the usual method?' he'd added cheekily.

'I pointed out that I wasn't asking for any further involvement if our joint efforts resulted in a pregnancy or looking for emotional involvement at any stage. I told him, if he agreed, I wouldn't divulge the name of the biological father until the child turned twenty-one. After that explanation and a reassurance my request wasn't about wanting money or support, he agreed and sheepishly delivered his gift of a container of sperm in a brown paper bag, after I'd calculated the exact time of the month I'd be ovulating.

I'd only been teaching in Marree for a few weeks when I found out I was pregnant, and I didn't see any reason to contact Barry. It wasn't as though he was going to be involved in my child's upbringing.

He'd just obliged by doing me a favour. He hadn't asked to be informed if the outcome resulted in my becoming pregnant. He'd told me right from the beginning of our negotiations our efforts may not succeed because he'd been checked out and found to have a low sperm count with sluggish swimmers.

It had just been one big hoot for him to do something so out of the ordinary. When my placement in Marree ended, I moved to Pimpinio to live with my widowed Auntie Margaret, being well aware there would be times I would need some support and backup. Margaret and her husband used to foster children before he'd been killed in a tractor rollover on the farm. She enjoyed having a baby in her home again—but this time for the long term.

I soon had employment at Horsham State School teaching third graders until Ken arrived in July, which makes him three months younger than you, Rose-Louise.'

'Gosh, this is quite a story! That sorts out the timeline. What did your parents think of it all?'

'I didn't tell them how my pregnancy came about or the father's identity, although I think they had a fair idea after Ken began to look so much like Barry. They had enough trouble processing the fact their unmarried daughter was going to have a baby. They didn't make me feel very welcome back in Wattle Flat after Ken was born, although they loved seeing photos of him and rang often to check on his progress. They travelled to visit us each Christmas and for all of Ken's important events.'

So unbeknown to their same biological father, two half siblings began life three months apart. The boy with red hair later grew into a young man who sported a russet moustache and beard and looked like a younger version of his father, and the auburn-haired girl with dark-brown eyes also resembled her dad. Although Barry had lived and worked near Clapper's Cove in South Australia all his life, the half-brother and half-sister grew up in different towns in Northern Victoria. The meeting of Rose-Louise Winter and Ken Johnstone turned out to be a momentous moment for both young people. Felicity felt thrilled for each of them and was astounded she was being blessed to find family connections previously unknown to her.

CHAPTER 16

When the notice in the newspaper announced Barry's death, Anna retrieved the slip of paper from her Bible where she'd written his name and address. She became very emotional as she told her menfolk the accident victim was Luke's biological father. They attended Barry's funeral service in the church and at the graveside but slipped away without explaining their relationship to anyone or going back to the golf club rooms for refreshments afterwards.

Acknowledging Barry's part in their lives was a big enough hurdle for Luke and Derek to absorb without immediately meeting the rest of his extended family. Sally had her final exams on the day Barry was buried, and because the identity of his biological father was of little interest to Luke, by the time Sally graduated and returned home for a holiday, Barry's death and Anna's revelation had become old news. So somehow she missed out on being told of Luke's paternity.

When Luke attended the funeral with his parents, several people concluded they must have been friends of Felicity or Barry. Unlike Ken, Luke didn't have red hair or fair skin and really didn't resemble

Barry in any way. He had brown eyes and dark-brown curly hair, and his skinned tanned easily. He looked a lot like Derek. There didn't seem any reason to tell anyone outside their family of Luke's relationship to Barry. They didn't mingle at the graveside and departed as soon as they'd paid their respects. The whole day was a bit of a blur as they huddled together supporting each other, oblivious to the curious stares that occasionally came their way.

'You are my real dad as far as I'm concerned,' Luke said to Derek. 'You're the only father I've ever known. Barry didn't know about me, and when he'd had too much to drink and went home with Mum, he probably never thought his actions could have resulted in her getting pregnant.

I can't see that publicly acknowledging him as my biological father is anyone's business, nor would it be beneficial to anyone but me—and then only if I was desperate to find out more about his medical history and the medical history of his family. It's a sensitive situation because I could be suspected of wanting to claim some sort of inheritance if I came out of the woodwork at the time of his death.'

Although Luke was curious to find out whether other members of Barry's family had neural tube defects, specifically spina bifida, he knew it could be a random happening. Anna had researched her own family, and no disabilities had been found. Luke resolved to follow the Clapper family history on Ancestry.com somewhere down the track, and he'd think about whether he'd contact Felicity sometime in the future.

They were never officially introduced, but Luke felt sure he'd spoken to Barry on more than one occasion when they were both queuing to buy refreshments at the canteen while attending football matches between Ardrossan and Wattle Flat at Maitland. Although not a player, Barry regularly attended football matches involving the local league, and likewise, Luke had often cheered his mates to victory if they played well and consoled them if they lost. Looking back, he was glad of those chance encounters (having recognised Barry from his photos in the newspaper), but he felt no real connection to him. He felt glad he had at least the opportunity to speak to him even though he didn't know at the time that they shared DNA.

As Luke's landscaping business expanded, he became well respected in the district, and people (including Barry, who had heard somewhere that he'd had been born with spina bifida) soon came to see him as a healthy young man running a successful landscaping business.

Felicity acknowledged Luke and his family's presence at Barry's funeral, little knowing Luke was fathered by Barry, and he would interact with her in the future.

*   *   *

At long last, the District Council of Yorke Peninsula agreed to set aside land to build a swimming pool. Felicity was particularly pleased as she had put the idea forward to the Wattle Flat Progress Association and gathered an enormous number of signatures from people who hoped it would happen.

Wattle Flat was a thriving town in the hub of five other towns all within a half hour's drive.

It took fifteen to twenty minutes to drive there from the Clapper farm. It was close to the ocean but not actually on the coast. Many of the nearby beaches were rocky and subject to visits from stingrays and other stingers. Felicity felt strongly that the town and district would benefit greatly from having a municipal swimming pool.

When she mentioned this idea to various townspeople, she'd met with mixed reactions ranging from scepticism to mild interest, and some people were even enthusiastic!

Many people held on to ideas from the past.

'We've always managed without a swimming pool. We can go to the beach if we want to go swimming. The idea has been presented before, and the council blocked it. They'll probably dismiss it again.'

These were the most frequent replies when she broached the subject with any of the locals. Most dissenters, when questioned further, found they were repeating mantras they'd learnt from childhood and grudgingly agreed they would support the venue once it was up and running.

Felicity didn't give up campaigning and could frequently be heard putting forward the reasons for having a swimming pool in Wattle Flat and how it would benefit all people on the peninsula in multiple ways. She was aware she was dealing with a large proportion of people who were steeped in apathy and negativity and who only partially accepted her.

'We have great opportunities for young people in this district to excel in most sports, but without a modern swimming pool, we will never give our promising young swimmers a chance to compete on the world stage.'

'So is that why you think we need a swimming pool—to train swimming champions? Surely producing elite footballers and netball players in the district is catering to our young people enough?'

'If we look forward to the future and plan ahead, there will be many benefits for all age groups. A swimming complex in Wattle Flat would provide job opportunities in both the building phase and when the pool is operational. It would give the town's young people a healthy alternative meeting place, keeping them off the streets and away from the pubs. Young mothers could have their babies safely taught to swim at an early age, and older children and adults who've never learnt to swim would also be catered for.

Water aerobic classes could be held for all ages. Besides which, going to the beach is not a good option when people grow older and are unsteady on their feet.'

'It'll be too costly. Where will we get the money?'

'I'm willing to donate a sum of money to start the ball rolling, in memory of Barry. As Barry had no children who bear the Clapper name, I think it would be great if his pioneer farming family could be remembered in this positive way. We will need to approach wealthy farmers and big business ventures to also sponsor the idea. If we can get the townspeople behind it, I'm sure they will invent innovative ways to raise money. Selling paving stones seems to be the way to go these days. Many surrounding towns have raised money like this. Family history plaques have sold for $1,500, and paving stones went for $50 when the townspeople of Minlaton were raising money to pay for a statue of Harry Butler, a famous local pioneering aviator.

There are grants we can apply for, and it would be great if the District Council of Yorke Peninsula comes on board with a land grant in a central position. My vision includes offices for people practicing supportive therapies such as reflexology, reiki, and Bowen therapy. Perhaps a physiotherapist could set up a practice as well, and maybe we should add a conference room. All of these businesses would bring in rent.

I envisage bringing busloads of schoolchildren to the pool regularly from all the surrounding schools. Because of Wattle Flat's central location, aged care facilities could help the mobility of their residents by exercising them in the swimming pool. Moving in water is far less painful for arthritis sufferers. I remember how my own mother met up with friends in a heated spa adjoining our local pool. She looked forward to the socialising as much as the pool's therapeutic value. There are so many ways our district—not just people in Wattle Flat—could benefit if we think ahead for future generations.'

After overcoming most of the hesitant reasons for not proceeding with the project and receiving one of the biggest government grants available, it wasn't long before the swimming complex began to take shape. With the cementing of the idea she had mooted, Felicity found keeping busy with fundraising helped keep her mind and body occupied. But from time to time, visions of the television footage of Barry's accident still haunted her.

She'd also had trouble sleeping, but these times began to recede as she got busier with the pool project.

Most of the townspeople came on board and were enthusiastic, but there were a few diehards who still declared it to be an unnecessary waste of money. (Many of these people were quite happy to see historic jetties in the district receiving extensive expensive repairs after being storm damaged time and time again!) Every money-making opportunity to fulfil Felicity's dream was explored. There were the traditional cake stalls, trash and treasure events, sporting challenges, straight-out donations, advance payments for commemorative plaques and paving stones, and many more. Country music concerts and local choral and drama presentations proved to be popular, and spectacular local gardens were displayed for small entrance fees.

The tender for construction was won by an Adelaide firm managed by a former Wattle Flat school student. Local tradesmen such as electricians, plumbers, and painters were all subcontracted, and they laboured alongside people with expert pool knowledge.

From the very beginning, the town benefited, with an influx of relatives and friends coming from outlying towns to view the project. Shop takings increased, especially in the supermarket and food shops, and the motel and caravan park were frequently booked out. Even in the very early stages of construction, it began to look like a win-win situation.

The planning committee, due to financial constraints and the size of the land donated by the council, decided to focus initially on creating a swimming complex catering for all ages with the requisite number of showers and change rooms and areas for pool equipment and maintenance. The rest could wait, they decided, at least for a little while. The size of the area set aside for parking was carefully calculated. Costs looked like escalating for a while when it was pointed out the pool needed to be heated and enclosed, at least during the winter. Having an all year-round facility for all ages was paramount, or ways of making money from the pool and being profitable would be lost if it was only available for use in the summer months. Gradually enthusiasm for the project gathered momentum, and although some corporate donations began to arrive, the windfarms and the mining companies were proving hard to persuade to support the project.

A small cafe inside the perimeter fence was planned to dispense hot and cold drinks as well as snack foods and ice cream. Felicity's additional idea of making it multipurpose with rooms for supportive therapies and a conference room was shelved as there were several halls in the town that could be utilised in this way. Sally was disappointed to find the planned room for a physiotherapist in the complex had also been discarded after she heard Luke telling their parents what a great facility he was helping to establish in Wattle Flat.

Luke had his quote for landscaping around the pool accepted and was eager to begin working there.

He planned to keep the area as uncluttered as possible, with easy-care low-maintenance plants and a large lawn which included several shaded areas. With the construction well underway, the committee received an anonymous donation stipulating it be used to build several sheltered areas with strategically placed seating where parents could keep an eye on their children in the water and a designated fenced-off area for passive adult exercise machines, which were becoming popular in many of the coastal parks.

At last, it seemed enthusiasm finally began replacing scepticism in Wattle Flat. Felicity also felt the attitude of the townspeople towards newcomers to the town begin to change. Most people, but not all, appeared to be more accepting of her. A stubborn group of long-term residents still held on to the belief that Felicity had something to do with Jack's premature death, but gradually they were being dismissed as troublemakers. *Was she now considered to be a local? Did it need her to request the building of a swimming pool, and following up by gathering hundreds of signatures from people who were in favour of the project to make this happen?*

If they were being supportive since Barry's death in the car accident, would they be less willing to see her as a person of value after a period of time? A niggle in the back of her mind surfaced intermittently, concerning what they thought of her; but for the rest of the time, she was undaunted by people's opinions.

While busy with the pool project, Felicity still hadn't given much thought as to how to best utilise the farm. She wasn't sure whether to lease again or sell it when the current three-year term ended. Apart from some cleared land around the farmhouse, there was a small paddock the leasing farmer couldn't use if his equipment proved too big to manoeuvre in such a small space. It had frontage on the main road and also along the accessing driveway. Felicity wondered if it could be used as an orchard for a selection of native trees or used for buildings of some sort.

A letter in the *Rural Times* eventually planted the seed of an idea that grew into reality on that block of land. It wasn't the first time Felicity had thought about people with disabilities. During her nursing career, she had watched the evolution of aids to assist people who'd had strokes, been injured in car accidents, or been born with less-than-perfect bodies. She'd also seen the lifelong effect polio had on victims and their families. The letter in the newspaper was appealing, as it called for more recognition for disabled people.

It stated in part: ***These days, more and more people with disabilities are getting out and about. They are no longer confined to their homes. Advances in wheelchair design, walking frames, and gophers are liberating, but more holiday venues are needed, where people with disabilities can be totally independent in a safe environment.***

Felicity had a light-bulb moment. Being fit and well, she couldn't imagine living with the physical challenges so many people were faced with each day. She knew if Barry had lived, his accident may have left him both physically and mentally disabled, and the lives of everyone around him would have changed dramatically. She decided to have five self-contained holiday cabins built in a garden setting in the two-acre site adjacent to the farmhouse.

It was one thing to make a decision, but she had no idea how many hurdles would have to be overcome before her dream became a reality! Rezoning, planning permission, and council approval were only the beginning. Looking into the possibility of receiving help and support from grants and volunteers also took time and effort. Access and parking areas would need to be available, and ramps with railings would be a priority. Although overwhelmed at times, Felicity remained excited and focussed on her new project. She intended to have her cottages especially fitted out for people with disabilities.

In the planning stages, Felicity read extensively and marvelled at all the ways mobility aids could be catered for in a modern dwelling. She planned identical units for people with disabilities, incorporating access for wheelchairs under hot plates and preparation areas, lowered work benches, and ovens that opened sideways situated close to heat-proof areas. There would be easy-to-access mixer taps, shallow drawers, and reachable pantry shelves and cupboards. Drawers would be installed instead of cupboard shelves.

As well as structural planning, she intended to select the many utensils now available to help arthritis sufferers and people with misshapen hands.

Bathrooms would feature raised toilets and handrails wherever they were needed. The showers without frames would be large enough to accommodate a chair. Mixer taps would be positioned opposite the shower rose (not underneath the taps) and also connected to a hand-held shower. Added structural support would be installed in the walls for all handrails. Hand basins would be free-standing to cater for wheelchairs. Felicity became aware that every fitting and utensil had to be evaluated and modified if necessary for elderly guests and people with disabilities.

She buttonholed Peter from time to time to listen to her ideas. He looked forward to her expounding her enthusiastic dream of value-adding to the farm income when they occasionally shared a cup of tea.

Wattle Flat townspeople were being reenervated as the swimming pool complex neared completion. Shops were expanding, and a walking track opened up. The township of Wattle Flat started taking on a new lease of life.

'The whole town's been injected with your infectious enthusiasm,' Peter told Felicity on more than one occasion. 'I'm sure that when your cottages are operational and added to the mix, they will be a big plus for the whole district.'

CHAPTER 17

Felicity knew she had to remain focussed and busy. She didn't want to slip into depression as she had previously when things were too hard to handle. With the building of the municipal swimming pool well under way and being managed by an energetic committee, she was eager for her planned units to receive council approval. Deciding she needed to focus on something else in the meantime, she started spring cleaning by clearing out at least one cupboard or drawer each day. She had once worked with a nursing colleague who did this religiously every day, and her home was always free of clutter.

Where to begin? Felicity knew she'd have to pack up all of Barry's things at some stage and take most of them to the op shop. She decided to take the very best of his clothes and possessions to an upmarket second-hand shop in a nearby town that sold articles for clients, taking a small percentage of the sale price as commission. Felicity enjoyed visiting that shop, and on Tuesdays, when all clothing was half price, she often arrived home with some great bargains— even better if the owner called her over to the desk and handed her a few dollars, telling her she'd sold some articles Felicity had brought in previously.

Cleaning out cupboards wasn't on top of Felicity's favourites' list, so she dodged the issue of Barry's belongings by cleaning the toilets and bathrooms instead. She was amazed at the amount of stuff that had accumulated in cupboards and drawers over the years. When she thought about starting on Barry's wardrobe, she became overcome by emotion. Sorting out shirts and jeans soon had her in tears, clouding her vision. She closed the wardrobe, sank down on their bed, and sobbed uncontrollably. It all felt too difficult.

Eventually she calmed down and was able to sleep for several hours. On waking, she was pensive for a while, then wondered, *Would Ken and Rose-Louise like something that used to belong to Barry?*

Felicity headed for the kitchen to sort out her thoughts over a cup of green tea. She often recalled the unlikely circumstances that brought Barry's offspring together with her in the restaurant in Horsham. How proud Barry would have been to meet them both, and how sad they had missed meeting him. They looked so much like him.

She knew she had to keep busy and not dwell on things that couldn't be changed. The kitchen cupboards beckoned. She set to work with renewed energy, and before long, she discovered the letter from Rose-Louise in the plastic shopping bag.

*   *   *

Gearing up for another country music festival, Horsham was in full swing, with Brian Letton, a featured artist, and many other prominent names appearing on billboards around the town. David Edgar appeared on the program for all three days, and his wife,

Meggie, was to read her original rhyming poetry at the poets' breakfast. Accommodation venues had increased bookings, and Rose-Louise prepared special restaurant menus to suit the country music theme. Bookings were essential. She knew March would bring increased business, so she was looking forward to taking a week's holiday early in April.

Her mobile rang, interrupting her thoughts.

'Hello, Rose-Louise, it's Felicity Clapper here. How are you?'

'I'm well, thank you. It's the country music festival in Horsham this weekend, and it looks like the restaurant will be booked out on all three nights. We've even taken reservations for Monday night as well. The motel is filling up as the festival brings people into town from all over Victoria and interstate, and not everyone arrives in a caravan or brings a tent. Many older folk like the extra comfort of motel accommodation. I'm busy, and at times, I'm exhausted by the end of the day. I will definitely be ready for my holiday break in a few weeks' time.'

'That sounds great. I loved visiting your restaurant. It's a welcoming venue, and the food was amazing. I've been cleaning out my kitchen cupboards and drawers and found the letter from you in a folded plastic bag. According to the postmark, it arrived when I holidayed in Yarrawonga. I had a friend living here minding my home, feeding the animals, and collecting mail. It seems your letter remained in the bottom of the bag and was put away in my kitchen drawer by mistake. Fancy meeting you in the meantime.

I'm calling to see if you'd be interested in having something that used to belong to Barry, as a sort of connection to your father.

I'm struggling at the moment to make a new start without him. It isn't easy with all his clothes and possessions around the house and farm. I can't imagine cleaning out the sheds out the back. There are generations of things I would classify as junk, but Barry kept everything just in case they came in handy one day. Peter, who used to be Barry's best friend at school, is my nearest neighbour and has agreed to lease from me for three years to give me breathing space. He's offered to help me clean out the sheds after seeding. I haven't a clue what most of the machinery does or even if it's in working order. Barry kept the farm side of things strictly to himself. I think he thought he had to prove he could manage on his own because his father didn't do much to build up his self-esteem.

It's Barry's clothes and things I'm finding distressing when I try to sort things inside the house. I'll contact Ken to see if he'd like something as well. I was wondering, if you had any time off soon, would you like to come and visit and maybe help me with some sorting?'

'That's a wonderful idea. Your timing is perfect. As I said, I have a week off in April, and I hadn't decided what to do with it. I'd love to come and visit then if that suits you.'

*   *   *

The opening of the swimming pool complex coincided with Rose-Louise's visit to Clapper's Cove. The whole town of Wattle Flat was buzzing with excitement. The beaches were deserted by the end of March, and now the townspeople could choose to swim and exercise in the municipal pool all year round. Bright-red geraniums and red standard roses provided a cheerful display outside the perimeter fence. The paving had been finished the week before the opening, and all the plants adjacent to the grassy area away from the pool were thriving. Inside the complex, set back from the saltwater pool, Luke had carefully chosen plants to provide shade, protection from wind, and for their stunning appearance.

He'd selected varieties with silvery, furry, or waxy leaves, choosing salt-tolerant species with a wide variety of colours. He was well aware that plants with fine foliage that dropped leaves could play havoc with pool cleaners and filters, and deciduous plants were not even considered.

When the site was being cleared and excavation was being done for the pool, there were heated discussions between conservationists and the pool planners about getting rid of several large gum trees just outside the pool complex perimeter.

Finally, they agreed to remove them as the investment in the pool was too great to risk large tree roots invading the precinct in the future. All invasive trees and shrubs were understandably excluded from Luke's list of plant selections.

The opening took place on a beautiful autumn day, and Rose-Louise caught some of Felicity's excitement as they toured the pool surrounds and inspected the exercise area.

'You must feel so proud to see an idea you instigated eventually come to fruition. What made you so passionate about Wattle Flat having a swimming pool?'

'When I was nursing, I worked a lot with people recovering from surgery and the elderly who found it too painful to exercise. I saw what a difference it made to them to be able to use a pool or spa. If children learn to swim at an early age, there are likely to be less drownings as well. The social aspect is important too, somewhere for young and old who aren't sporty people to meet, rather than gather on the streets or frequent hotel bars.

So many country towns are dying. We're lucky in Wattle Flat all our shops are occupied, but there's no guarantee they'll stay that way. Because the town is situated on Yorke Peninsula like the hub of a wheel, half an hour from several surrounding communities, I felt it would be a big plus for the town to have something to offer everyone, even if they're not athletic. You never know, we might produce an Olympic gold medallist like Dawn Fraser in a few years! At the moment, swimming is probably one of the only local sports where the people of Wattle Flat haven't produced a champion.'

'How did you manage to persuade them?'

'I just thought it was worth a shot. I had nothing to lose if I stuck my neck out. I think I have finally been accepted into the community now because of my passion for this swimming pool idea. It seems the younger generation, those with children in preschool, were my strongest supporters. They thought up heaps of innovative ways to top up the grants we were able to get. They baked, sewed, and invented all sorts of reasons to have parties to raise money.

Elderly people were also very helpful. Many of them had enjoyed swimming over the years but now found it hard navigating through the sand and rocks on our beaches, not to mention the need to watch out for stingrays, stingers, and razor fish.

The older folk were also very aware they could get into difficulties if they swam alone at the beach, and they couldn't always find an able-bodied younger person to accompany them during the day.

The middle group of people have been busy earning a living, but they dug deep into their pockets when the hat was taken round. In the end, the whole community has pulled together, with a great result.

Local tradespeople have been employed wherever possible. The pool contractor established his business in Adelaide but had gone to school in Wattle Flat. The plumber and electrician both grew up here. Luke, a local landscape gardener, has done an amazing job at a reasonable price. He's probably generated a lot of business for himself out of this project. I, for one, will be using him to put the finishing touches on my next project, which is now at the council offices awaiting approval.'

'Do you have more community projects in the pipeline?'

'No, this is a private venture . . . although I'll gratefully accept any donations and grants if they come my way. When Barry died, he left me his superannuation as well as the farm and more than enough to live on. I'm not too old to return to nursing if I choose to do so, and I have a small massage business where I can select whenever and how often I want to work. I envisage using Barry's superannuation to build holiday units to cater for the elderly and for people with disabilities.'

'What a wonderful idea.'

'I think it's great how people with disabilities are accepted and catered for in the community now and how terms such as *spastic*, *cripple*, *defective*, and *retarded* are now viewed as inappropriate. Those names were often used in a derogatory manner and were stigmatising and patronising. Apparently they were based on medical meanings and not meant to offend anyone, but that's not how it played out over time. Originally, spastic referred to people with cerebral palsy. Someone who had difficulty walking or had been injured was labelled a cripple, while people with problems who didn't fit into either of those categories were often classified as defective.'

'Yes, I'm certainly more comfortable referring to people as being disabled instead of any of those other terms.

Some words used by our members of parliament recently really make me cringe, and we'd be better off without those politicians too! When do you expect to hear back from the council, and do you think they'll raise any objections?'

Much to Felicity's amazement and delight, the approval for building her proposed units was finalised by the end of the month.

CHAPTER 18

Ken was determined to keep in touch with Rose-Louise, so he had a meal in her motel restaurant at least once a month. He had no hesitation recommending the venue to friends, especially if they were looking for somewhere to dine on a special occasion. Ewen escorted his parents to a meal there for his father's seventy-fifth birthday, and they were greatly impressed by the whole package: the food, the venue, the service, and the fact that Rose-Louise as manager greeted them as though they were very important guests. Jenny and Auntie Margaret dined there regularly until Margaret became too frail to enjoy eating out. Jenny also introduced friends from the CWA and the craft group to the fine food served at the thriving motel restaurant.

Soon after Margaret signed her farm over to Ken, she moved into the Lutheran Retirement Village, where she happily spent her final years with people her own age, being well-cared-for in a sheltered environment. Jenny remained on the farm with Ken until her mother slipped on wet concrete steps and broke her hip, and her father asked if Jenny would return to Wattle Flat to help him care for her. Ken knew he needed to start fending for himself sometime soon. He'd taken a fair bit of flak from his mates over the years because he still lived with his mum.

'My moving out could be a very good idea. It will mean you'll need to become more independent. I feel like I've been cramping your style with the young ladies of the district by still living here. With me off the farm, maybe you'll find a nice girl, settle down, and produce some grandchildren for me to spoil and come and visit occasionally.'

Ken hadn't been able to take time off away from the farm in April when Rose-Louise spent a week staying with Felicity on the Clapper property. It had been hoped they could travel over to South Australia together.

'I'll drive there as soon as I can after the wheat crop is in the ground. Something personal of Barry's would be great to keep—like his favourite hat, wallet, or boots. I wouldn't mind having a look at some of his tools as well, if that's OK with you?'

Finally, the cottages were all but finished. The site would be cleared of building debris by the end of the week, the lawns mowed, and flowers placed in each of the units. Felicity was thrilled by the way they'd turned out. She checked the fridges to see they were stocked with long-life milk and cold water and saw that tea and coffee sachets were in plentiful supply. The bathrooms had been equipped with soap, tissues, and toilet paper the day before.

The opening was advertised in the *Rural Times* and on Gulf FM radio, and flyers had been left in many of the local shops. A marquee was fully equipped with refreshments ranging from tea and coffee to cool drinks, an assortment of sandwiches and home-made biscuits, and several traditional sponge cakes topped with strawberries and cream.

Although designed as a private venture to value-add to her farm and bring in extra income, it had generated support from the townspeople. Many Wattle Flat townsfolk and even some people from neighbouring towns showed interest in attending on the opening day to see what the buildings would offer to future guests with disabilities.

Nestled in among the trees, where the ground was rocky and only sparse vegetation struggled to grow, the five self-contained cottages were fully equipped for elderly people or people of any age with disabilities. They featured ramps and non-slip surfaces and wide access doorways and ample space to manoeuvre walking frames, wheelchairs, or motorized scooters (commonly called gophers) in all the rooms. The two-bedroom units were designed for privacy with ease of movement for a carer, as well as for someone elderly or with a disability. Each stand-alone unit had its own carport enclosed on three sides, with plenty of room to move mobility aids in and out of vehicles.

Felicity invited both Rose-Louise and Ken to the opening of her project. They opted to share the long drive this time. This event would be a turning point in all their lives. As Luke had become more of a friend than a subcontractor, he was also invited to attend and was asked to bring his parents and sister with him as well. Sally showed interest (as a physiotherapist) and wanted to learn more about the innovative venture and felt proud of the job her brother had done with the landscaping.

*   *   *

Derek and Anna were keen supporters of the old-time dance club that met every fortnight in a different venue on the peninsula. Felicity also wanted to go dancing and invited Peter from the next-door farm to go with her.

'I feel a bit uncomfortable going out with a woman who isn't my wife,' he'd told her when she invited him the first time.

'This isn't going out together. We're not going on a date. I'm just asking you to be my dance partner. It'll do us both good to get out and about a bit more.'

When Peter moved back to his family farm near Clapper's Cove to try and make it a profitable entity once more, he and his wife had corresponded frequently by email and telephoned often. But as the weeks turned into months, they seemed to have very little to say to one another, so they connected less often.

Peter proved to be a tower of strength for Felicity whenever she needed advice or assistance. He made himself available with his trusty tractor and front-end loader if she wanted to move heavy objects, and he happily taught her about farm procedures.

With Barry, it had been very different.

'I'm happy to have you helping me pick rocks, pull out weeds, and dig out the sandy soil from newly dug post holes, but not drive any machinery,' he'd said on more than one occasion.

Felicity remembered those *'bloody'* post holes when Barry instructed her to get down on her hands and knees and dig loose soil out of them with a sardine tin! Attaching the cyclone wire to the timber posts with staples was frustrating too. The head of the old hammer she had been given to use kept separating from its handle. After having this happen for a third time, in a fit of frustration, she'd thrown it out into the paddock, where it was never seen again. As you can imagine, such rebellion wasn't met with approval, but it produced great satisfaction at the time.

The exception to Barry's rule about machinery was to allow her to feed hay out to the cattle using the Massey Ferguson tractor, which had prongs on the front of it to carry the hay. His instructions were typed out and laminated so she wouldn't forget anything. They returned to her like a mantra whenever she climbed into the driver's seat.

Check the oil and water levels.

Release the foot brake.

Make sure the stop knob on the left is pushed right in.

Make sure the gear lever is in neutral (middle position).

Start engine with key and set revs at 800.

Select gears, using big and small gear levers.

Felicity was terrified she would do something wrong, and that would be the end of her contributing to helping Barry with farming tasks. What's more, those instructions were just the beginning. They continued:

To lift the bucket, move the pink lever by left leg forward, and outer right-side lever right up, and inner right-side lever right down. Then pull outer grey knob lever down (near steering wheel).

Select high first gear.

To lift the rear prongs, pull pink lever by left leg upright and outer right- side lever all the way down. Then use only inner right-side lever to raise and lower prongs.

Finally, with her confidence growing each time she used the tractor, she'd asked to help in other ways on the farm as well. Only once had Barry allowed her to drive the header but only for one lap of their smallest paddock, and one other time, she drove the tractor, pulling the slasher for a short distance. But there was a problem— Barry travelled on the back of the vehicles both times, as though he was waiting for her to get into difficulties.

She knew she'd managed well but soon decided that constantly having to request to be included in farm activities wasn't worth the effort. Except for occasions when Barry couldn't legally operate on his own, such as burning paddocks prior to seeding, Felicity's contributions were limited to working in the house and garden. She could never understand why Barry felt so compelled to manage everything on his own and only reluctantly accept help.

'Oh, there were also written instructions on how to stop the tractor after I'd fed the hay to the cattle,' she'd continued telling Peter.

*To finish, push inside lever down, then push pink
lever forward, then push right-side lever upright.*

*Pull out stop button and push back in when motor
stops.*

Select neutral on both gearbox levers.

Although these anecdotes seemed funny when she recounted
them to Peter, her frustration had been very real at the time. Under
Peter's guidance, she was achieving a great deal and had become a
more capable contributor to the workings of the farm she'd inherited.
Her stress levels were almost non-existent, and she felt more fulfilled.
She was feeling happy and content for the first time in years.

*   *   *

Luke was comfortable with who he was. He had loving parents and
a sister who used to be a pain in the neck when she was growing up
but had now become an intelligent, independent young woman. Luke
felt proud of her and didn't hesitate to recommend her as an excellent
physiotherapist who was especially tuned in to people with disabilities.

His paternity was of no interest to him. He was pleased to be
employed by Felicity doing the landscaping for her cottages. Not once
had he felt the need to divulge the identity of his biological father to
her. He didn't look like Barry at all, but rather he resembled Derek with
similar mannerisms and the same dark-brown curly hair and brown eyes.

Because of the hurdles Luke had faced with his health challenges,
he was probably more understanding of people with disabilities than
someone whose health had only been subject to childhood illnesses.

He wasn't looking for opportunities to tell anyone his biological father's identity, and very few people knew of the disability he dealt with every day. Luke was intensely loyal to the parents who'd been with him all his life, who'd educated him and set out good values for him to follow. And he was proud to acknowledge his success as a landscaper, living in a unit he owned in a town of his choice.

There were no speeches or formal opening of the Clapper Cottages. Visitors and townspeople viewed the units and their facilities and took home one of the strategically placed advertising brochures. People milled around before gathering in the refreshment tent.

When Ken first heard about Felicity's idea to build cottages on the small paddock near the farmhouse, he offered his computer skills to make posters and flyers. He took photos and gathered information when he visited Felicity, and she regularly emailed him progress photos as the building progressed. The resulting work was stunning, and there were even enquiries from people wanting to know who she'd employed as her graphic artist. She knew a professional approach to her business was necessary for it to be a success. Felicity was lucky the farm boundary was close to the new swimming pool complex and Wattle Flat township. Proximity to both would help promote her new business.

Felicity gratefully accepted an offer from Rose-Louise to help with the refreshments. Rose-Louise was the perfect hostess for the occasion due to her restaurant experience. She added subtle touches to the table decorations and made sure all their visitors' refreshment needs were met. Felicity felt proud that her new stepfamily were part of her value-adding venture, especially since the Clapper Cottages were built on part of the farm she'd inherited from their father.

Rose-Louise chuckled to herself when she overheard one elderly lady saying to her companion, 'Those two, the graphic artist and the woman serving afternoon tea . . . they remind me of Barry Clapper. I wonder if they are distant relatives.'

Ken and Rose-Louise didn't announce to anyone if or how they were related or their connection with Felicity. It was pretty obvious because of their similar appearances and their likeness to Barry that they were connected to the Clapper family in some way. Although speculation was probably high among the town gossips, there were no direct questions. Ken and Rose-Louise agreed telling Felicity about Barry being the biological father of both of them was all that mattered. As Luke hadn't divulged his personal discovery to Felicity, or anyone else, the two groups of half siblings were unaware they were linked by DNA. Only Luke's parents knew of his Clapper connection.

*　　*　　*

There was instant chemistry between Ken and Sally, and after spending some time glancing surreptitiously at each other in-between directing people to parking spaces and explaining features in the cottages, they ended up chatting together for much of the afternoon.

It was the beginning of what would happen in the future. They made sure they exchanged email and postal addresses and phone numbers.

Felicity, Rose-Louise, Luke, Ken, and Sally explored a walking trail at the rear of the farm on Sunday morning, the day after the excitement of the official opening of the cottages. (Ken asked Felicity to extend an invitation to Sally and her brother to join them, as he wanted to further explore his unexpected feelings towards Luke's sister.) They enjoyed the relaxing walk as the trail meandered between the sandhills along the clifftop before returning them back to the main road near the cottages. Felicity was hoping some of her able-bodied guests would be able to follow the same route in the future.

They were all thrilled to learn there were already seven future bookings made on the opening day. Rose-Louise and Luke discovered they had instant rapport also, but while Ken and Sally sought opportunities to be alone, Luke was determined to maintain a brother/sister relationship with Rose-Louise. He needn't have been concerned, as for several months she and Ewen (Ken's farming friend in Pimpinio) had been inseparable. Ewen would have travelled with her to the opening of the cottages, but he'd agreed to be a groomsman at a Longerenong College mate's wedding on that weekend.

There was no doubt Ken found Sally attractive. He loved her silky blond shoulder-length hair, blue eyes, and fair complexion, and the fact her slim body had curves in all the right places was appealing to him as well. They discovered they had so much in common, being able to talk about meaningful topics as well as sharing a love of the outdoors and exercising.

Sally appeared to be smitten also. Ken and Rose-Louise spent three days on the peninsula before Ken returned to Victoria, and he spent as much time as possible with Sally. He met with her after she finished work for the day, and they talked together well into the night at the local club until it closed. Ken had often dated in college. He was good-looking and clean-shaven in those days. Since he had taken up the challenge to grow a beard and moustache to raise money for a new ambulance needed in the Horsham district, he looked very distinguished. He talked to Rose-Louise about his feelings for Sally.

'I've never felt like this before. Is it possible to be in love with someone after only knowing them for three short days? Sally's a great girl and so easy to talk to about anything at all. But the logistics of a long-distance romance are more than a little daunting. It's too far to drive for just a weekend.'

'Anything is possible. I don't think there are any set rules regarding falling in love! Keep in contact as often as you can and see what eventuates. With emails and texting and mobile phones, it's easy to keep in touch these days. If Sally feels the same way, you'll work out something so you can be together. Both she and Luke are lovely people. It was weird seeing you and Luke together. You walk in the same way and flip your hair from your eyes in a similar way as well.'

'That's interesting. Did you know you have a mole on your cheek in the same position as Luke? That's strange, isn't it?'

Felicity also noticed the similarities between the two young men and even the matching moles on Rose-Louise and Luke, but she dismissed them as coincidences and not of any importance. Finding out that Ken and Rose-Louise both had the same father, who just happened to be her deceased husband, was incredible enough. She could be excused for not even contemplating there could be any more of Barry's offspring, especially knowing his poor fertility history.

Once Ken arrived back on his farm, he found his thoughts frequently drifted back to Sally and the myriad thoughts and ideas they'd exchanged in just a few days spent together.

Luke hadn't told Felicity that Barry was his father. He wondered when or even if there would be a right time for the revelation. Likenesses between Ken and Rose-Louise, and photos of Barry, left no doubt they were related somehow. Only Felicity, Ken, and Rose-Louise knew how they were related but not that Luke was linked to them in the same way.

Somewhere along the line, because she had taken her final exams in Adelaide on the day of Barry's funeral, Sally missed out knowing about Luke's origins. Because it had been of no significance to Luke, he'd never thought to mention it to her.

It wasn't long before Ken told her, during one of their in-depth conversations, about his parentage and how he was linked to Rose-Louise. Sally was fascinated but still had no inkling she would discover a further link about their biological origins further down the track.

CHAPTER 19

The township of Wattle Flat was thriving. It seemed the construction of the municipal swimming pool had united the town and had brought many more visitors to the district. The apathetic haze that had encompassed the community for so long seemed to have dissipated. Bike racks were installed in strategic positions adjacent to the shopping centre, and the gardens down the middle of the main street were revamped. An opportunity shop was set up, and all profits were being directed to the local community fundraising as well as supporting the Royal Flying Doctor Service.

Volunteers emerged from nowhere to staff organisations such as Yorke Peninsula Community Transport and to keep the Health Bus on the road. These greatly valued services ferried elderly people to specialist doctors' appointments in Adelaide at a minimal cost, using volunteer drivers and carers.

The progress association was being swamped with ideas to keep the town moving forward. A central venue was acquired and staffed by volunteers to sell local produce and craft products. The variety of items for sale at very reasonable prices was mind-blowing. The support of the townspeople for this venture continued to be amazing, and many visited the centre to socialise or just to enjoy a cup of tea or coffee. The information centre was renovated and upgraded, and more staff were employed.

The mobile blood bank visited Wattle Flat regularly, and Felicity, Peter, and Luke were all registered donors. Peter and Felicity were both O+, the blood type most frequently found in the community. Luke was A−, which wasn't common in many people, and the blood bank's records showed there used to be one other person in the district with the same blood type, but the donor, Barry Clapper, was deceased.

*   *   *

Over the years, with advanced methods of farming and the need to cover vast distances quickly, many of the young men and women in the Wattle Flat district obtained their pilot's licences, and some, after a good season, even owned their own planes.

Andrew Brown had been one of the younger generation of pilots flying on Yorke Peninsula. He often took paying passengers to help cover the cost of his fuel. Felicity remembered Barry taking several flights over the district supposedly to check on crops, but he'd told her, 'The flights were supposedly to check on the condition of crops, but that proved to be secondary to experiencing the freedom and joy of being in the air, high above the everyday world.'

Many photos were taken over the years, and when it was fashionable and easy to carry video cameras on holiday or to important events, many flights were recorded on tape. Some were reviewed afterwards, but often they were carefully stored to be looked at some time in the future. (Felicity felt guilty for doing the same thing with books, saving them to read when she was old but forgetting her interests could change and that the print might be too small by the time she was ready to read them.)

A combination of history enthusiasts, members of the camera club, and other interested townspeople joined forces to sort out community photos and videotapes and catalogue them. Twelve months down the track, they had enough to stage an exhibition open to the public for a whole weekend in the senior citizen's club. They planned to exhibit all types of photos—some regular sized, some huge enlargements— and have videos playing continuously. Some were even displayed in photo books and as canvas prints. There was excitement in the town as many townsfolk unearthed long-forgotten photos and submitted them for selection.

Felicity hadn't ever wanted to personally learn how to fly but had repeatedly asked Barry to tee up a flight for her with Andrew Brown, but it never happened. Instead, she entered and won a competition at the Maitland Show that offered a flight around the district as first prize. She was gobsmacked and so excited to be able to see far away across the paddocks of crops to the coastline. She remembered recording in her diary:

Although the flight only lasted a quarter of an hour, it was one of the highlights of my life.

There were advertisements about the upcoming photographic exhibition in the local newspaper and flyers in many of the shop windows. Felicity marked her calendar boldly with a black text, as she was determined not to miss the event.

In the same edition of the *Rural Times* as the ads, an article also gave a brief account of Jack's death in their *'What Happened Many Years Ago?'* section.

This revived discussion among the older town gossips, who were glad to have something to share with newcomers to the town. They presented the story as an unsolved mystery, which may have even been a murder, and Felicity as their prime suspect! The gossips—both men and women—were eager to point out to anyone who'd listen that the cause of Jack Clapper's death had never been satisfactorily resolved. For a few weeks, Felicity remained the target of quizzical looks as the gossips again relished discussing the possible ways Jack could have died and Felicity's possible involvement apart from discovering his body tangled in barbed wire face down in the tidal pool in Clapper's Cove.

*　　*　　*

A week before the exhibition, Felicity received a phone call from Ken. After a few polite enquiries about her health, her cottage business, the state of the crops in the district, and the current weather, he finally came to the reason for his call.

'I was wondering if you have a vacancy in one of your cottages next week. If so, could I please make a reservation for a few days, from next Thursday evening until Tuesday morning? I've heard there's to be an exhibition of historic photos in town and thought if I visited over the weekend, I might also be able to spend some time with a certain young lady I met recently. Jenny has people staying with her over that weekend as well, and her house will be bursting at the seams, so she doesn't need me sleeping in a swag in her lounge room.'

'You're out of luck in regard to renting a cottage for that time. They're booked out that week, but I would love to have you stay with me. I can give you the bungalow out the back, and you can come and go at whatever time you choose.

Sally has popped in to say hello from time to time and always asks if I have heard from you recently. She's a lovely lass. Am I correct in presuming she's the certain young lady you're referring to?'

'Yes, Sally and I have been in contact fairly regularly. It's a long drive to Yorke Peninsula, but I'm really looking forward to a break, and Ewen said he'd keep an eye on things here . . . if he can spare time from seeing Rose-Louise. They're definitely an item, and I'm sure there will be an announcement from them in the near future.'

'I'm so glad to hear Rose-Louise is happy and looking forward to a future with Ewen. She's worked so hard. She deserves to have a supportive partner in her life. I'll be happy to contribute towards her wedding expenses when the time comes, if she'll let me.'

*　　*　　*

The exhibition of photos was a great success. People came from miles around. Some came to see the advances made in photography over the years, while some visited to see how their old photos, packed away for years, had been displayed. Everyone gladly donated a gold coin towards the renovation plans for the preschool centre, whose brainchild it had been to put the exhibition together along with the cooperation of the photography club. There was talk afterwards about keeping most of the photos in the local museum as a permanent historical record. The museum was a fascinating place to visit. Its collection of local history could keep a visitor enthralled for several hours. It had been mooted that the next town challenge would be to find a more spacious venue so exhibits could be less cluttered and better displayed.

Ken drove into town, looking forward to meeting up with Sally, who planned to visit the exhibition with her parents after an early lunch at home. She'd wanted to get to Wattle Flat sooner but had agreed to see some private patients during the morning. She and Ken scanned the exhibits superficially to justify their reason for meeting there then slipped away to the bakery for sticky buns and coffee. They intended to spend as much time as they could together, but both had responsible occupations and were conscious of time and the miles usually separating them.

Anna and Derek watched them as they slipped away.

'They make a handsome pair, don't they, Derek?' Anna commented. 'This is the first boyfriend Sally seems to be totally in tune with. Ken and Sally both look relaxed and happy.'

'It's good to see them enjoying each other's company. Sally deserves to be happy. She's such a caring person. If anyone ever hurts her, they will have to deal with me. If there are good-looking grandchildren in the future, that'll be a bonus. As for the trend these days of not bothering about getting married, I'm not sure how I would deal with that idea.'

'Let's deal with that hurdle if or when it happens. They only met a short time ago. Right now, they only have eyes for each other. We can only hope that if they are meant to be together, they will sincerely love one another.'

'I just hope both our children will be as happy in their chosen relationships as we've been in ours. We sincerely want good health and happiness for each of them.'

Sally and Ken were free of commitments for the rest of the weekend. On Monday, Sally had a booking at the mobile Red Cross blood bank. The large vehicle had a regular parking spot whenever it visited, next to the sports store in the main street. Sally had been donating blood ever since her first year at university.

'Ken, do you know your blood group? Have you ever given blood?'

'No and no are the answers to those questions.'

'I have an appointment at ten o'clock on Monday morning. Why don't you come and give blood too? They always welcome new donors. It's a good way to find out your blood group, and it's certainly a worthwhile cause.'

That was how Ken came to find out that his blood group was the rare A−.

'That's pretty cool. My brother, Luke, is the only other person I know with A− blood! Maybe you are brothers,' she added flippantly, not knowing she'd stumbled close to the truth.

*   *   *

Felicity and Peter met up at the photographic exhibition. They'd viewed all the exhibits separately, but both of them, for some unknown reason, drifted back to the same section more than once.

'Peter, is this video taken from a plane flying over my farm? The area looks familiar. Isn't that the tidal inlet near Clapper's Cove?'

They stood watching while the video played over and over. What they were seeing dawned on them at the same time. The video took them down the coast over Clapper's Cove before going back to Wattle Flat, passing over the cove again on the return journey.

'Look, Peter. It's hard to tell exactly, but in the first section, it looks like there's someone hanging on to a big sheep tangled up in a roll of barbed wire. A bit later, we see the sheep clambering up the path to the clifftop.'

'Yes, I see what you mean. That's probably why we can't see the sheep later on. But it looks like there could be a person lying in the water at the entrance to the cove.'

'That looks like the place where Jack died. Could this be a video of what actually happened to him? It was probably filmed by a passenger in a small plane flying over the area. Could the unsolved mystery of his death be here on this video?'

'Look, if that's Jack in the video, he may have seen a sheep tangled up in that barbed wire and gone down to investigate. He would have left his trike on the clifftop while he clambered down the cliff to try and free the stupid animal. Just as he managed to get the sheep untangled, the roll of wire could have sprung back and tangled around him, at the same time knocking him face down into the shallow water of the tidal inlet.'

The video ended at that point before starting over again. Felicity suddenly went pale and began to shake uncontrollably. Peter took her hand and pulled her closer to him, turning her round to look directly at him.

'I've always believed that's what must have happened. I knew you were innocent of any involvement in his death. Jack could be a controlling old bastard at times and had a lot to answer for the way he treated Barry. My old man was controlling too and wouldn't listen to any new ideas. That's why I left home. Maybe now those gossiping old biddies who can't resist stirring up doubts from time to time will be silenced forever.'

'Look, Peter, it says here on this card it was filmed by Joe Wilson, a passenger in Andrew Brown's plane . . . and the date of the video is the same day Jack died. Joe was renowned for taking lots of videos and storing them to catalogue later. I believe he handed a box of videos to the committee to make a selection, and they may have randomly selected this one, knowing all his videos are worth looking at but hadn't been aware of its significance.'

Felicity felt warmth flood through her as Peter supported her, holding her close to his body. It felt so good to finally be believed! Someone found a chair for her, and she was brought a glass of water.

One of the exhibition's organisers arranged for the video to be carefully removed and handed into the care of the police. Later on, the actual time and date were checked and verified against the pilot's records. From then on, things were a blur for Felicity. She felt overwhelming relief knowing there was proof of her lack of involvement in Jack's death. Although she'd always known she was innocent, it seemed amazing to be vindicated in such a public way.

The gossips were silenced but failed to apologise, hoping they could fade into anonymity. But most people knew who they were. The *Rural Times* published an article the following week about how, in an extraordinary coincidence, the video shown at the photographic exhibition had been seen by Felicity, the daughter-in-law of Jack Clapper, whose death had unknowingly been caught on an amateur video. It had been an extraordinary coincidence.

The headlines had read, ***Video Verifies How Local Identity Died by Misadventure.***

*   *   *

Felicity was becoming more and more attached to Peter, who in turn was increasingly supportive and helpful. As dancing partners, they were out together every fortnight and soon began sharing an evening meal prior to each event. Peter's contact with his wife had dwindled to when they rang each other only to discuss business. She had taken in a schoolteacher as a boarder, who was frequently mentioned during their conversations. Peter had gleaned the impression he'd become more than a boarder. This fact was verified when he spoke to his son from time to time.

Love developed steadily between Felicity and Peter, growing out of the mutual respect they had for each other and the passion they shared for their farms. Both their lives and farms were benefiting from their happy relationship. It was evident to everyone who knew them they were well suited for one another.

Rose-Louise, happily in a relationship with Ewen, was very pleased to see Felicity so content, and everyone was glad the mystery of Jack's death had been cleared up. They knew it must have been horrible living under a cloud of suspicion, even though the cloud was mainly kept fluffed up by malicious town gossips. They agreed it was time Felicity had some decent breaks after all she'd had to contend with.

Ken and Sally had probably glanced at the video as they skimmed the exhibition, but neither were familiar with the layout of Felicity's farm, so it had no significance them. Their interest in the photos and videos had only been an excuse to spend more time together.

At last, with the mystery of Jack Clapper's death finally solved, relief and resolution was felt by many people in the small close-knit community.

CHAPTER 20

It was during the unseasonable wild weather that wrecked many of the jetties along the Yorke Peninsula coastline that Luke, the cherished son of Anna and Derek and beloved brother of Sally, lost his life. All planes were grounded, so the Flying Doctor was unable to assist in his transportation. Although rushed to Adelaide by road ambulance, by the time he arrived, his fight for life was nearly over. Ironically, A− blood, donated by his half-brother Ken, was unsuccessfully used to try and stem the tide of his burst aneurysm. Luke had been only twenty-two when he died.

Luke's aneurysm had been a silent killer. He didn't know he'd been harbouring a potentially lethal invader. His assailant came out of the blue, and as the host, Luke didn't stand a chance. He was shopping in the supermarket buying milk when it happened. It came on so quickly. Other shoppers heard him cry out in pain. He staggered and lurched against the grocery shelves before he slumped to the floor clutching his head and saying he was feeling very dizzy and the pain in his head was unbearable. An employee felt his rapidly racing pulse as she made him comfortable on the floor, while another dialled for an ambulance.

All volunteers rostered for ambulance duty that day lived within the town boundaries and were at the ambulance station in a matter of minutes. Sadly, their swift response wasn't enough. Luke needed urgent specialist care in Adelaide.

All air traffic was cancelled, including the Flying Doctor's specially equipped plane. Due to the gale force storms lashing the whole of the state, Luke had to travel the two and a half hours by road ambulance. With the storms raging, whipping up gale-force winds and torrential rain, the hazardous journey would have been extremely uncomfortable.

It was cruel to have this happen to such a fit young man who exercised regularly, ate a healthy diet, and didn't smoke. The only glimmer of comfort from Luke's death was the fact he carried an organ donor card in his wallet, authorizing the use of his organs and tissues for transplant purposes. Passing away in the Royal Adelaide Hospital meant this wish could be fulfilled to its maximum degree, as there was no need to transport his body large distances for organ retrieval before returning him to his family in Ardrossan.

Anna and Derek both had *organ donor* printed on their driver's licences and had persuaded Sally and Luke to join up as well. They were told one person donating their organs and tissue could change the lives of more than ten people. It is such a worthy cause, and Australia's successful outcomes from transplants rate very highly worldwide. The most commonly transplanted organs are kidneys, livers, and lungs. (South Australia's Queen Elizabeth Hospital had the first successful Australian kidney transplants from both live and deceased donors.) A donor could pledge his organs, but the harvesting wouldn't happen unless the next of kin also agreed. Anna and Derek knew there were usually about 1,500 people on Australian organ transplant waiting lists at any time each year, so when the call came from the Royal Adelaide Hospital for verification of Luke's wishes, they didn't hesitate in giving their endorsement.

Everyone who knew Luke was greatly distressed to learn of his untimely death, his family most of all. Derek and Anna were also faced with the dilemma of whether to reveal Luke's paternity privately to Felicity and Sally or not at all, knowing his secret could go to the grave with him.

'If he'd intended telling anyone, surely he would have done it by now,' declared Anna. 'He had many opportunities when he could have broached the subject.'

'I think he would have told Felicity eventually.'

'We know Ken and Rose-Louise have the Clapper genes, but does anyone know exactly how they are related?'

When Ken told Sally that he'd been brought up by his unmarried mother and grown up on his great-aunt's farm at Pimpinio, she hadn't questioned him about his paternity. It didn't seem like an important issue. It never occurred to her the two young men, who didn't look at all alike (one of them her brother), shared the same biological father.

As Sally and Ken deepened their relationship, Ken decided he would tell Sally about his origins and his subsequent relationship to Rose-Louise when an opportunity presented itself. By the time Luke died, Ken hadn't found an opportunity to tell Sally how he was related to Barry.

All Derek and Anna knew was that Rose-Louise and Ken were related to Felicity by marriage, but they didn't know how. They also knew Barry had been Luke's biological father, but that was all.

Felicity knew of the blood relationship between Rose-Louise and Ken, that they shared the same biological father. She'd also heard the account of how each of them grew up with different mothers. And even though she'd noticed the similarities between Luke, Ken, and Rose-Louise, she hadn't guessed Luke's relationship to the Clapper family.

Finally, Anna and Derek decided to talk to Felicity. They felt Sally should be told about Luke's origins as well, as she'd become distressed on each occasion after Luke's death when she noticed how Ken walked and how he brushed hair away from his eyes. They reasoned if she knew how the young men were related, she might cherish the similarities instead of resenting seeing them being enacted by someone other than her deceased brother.

Anna and Derek visited and talked to Felicity soon after Luke died, and they showed her the slip of paper in Barry's handwriting that had lived inside the cover of Anna's Bible for more than twenty years. This was the only connection Anna had to back up her word that Barry had fathered Luke. Just on a whim, they brought his blood group card with them as well.

After Felicity told them Barry's rare blood group matched Luke's, they'd expected her to challenge them because of Luke's distinctly different colouring. They knew Luke hadn't followed through with any investigations into the Clapper family with regard to his spina bifida. Felicity was amazed to be told about his disability and medical history, but she couldn't throw any light on any Clapper family connection with it.

'I don't think anything will ever surprise me again after hearing your revelations.

I don't know whether you know or not, but Barry was also the biological father of Rose-Louise and Ken! Three children with three different mothers from a fellow who once had sleepy sperm.

Not a bad effort, don't you think? Barry left me a ready-made family who've been willing to have me in their lives. A pity he didn't know about any of them. He'd have been so proud of them all!

It's so sad we've all lost Luke. He overcame so much to become a well-respected tradesman. This also explains why he was so passionate about my project to provide holiday accommodation for people with disabilities. The landscaping he did around the cottages will constantly remind me of the wonderful young man he was and will perpetuate his memory.'

The whole saga seemed almost unbelievable.

The family felt unsettled during Luke's funeral. It seemed wrong to bid farewell to someone so young and watch him being lowered into a grave. It was devastating. (He was the third young person to die in as many weeks on Yorke Peninsula. A promising young female student had died during an asthma attack, and the only son of a local farmer couldn't be revived after his car veered of the road near Port Rickaby and slammed into a tree, burst into flames, and trapped the sole occupant.)

At Anna and Derek's request, Felicity invited Rose-Louise and Ken to meet them with Sally at their home before the undertaker arrived to finalise funeral arrangements. They were all told there was something about Luke they all needed to hear. After they arrived, they waited expectantly while cups of tea were handed around. They wondered why they were all asked to meet together when it was more usual for just immediate family to grieve together at such a time.

Derek began, 'You're probably puzzled to be asked to meet us prior to Luke's funeral. What we're about to tell you we've mulled over and decided it's important and needs to be told. We could have let this knowledge be buried with Luke, but we're quite sure he would have told you all eventually. If we didn't share this information with you, we decided we wouldn't be fully acknowledging Luke for the person he was and had become.'

Anna continued, 'You may not have known that Luke carried a disability with him every day. He was born with spina bifida, and the neural defect in his spine was repaired soon after his birth. He was brave and courageous and lived life to the fullest, at least within the boundaries of some daily physical limitations, but he never made a fuss or traded on having a disability. Yesterday, while we were visiting Felicity, she told us that her husband, Barry, was the biological father of both Rose-Louise and Ken.

We could see from your likenesses you were related in some way, with a resemblance to Jack Clapper, but hadn't known how you were connected. The rest of Luke's story, with Derek's blessing, is to tell you Luke's biological father was also Barry Clapper!

This means Luke was also a half-brother to both Rose-Louise and Ken. Too much to assimilate? I am not proud to say that Luke was the product of a one-night stand. To have sex in this way was quite out of character for me, without being emotionally involved, and it hadn't happened before or since. I knew Barry, but we never dated. We met up at a dance soon after his first wife, Jane, had left him. At that time, my partner of many years had finally admitted he didn't ever want a family, nor was he interested in getting married. Without consulting me, he'd applied for and been accepted for an interstate position in the police force.

Barry and I both had too much to drink after the dance, and he stayed with me overnight in my little flat over the bread shop in Port Vincent. Although we exchanged names and addresses intending to get in touch again, we never did. I could see no reason to tell Barry about my pregnancy. It hadn't been planned, and I wasn't going looking for maintenance or any other support from him. Contacting Barry about my pregnancy would only have brought complications to both our lives.

I met up with Derek on the day my doctor confirmed my pregnancy. Derek and I used to go to school together, but we'd gone in different directions afterwards. I always liked and respected him, and after meeting up with him again, we started dating. Derek knew I was pregnant right from the time we started going out together, and I told him the full circumstances. When he proposed to me, he promised to accept the baby unconditionally as his own. I didn't tell him the identity of his 'son's' biological father, and Derek never asked. Derek was a wonderful father to Luke. Even when we found out Luke would be born with spina bifida, he didn't waver in his decision to marry me.

Luke had no interest in finding out the identity of his other father, but when Derek and I read about Barry's death, we decided to tell him. We felt it important for Luke to attend the funeral. Over the years, Luke had apparently enjoyed speaking casually to Barry at a couple of sporting fixtures, so if he chose to go, he wouldn't be attending the funeral of a complete stranger. After being told about his connection to Barry Clapper, Luke had spoken to Derek with conviction, making his point of view very clear.

Speaking firmly, he'd said, 'As far as I'm concerned, you will always be my father—the only father I've ever known. I doubt if anyone would believe Barry Clapper was my biological father without the verification of DNA testing anyway, because of his different hair and skin colouring.

Because Barry didn't know about me, I can't see that publicly acknowledging him as my biological father is anyone else's business! My newly discovered knowledge is only valuable if I want to find out more about the medical history of Barry's family.'

Derek continued the conversation. 'If everyone agrees, there's no need to feed the local gossips with the information we've shared with you today. Anna and I have decided it would be better to keep this information to ourselves, unless disclosing it would benefit one of us in the future. By the way, in case any of you are wondering, Luke's unit has been left to Sally to live in, rent, or sell as she sees fit. The proceeds from the sale of his equipment and the money he's accumulated in a bank is to be divided equally between the upkeep of Felicity's cottages and the Spina Bifida Society.'

CHAPTER 21

I t wasn't meant to happen, but distress combined with caring had brought them together. In retrospect, looking back from several years down the track, everyone could see the timing was fortuitous. When Sally's pregnancy test was positive, Sally and Ken were shocked, and even though their grief over Luke's sudden death felt overwhelming, the promise of new life put hope and positivity back into many lives. Although Sally had been deprived of the opportunity to tell Luke she loved him, Sally and Ken were both glad to be distracted from continuing to have Luke's death as the main focus of their thoughts.

Luke's death had left Anna and Derek feeling shattered. Despite the obstacles placed in his path during his short life, Luke had coped well and excelled in his chosen vocation. Derek was proud to have been his dad and had loved him and Sally equally. Derek and Anna were glad their marriage stayed firmly on track through all their challenges. They grieved together and tried their best to understand how it must feel for Sally to have lost her brother, her only sibling. Although Rose-Louise had only met Luke a couple of times, she greatly admired his handiwork, both at the swimming complex and the cottages. She was surprised to learn he dealt with a disability on a daily basis and grieved for the young man she hadn't been able to acknowledge as her half-brother. She grieved as well for his sister and parents and for Felicity and Ken, who'd only learned the full story of their relationship after Luke's death.

Ken carried a heavy burden. He too hadn't had a lot of contact with Luke, but he loved Luke's sister and hoped to marry her one day. Their relationship had blossomed from the first time they'd met. He mourned the loss of Luke, of not being able to acknowledge him as his half-brother and potentially as a future brother-in-law. He was at a loss as to how best to support Sally and help her work through this terrible time.

For her part, Sally was in a daze. It all seemed so unreal. At any moment, she expected Luke to walk in the door with a cheery greeting or to phone or email her. She could see everyone, including Felicity, was stunned by Luke's death, and they were dealing with their loss in different ways.

Felicity grieved for Luke's family. She'd loved and respected Luke even though she'd not previously known they were related. She was proud to have employed him to landscape around her cottages. Luke's passing had reduced her newly acquired stepfamily by a third, but she would cherish the living legacy he'd left behind.

Perhaps Sally's pregnancy had been inevitable, although definitely not planned. After a series of deaths, to be able to rejoice and look forward to a birth certainly lifted everyone's spirits. In supporting each other while they shared their grief, Ken and Sally had completely forgotten to take precautions. It turned out that Sally had conceived shortly after Luke's passing.

Sally and Ken had known they always wanted to be together, right from their very first outing together. They made plans to get married but kept them secret. Ken wanted to have an engagement ring especially made to a design Sally had seen in a magazine and particularly admired. They'd planned on marriage and then a child, but now their plans had been reversed. Just the same, they knew they would manage with family support and would take things in their stride.

While still keeping wedding plans on the agenda, they decided to plan the event for about three years down the track. Derek and Anna could see their logic and supported their decision, even though they had reservations about it at first. Sally decided to seek a position as a physiotherapist in Horsham or somewhere in the surrounding district and move in with Ken on the farm at Pimpinio. It was only a matter of weeks before she secured a job in a private practice based at Horsham Hospital and was packing up her things, ready to move south-east. Anna was filled with mixed emotions as she helped her only daughter prepare for the move.

Despite their continuing grief, they knew keeping busy would help ease their pain. There was so much to organise in the short time before the baby's arrival. Sally met other expectant mothers when she started attending antenatal and exercise classes. Ewen's parents helped by directing her to a well-regarded doctor who had been delivering babies in Horsham for over a decade. Sally booked into Horsham Hospital for the birth and cited Ken and Anna as her support people. Anna was ecstatic.

'How about that? Our daughter is about to have a baby and become a mother and we'll be grandparents! Makes me feel old even thinking about it. Sally has asked me to be present at the birth, along with Ken. What a privilege, and how times have changed.'

'Yes, I remember not being allowed to be with you when Luke and Sally were born. I'm glad they've got rid of that idea. I hated knowing you were in pain and not being allowed to be there. Let's hope it all turns out well for them. I have no doubt they're well suited to one another. They certainly have my blessing.'

Sally intended to work as long as she could prior to the birth. At times, she felt overcome by the myriad of things that needed to be added to her to-do list. Cementing and building their relationship was a priority for both Sally and Ken. Sally knew there would be challenges in moving into a family home where Ken had lived all his life. Luckily, Ken was a forward thinker and willing to consider changes to lifelong living patterns and to even make some structural modifications to the old farmhouse.

The birth of the baby helped everyone heal. Luke had left them forever, and they would miss him in so many ways, but they knew he would want them to rejoice in the upcoming event. Anna was cherishing every moment she spent with her daughter before Sally embarked on her new life with Ken and the baby they were expecting together. Things were very different from when Anna and Derek were married. No longer was there such a stigma attached to giving birth outside marriage. Some couples decided not to get married at all, regarding a wedding as a waste of money that could be better channelled towards buying a house. Others declared that receiving a marriage certificate wouldn't make any difference to how they felt about each other. Marriages of different religions were accepted as nothing out of the ordinary, and different nationalities were marrying far more often than ever before.

In 1953, the government supported forced adoptions of all babies born to single mothers, even if the mother had parental support to keep her child. This was done in the so-called best interests of the child. This horrific state of affairs lasted for thirty-four years. Rose-Louise, Ken, and even Luke could have been victims of this barbaric law if their mothers hadn't been absolutely positive about wanting to keep them and had the financial means and assistance to make it possible.

By 1973, single mothers who were not entitled to receive a widow's pension were finally granted a supporting mother's benefit, making it easier for them to keep their babies.

Much publicity was also given over the years to the stolen generation, when for sixty years, until 1970, the government condoned taking aboriginal children from their natural mothers, supposing they were giving them a better life with a Christian upbringing in institutions or by being adopted into a white family. Much less noise was made during this time about children taken from single mothers, who then suffered a lifetime of anguish at being pressured to have their babies removed from their care and put up for adoption.

Ken and Sally decided to put off their wedding plans until well after their baby was born. They understood it would be a huge upheaval, welcoming a little person into their world and sharing a home together. There would be time later to plan a wedding complete with a ready-made page boy or flower girl! Sally wasn't fazed about moving to country Victoria and looked forward to living on a farm even though she knew they would need to make many adjustments to their lives. Because of Luke's disability, they asked Felicity to investigate the Clapper history to see if there were any references to medical conditions.

'There was nothing among Barry's papers out of the ordinary or even in Jack's spasmodic family records. I didn't find anything on Ancestry.com either' was Felicity's prompt reply.

As Barry had been a party to Rose-Louise's and Ken's beginnings and they were both healthy, they concluded Luke's disability was probably not due to any heredity factor. They opted not to find out the sex of their baby when Sally had her routine ultrasounds, but learning that there was no indication of any neural defect was a great relief to everyone. Anna and Derek were particularly relieved. They knew they'd been lucky Luke had been a boy. It would have been more difficult for a girl to grow up needing regular catheterisations.

Anna and Derek were facing huge adjustments as well. They missed having Luke and Sally share an occasional meal or drop in for a visit out of the blue. They kept in touch with Jenny, who by then was caring for her elderly parents full-time in Wattle Flat. They persuaded her to employ a sitter and accompany them, with Felicity and Peter, to the fortnightly dances. They took it in turns to meet at a different hotel or club for a meal before sharing one vehicle instead of taking one each.

Felicity and Peter had an open invitation to visit Sally and Ken at any time, while Sally's parents visited them whenever Derek had holidays. He enjoyed helping Ken with farm chores and pottering in the garden, especially the vegetable section.

Derek concentrated on growing carrots, potatoes, silver beet, beans, and peas rather than cruciferous varieties such as cauliflower, cabbage, and Brussels sprouts that required regular spraying to prevent disease and pest damage. His pet project was to add new trees to the orchard for the young couple to celebrate every major event Ken and Sally shared. He'd planted a beautiful peach tree when Sally moved into the farmhouse with Ken and was sourcing different types of citrus trees for when their baby arrived.

Derek helped Ken build a new enclosure where the poultry were shut in each evening to keep them safe from foxes. Anna delighted in the morning chore of letting the squawking birds out to roam freely around the farm all day. She collected the eggs and restocked the feeders with pellets, marvelling when some of the eggs were still warm. There were usually the same number of eggs each day, in slightly different shades of brown and white.

When they multiplied more rapidly than could be used in all manner of recipes, they were carefully packed in recycled egg cartons and taken in to the Uniting Church hall to be distributed to needy families or be used in the preparation of healthy meals made available to elderly pensioners twice weekly.

Anna helped by taking over many of the housekeeping chores when she visited the Pimpinio farm, and she enjoyed exploring the shops for treats for both her daughter and the coming baby. She was amazed at the amount of equipment deemed necessary to look after a modern baby and the variety of brightly coloured educational toys available in all the shops. She couldn't resist buying a soft, cuddly teddy bear, noting how different it felt from the toys that had been packed tightly with stuffing when Luke and Sally were small children.

Sally's physiotherapy skills were greatly appreciated in Horsham. As she continued feeling healthy and able, she worked happily until she reached thirty-six weeks' gestation. Sally wanted to have a month to wind down from her professional working mode, focus more on the coming baby, and prepare one of the smaller bedrooms as a nursery, complete with a rocking chair she intended to use while breastfeeding. She'd cautioned many mothers-to-be not to work too long and become overtired and run down before they gave birth. She knew she would be foolish if she didn't take her own advice. She was given a send-off from work with a baby shower and brought home a wonderful mixture of both essential and frivolous goodies.

Sally added three tiny jackets and matching bootees to the articles of clothing Felicity and Anna had knitted. Jenny and Rose-Louise were excitedly amassing wardrobe items too, and temptation often led Sally to buy bibs with quirky messages embroidered on them. Not knowing the sex of their baby didn't unduly concern them. They didn't intend sticking to the strict 'pink for girls' and 'blue for boys' guidelines and definitely didn't adhere to the idea of clothing a baby in navy blue, red, khaki, or black! The colour of choice for the nursery was a delicate pale peach, combined with a scattering of light greens and blues. Altogether it was a very appealing, welcoming space, with the restored rocking chair taking pride of place near the window, where bright sunshine often poured into the room.

Although it was tempting to want everything new for a first baby, Sally gratefully accepted gifts of second-hand clothing and equipment. Some clothes had never been worn, as clothing gifts given out of season were often too small by the time the next suitable season arrived. Babies often seemed to grow overnight, and actually estimating some children's rate of growth could be classified as an extreme skill.

Anna and Derek bought a pram for the new baby, taking into consideration it would be loaded in and out of the boot of Sally's car whenever she ventured into Horsham. Size and weight and durability were all taken into consideration. Sally asked her friends for advice on the best brand to buy, planning to have it last for more than one child and to safeguard against being swayed by persistent sales talk.

Jenny purchased the baby capsule, a very pricey item she was glad to fund, enabling the new parents to have the safest capsule on the market. Baby car seats had to meet so many regulations. Anna marvelled that when her babies were small, they all survived travelling in a Moses basket, sitting on the back seat of their car, sometimes anchored with a webbing harness.

Friends and neighbours gave Sally and Ken a baby bath and change table, a cot with an allergy-free mattress, and a high chair. Sally discovered a sturdy playpen up in the rafters of the main garage that she decided would be great to use outside on the lawn on suitable occasions. This would keep the dogs from being too playful and smothering the new arrival with slobbery affection.

Soon after she moved to Pimpinio to live with Ken, Sally found a treasure trove of baby and children's clothing and toys packed away in trunks in one of the sheds adjacent to the garage. Jenny recognised the items Auntie Margaret had loaned her when Ken was a baby, things left over from before her husband passed away when they'd been foster parents.

She also found a selection of baby clothes packed securely in pale-blue tissue paper. The jumpsuits were mainly white, though several were blue. There were three little cardigans with matching caps and a tiny pair of shoes with soft soles. As well as clothing, she found a striped bunny rug and a couple of cloth nappies. A woollen shawl that had taken Jenny nearly six months to knit was preserved in the package and, miraculously, hadn't yellowed greatly with age. Jenny remembered putting the clothing away, feeling it was part of her early history with her son. She'd been reluctant to throw anything away but wondered if any of it would ever be used again.

The surprising items that had everyone feeling a little puzzled for a while were copies of *The Age* and the rural newspaper *The Weekly Times*. Both Victorian newspapers were printed on the same day. Then the penny dropped—they held a record of events, both local and further afield, of things that happened on the day Ken was born. Sally was fascinated by everything she discovered, forgotten treasure that had been lovingly wrapped and stored in a safe place.

Felicity often travelled with them when Anna or Jenny visited, treating herself to a week's stay at the motel where Rose-Louise ran the restaurant. Jenny felt happy to help out from time to time with menial tasks and soon was officially listed as a casual employee. The restaurant increased in popularity in Horsham and the surrounding district, and soon there were plans to renovate the kitchen and expand with an entertainment area.

*   *   *

Peter kept busy running both his and Felicity's farms, so it wasn't feasible for him to accompany her to Horsham for more than a few days at a time a couple of times a year. By combining their machinery, they had cut down on repair costs and maximised their productivity. He'd become Felicity's constant companion and a frequent visitor to her home—and not only to consult about farm matters.

His wife still lived interstate and was rarely available when he tried to contact her. She'd only visited the farm near Clapper's Cove once since Peter had returned there. It hadn't been a successful visit either, as the toilet blocked up and couldn't be cleared until late the next day. She was full of complaints about the house being cold and draughty and the poor mobile phone connection. Wet weather with high winds didn't improve anybody's mood either.

He was thankful she insisted on sleeping in a guest bedroom, citing she had caught a cold and didn't want to share it. Peter felt awkward and on edge for the whole length of her visit. Felicity felt the writing was on the wall in regard to Peter's marriage but was wary of being thought of as the other woman.

CHAPTER 22

Thousands of lightning strikes arced across the sky. The deafening noise of the wind and thunder made conversation almost impossible. The rain lashed the buildings in stinging sheets, and hail piled up in doorways and under verandas. This wasn't meant to happen just as most of the wheat crops were ready for harvesting. With the header serviced, the grain bins in position, and the emergency firefighting unit filled with water, Ken was well prepared for the harvest. It looked like the best crop he'd grown in years. He started on his northern paddock after he'd tested the moisture content of the grain to make sure it would meet the rigid conditions for delivery to the grain storage silos near Horsham. From the time the grain came into head, the crop had promised great returns—until the storm came.

Western Australian crops suffered millions of dollars in damages as hailstones the size of golf balls pounded the ripening grain into the ground. With unrelenting ferocity, the storm caused indiscriminate destruction along its path into South Australia before raging into Victoria. Many trees were uprooted, and several houses and sheds were flattened or lost roofs. Flying debris was everywhere, and people were cautioned to stay inside. Briefly, Sally recalled she'd been amazed to learn that many animals gave birth during thunderstorms, wondering why they made such a choice.

Along with the niggling pain in her back, as her waters broke, she had her answer.

'They probably didn't have a choice either!'

Michael Luke Kenneth Johnstone entered the world three hours later, in Horsham Hospital where the emergency generator had been operating for half an hour.

It would be some time before the extent of the damage to power lines could finally be assessed and electricity restored to the town. Luckily, Sally had packed her suitcase with everything she needed to take to hospital and stowed it safely in the boot of her car several days previously. They'd chosen her cherished HJ Holden as transport as she could get in and out easily, and it had already been fitted with the baby capsule. When her pains were six minutes apart, Ken and Sally began debating whether to brave the storm or wait a little longer, as the wild weather wasn't showing any sign of abating.

'I thought first babies are supposed to be late, not one week early,' Sally protested.

'I'm glad we can get to the garage without going out in the storm. I'll call your mum while the nursing staff are admitting you and assessing your progress. I doubt very much if she will be able to get here in time to see her grandchild born now. She intended to drive here the day after tomorrow. I don't think it's wise for her to be travelling in this wild weather anyway.'

Anna returned home after a quick dash to the shops for some bread, just after Ken called and left a message on her answering machine.

'It's Ken here. It looks like today is the day you are about to become grandparents.'

Anna and Derek had heard the storm warnings and seen the devastation caused as it tore across South Australia. Luckily, it bypassed Yorke Peninsula but flattened crops further north. A freak mini-tornado ripped through the edge of Ken's most northern paddock at Pimpinio, but luckily, he'd harvested his wheat crop there two days previously. Although trees on his fence line were torn out, he'd escaped any other major storm damage. Some of his neighbours were not so lucky, where their field bins were overturned and grain scattered by the wind before having a heavy deluge dumped on it.

Felicity was visiting Jenny when Ken phoned to let her know Sally was in labour. They'd become firm friends and visited each other frequently and had shared many cups of tea together. They were both excited to hear it was all happening for Sally.

'Are they hoping to have a boy or a girl?'

'Do you think the baby will have Ken's hair colour?'

'Probably the answer to both our questions is that they don't really care. They just want Sally to give birth to a healthy baby without intervention of any sort. She hopes she won't be needing forceps or caesarean delivery.'

'Her doctor and the midwifery team are said to be very competent.'

'Yes, and she's been healthy and active all through her pregnancy. I can't wait to see the baby. Fancy us being grandparents. I hope Barry, wherever he is, can see the wonderful legacy he left us.'

Michael Luke Kenneth Johnstone was born healthy, with a sprinkling of pale gingery hair, and everyone rejoiced. 'Awesome' was Ken's description of seeing his son slither into the world and utter a shrill cry. He felt extremely privileged to be with Sally all through her labour, even if all he could do to help was rub her back and give her sips of water or have her squeeze his hand. They cherished their time together holding their son straight after his birth, and as soon as they were alone, they checked to see he had all his limbs and fingers and toes and little boy bits.

When he was taken away to be weighed and cleaned up, Ken produced a beautiful engagement ring featuring a solitaire diamond supported by three slim finely crafted gold shoulders on either side joining it to a diamond-patterned eighteen-carat gold band. He gently placed it on the fourth finger of Sally's left hand. She promptly burst into tears, realising he'd remembered the engagement ring she'd admired in a magazine soon after they'd first contemplated getting married.

'I don't have anything to give you to celebrate our son's safe arrival,' Sally sobbed.

'You've just delivered our son safely. There's nothing better you could give me,' Ken replied. 'Right now I feel as though I'm the luckiest man in the whole world.'

Still, amidst all the excitement, there was a little sadness too, as they remembered Luke, who would have been a wonderful role model and uncle to the little boy.

As Derek was unable to leave his work commitments at short notice, he arranged to have Anna travel to Horsham with Jenny and Felicity. Anna took up residence in the spare room at the farm, while Felicity and Jenny opted to stay in a unit at the motel, allowing Sally and her mother to explore and enjoy their new roles for the first week together. They planned to visit daily and do laundry and shopping. Derek drove up to Pimpinio a week later. In the meantime, he proudly announced his new status to all and sundry, as though he was the only person who had ever become a grandfather.

Rose-Louise was pleased to have Jenny and Felicity as guests. She enjoyed every minute of their newly discovered shared-relative status. She soaked up information about Barry and was still amazed to think he had unknowingly fathered three offspring. Felicity often pondered imaginary situations, visualising Barry's astonishment as first one, then two, and finally three young people arriving at the farm to meet him. She also wondered if Jack's controlling attitudes would have mellowed if he had met his grandchildren.

Felicity felt blessed. She had always known her chances of getting pregnant were slim, especially when coupled with Barry's low fertility. After being resigned to being childless, she was overawed to find out she had three stepchildren.

On the day before Sally returned home, Felicity and Jenny were like a couple of whirlwinds, helping Anna give the farmhouse a quick spring clean and the garden a watering as well as rearranging and combining the many sheaves of flowers that had overflowed from Sally's hospital room. They baked bread and cakes and casseroles, determined to make the new mother's settling in time as smooth as possible.

When Sally and Ken were selecting a name for baby Michael, they decided that one meaning 'a gift' was most appropriate. As there were very few births that month in Horsham Hospital, Sally opted to stay for five days until her milk supply became well established. Although Anna and Jenny offered to help with advice from their own experiences, Sally wisely felt she would be less overwhelmed by being under medical and expert nursing care during this time.

This decision allowed her to cope more privately with the baby blues on her fourth postpartum day, when her hormones were sorting themselves out. (Twenty years on from when Jane had delivered Rose-Louise and had been devastated by feelings of rejection for her baby, the condition of postnatal depression was widely recognised, acknowledged, and treated early without any stigma being attached to the affected mother.)

On the day of his son's homecoming, Ken drove to the hospital early, in time to help with bathing his precious son.

He felt extremely proud of Sally. She'd managed so well over the months since the overwhelming loss of her brother. Her unexpected pregnancy, and subsequently relocating and starting a new phase of her life in another state on a farm, introduced enormous changes in her life. She'd had times when she felt overcome by the extent of the upheavals she'd faced, but mostly she'd sailed through the ups and downs and her pregnancy without too many hiccups. Family support and Sally's own sunny personality contributed to how she had quickly become part of her new community. Working in the capacity of a much-needed physiotherapist at Horsham Hospital definitely helped with her assimilation.

Michael arrived home, snug in the baby capsule that would accommodate his travelling needs for many months to come. No longer did newborns travel in bassinets that were occasionally harnessed into the back seat of cars. He slept all the way and still stayed asleep when the capsule, with its precious cargo, was carried into the farmhouse to the room prepared for him adjacent to his parents. Anna greeted her daughter with a welcome cup of tea. Sally couldn't believe how tired she'd become while travelling the short distance back to Pimpinio and gladly opted for a sleep before Michael woke up and noisily demanded to be fed.

Ken and Sally were more than a little scared by the realisation they'd be responsible for the small person in their care for all the formative years of his life, but together they were determined to do the best they possibly could. Another new phase of their lives had begun.

Gradually, the excitement settled, and a routine of sorts was established as much as it could be with the ever-changing scenario of a growing baby in the house. There was no doubt who ruled Sally and Ken's world now. They became besotted parents who couldn't wait to share every small milestone with anyone who would listen.

Baby Michael was two weeks old when he had his first official outing joining a small gathering of friends and relatives at Ewen's family home to celebrate the engagement of Rose-Louise and Ewen.

Although Sally and Ken enjoyed being showered with love and care by Sally's parents and Ken's mother, they admitted to each other they were glad when they finally went home soon after Rose-Louise and Ewen's engagement celebration. Jenny left with Anna and Derek, and Felicity stayed on longer than she'd planned to help Rose-Louise.

Ewen had been strutting around as proud as a peacock for weeks but wouldn't tell anybody exactly what he was so pleased about.

He didn't fool anyone because Rose-Louise was wearing a huge smile that brought sunshine and laughter to everyone who came within range. Together they'd selected a beautiful 2.1-carat round-cut ruby engagement ring, with three graduated diamonds on either side merging into a yellow gold band. As Rose-Louise hadn't previously worn a ring of any sort, she was very conscious of it on her finger, especially if it twisted round so the stone was visible when she looked at the palm of her hand.

Their engagement party was low-key, with friends and neighbours providing all manner of food delicacies. It ended up being a wonderfully happy event. Extra chairs were rediscovered in the old shed near the garage, dusted down to remove a myriad of spiders and their webs, and set out on the lawn. Shade cloths were strung between trees, and a bar was placed at one end of the veranda loaded with cold drinks and an urn for hot drinks at the other end.

'Oh, look at those pavlovas. They all have different toppings and look totally amazing,' Anna remarked to Derek.

'I'm going to make an impression on that plate of sausage rolls first,' he replied.

A table set aside for presents soon overflowed with gifts of all shapes and sizes. Having lived most of her life in a caravan or motel room (when she took over the management of the motel restaurant), Rose-Louise was looking forward to living in a larger space.

Ewen's parents were thrilled when Rose-Louise and Ewen finally announced their engagement. Their new house in Horsham only required a concrete driveway and paths before they could move off the farm into town. On each trip into Horsham, the boot of their Holden was loaded with boxes of necessities to start the next chapter of their lives. New furniture and appliances were awaiting delivery, and their excitement nearly equalled that of the newly engaged couple. It was fitting that their time to move coincided with changes in their son's circumstances, giving him freedom to pursue his dream of running his own farm and, hopefully in the future, to provide them with grandchildren.

Rose-Louise and Ewen were to take over the hundred-year-old farmhouse, with its large rooms featuring bay windows, wood panelling, and tin ceilings and housing heavy furniture that was far too tall to fit into a small modern home. Built of brick, with wide verandas on all four sides, it was a gracious home, surrounded by a garden of shrubs and trees.

Rose-Louise was delighted to find a beautiful rose garden paved with bricks surrounding a courtyard as well as bordering the path from the laundry to the enormous Hills Hoist clothes line.

Ewen had fond memories of swinging from that clothes line when his parents weren't around, and he also remembered when a cover had been fitted over it, resulting in the shady area being used for entertaining. Ewen's parents installed the rotary clothes line soon after they gained popularity in the early fifties, replacing clothes lines hung between two posts and propped up in the middle by a stick. (Rotary clothes lines had been invented and patented in Adelaide by Gilbert Toyne in 1926 but were only sold in small numbers until the early 1960s.) Lance Hill's compact rotary line consisted of wire and metal tube with a cast aluminium winding gear. His first batch was made from the underwater boom hung under Sydney Harbour Bridge to catch enemy submarines during World War II.

Papers were being drawn up to hand the farm over to the newly engaged couple on their wedding day. However, Ewen had his parents' blessing to begin upgrading the bathroom and renovating the kitchen as soon as he could secure a tradesman willing to do the job. The bathroom became more user friendly with the installation of a large two-person bath, enlarged shower recess, room for a chair, and a new vanity unit with two basins and a wide mirror. But what Rose-Louise liked best was that the door was repositioned so the bathroom could be accessed from a tiled area, not a carpeted hallway.

The tired farmhouse kitchen demanded attention too. The ceiling was lowered and a skylight installed, angling it from the space left in the roof where the old wood stove had faithfully served the family for as long as Ewen could remember. Easy-to-clean cupboards and benchtops were installed, along with a new cooktop and oven, a double sink, and a new two-door refrigerator. All the doors that had opened into both the kitchen and the bathroom were replaced by sliding doors. Non-slip, easy-care tiles replaced lino in both rooms. Despite the upgrading of all the facilities, the hundred-year-old farmhouse still retained its old-world charm and warmth.

They inherited lots of the furniture from Ewen's parents, who were looking forward to updating everything when they moved into their new house in Horsham. They knew the younger couple would cherish the beautiful wooden wardrobes with their mirror inserts, the gnarled dressing tables and sideboards, and most of all, the wonderful old player piano that graced the living room.

Ewen had learned to play the piano for a few years but preferred to beat out a rhythm on the drumset that lived in the disused, mouse-proof barn some distance away from the main house. Felicity was invited to sift through the music she discovered in the music stool and was looking forward to having friends sing around the piano from time to time.

*   *   *

When Rose-Louise was still a little girl, Jane had told her the reason for her name. When she'd visited the Clapper's farmhouse for the first time, there were very few roses still thriving, but a deep-red bloom with a wonderful perfume had survived on both sides of the steps leading up to the front door. Felicity hadn't been able to find out what it was called but guessed it could be one of a group of heritage or old-fashioned roses. Roses lacking in fragrance didn't have the same appeal to her as those with a distinct perfume.

Rose-Louise had a favourite rose and looked forward to planting some modern scented varieties where older ones had died off. She knew the area had to be specially treated and rested so the new plants would remain healthy. Ewen gave her two Joyfulness tea roses when he proposed to her, and they accurately illustrated the couple's feelings for each other. Rose-Louise knew the colours of the blooms would change as they aged into various pastel shades of apricot, cream, and pink. She hoped to nurture strong healthy bushes and produce many long-stemmed roses with beautiful fragrance for many years.

Far from feeling their euphoric state was being overshadowed, Sally and Ken were pleased to have the focus shift away from them for a while. They were happy for Ewen and Rose-Louise, and Felicity fussed about like a clucky mother hen. She was proud to be accepted as surrogate mother and silently thanked her deceased husband over and over for gifting her three wonderful young people, who had already shared important events in their lives with her. There were times she felt she was living in a dream, and any moment she might wake up alone again.

CHAPTER 23

Felicity didn't want to wait any longer. She'd already been away for ten days more than she'd planned. She acknowledged that Peter had been amazing—uncomplainingly looking after her farm as well as his own and also keeping an eye on the tenants in the cottages. He'd been in her thoughts constantly, and she wondered whether he thought of her often as well. They had agreed not to call or text while Felicity was away from home. They both needed to examine their thoughts and feelings unencumbered by direct contact. They knew they were strongly attracted to each other but were very conscious of the fact Peter was married and all that it entailed.

Neither Peter nor his wife felt as though they were married to each other any more. Peter still found it hard to make contact with his wife, and several phone calls from his son made reference to the fact she had a regular male escort and was making no effort to hide their friendship. He'd intimated on several occasions that when his mother's friend visited them at the farm, he'd stayed overnight.

Peter's wife knew he helped Felicity on her farm, and whenever they did happen to speak, she kept making snide remarks about her husband's partner. After her disastrous visit, when Peter could see no evidence she was suffering from a cold but had still insisted on separate beds, he began to decipher her hidden message.

Felicity sensed what was happening before realisation hit Peter. She understood his turmoil, knowing he took his marriage vows seriously. As she watched his struggles, she made sure she didn't allow her growing feelings for him influence the decisions he needed to make.

'I never wanted to live on this godforsaken farm,' Peter's wife had declared after the disaster of the blocked toilet during her first and only return visit.

'Why don't you sell what's left of it? And why on earth did you think it necessary to lease that widow's farm down the road when there's so much that needs to be fixed up here?'

Peter tried to tell her about his deep connection to the family farm where he'd grown up, but she adamantly stated she didn't ever want to live there again. He was sure the farm he'd established, where they'd lived together and raised their two boys, would be well cared for, being managed by their older son. The questions he was mulling over ranged from *Why is it so important to me to make this family farm profitable again?* to *Am I running away from my marriage by wanting to stay here, knowing my wife doesn't want to move to South Australia?*

Peter also asked himself, *Is my wanting to stay on the family farm influenced by my attraction to Felicity?*

Peter was very fond of Felicity and admired her determination to encourage the local community to think outside their square and embrace the idea of having a swimming pool built in the town. Spending some of the money she'd inherited to establish accommodation units for people with disabilities greatly impressed him as well. Deep down, he began to experience feelings he identified as being much more than affection. He kept thinking of her all the time, many times during the day, and if he awoke at night, his imagination took hold and went in many erotic, fanciful directions, which caused him to feel quite embarrassed at times!

He felt guilty at first, but after a while, he accepted his true feelings—that he no longer wanted to be married to his wife. He wanted to be with Felicity full-time. Armed with a new confidence, he eagerly awaited her return after Rose-Louise had rung to tell him Felicity was on her way home.

Felicity's feelings were in turmoil too. She wasn't comfortable to be seen, especially by the narrow-minded gossips of Wattle Flat, as the other woman in a relationship with a married man. It had made sense for them to travel together into town to go shopping or to go dancing and sharing a vehicle from time to time, and the gossips had gone into overdrive. Not being approached or criticised openly gave Peter and Felicity no chance to offer an explanation, and the gossips probably wouldn't have believed them anyway. The truth might have spoilt a good story!

She knew without doubt she was in love with Peter and had sifted through all the scenarios that may have been influencing her thinking.

Was she just lonely?

Did she want to spend the rest of her life with Peter?

Would his two boys accept her as Peter's wife if he were to divorce their mother?

Would Rose-Louise and Ken embrace the idea of their newly found stepmother wanting to remarry?

In laying out her thoughts like this, Felicity could clearly see what she wanted for the rest of her life. She knew that if Peter asked her, she would accept his proposal.

Felicity knew it wasn't a wise thing to do, but once in the car, she was determined not to break up the trip with an overnight stop. But before setting out, she set herself some ground rules for the drive home.

1. If she yawned five times, she would get out of her car and walk around for a while.

2. She would drink plenty of water.

3. She would eat grapes and chocolate to help keep herself alert!

4. She would play the CDs she'd collected but never played over the years.

5. She would make frequent stops, at least every two hours (her aim to drink plenty of water would probably make those stops very necessary).

6. She would eat a healthy meal at least twice during the journey.

Although she knew it would take between seven to nine hours to get home, depending on her speed and the highway she chose to travel, Felicity knew that with frequent stops, it would more likely take nearer to twelve. This was especially true since she started yawning just half an hour out of Horsham and religiously walked around her car several times.

She'd said her goodbyes to Sally and Ken and admired baby Michael again the previous day. Rose-Louise hugged her, and they were both tearful as Felicity set out from the motel after a very early breakfast.

*   *   *

On the Pimpinio farm, seasons changed and produced some great harvests, some that were mediocre and one that was wiped out by hail. Ken and Sally prospered, and Michael grew into an active toddler with a mischievous grin. He idolised his father, and Ken was entranced by the way he tried to copy all his mannerisms. Far from being annoyed—as Jack had been with Barry—Ken enjoyed seeing Michael sitting beside him, pulling on his little boots and searching for his hat, before going outside with him to inspect the crops.

Michael's favourite toys were replicas of farm machinery. Some had been stored away since Ken played with them as a small boy. Sally loved her two 'farmers' and was thrilled to have the younger version act as a two-and-a-half-year-old page boy at their wedding.

Sally was a radiant bride, wearing a beautiful pale-cream crystal-satin full-length gown. The bodice featured a five-metre lined train, attached at the back from her shoulders and edged with tiny seed pearls. The long sleeves were pointed along the back of her hands with the same edging. Sally had employed a professional dressmaker to make her wedding gown but had fashioned her own circular veil, which she connected to a hollow pillbox covered in matching crystal satin. She had spent hours laboriously stitching seed pearls around the headdress circumference. She looked absolutely stunning as she walked down the aisle attended by Rose-Louise. Michael played his part to perfection, and Sally's apprehension as to how he'd behave proved to be unnecessary.

Anna, Derek, Jenny, Felicity, and Peter all travelled to Horsham for the happy occasion. So much had happened to unite them as a family in the last few years, and they were all happy and proud to be part of Sally and Ken's wedding celebrations.

They held the reception at the motel restaurant, where Rose-Louise excelled in making their day run smoothly. As Sally and Ken were married in mid August, the crop was in the ground, and they were able to take a break before haymaking and harvesting. Anna and Derek stayed on to mind Michael and the farm while Sally and Ken went to Western Australia for their honeymoon. Minding Michael was bittersweet for them as it brought back memories of Luke at the same age. Although many months had passed since Luke's untimely death, the pain of losing the son they were so proud of was still raw.

Exciting news followed a few months later when Sally and Ken announced they were expecting a baby girl—probably conceived on their honeymoon.

Ken and Sally's wedding was the final event in the motel restaurant before it closed temporarily for renovations. The management planned to add a function room and a smaller dining room, catering for between thirty and forty people, built apart from the main restaurant and suitable for private parties. Rose-Louise resigned and took up a temporary position at the Returned Servicemen's Club in Horsham, although she still worked in the restaurant three days a week. After managing the motel and restaurant for several years, she was glad to wind down to have less responsibility and better hours.

They limited their wedding celebration to close family and intimate friends. But that didn't stop other friends and acquaintances from sending presents and best wishes. They'd become a popular couple in the district and often attended events with Sally and Ken. They were lucky to be the first couple to have a wedding reception in the new function room. The new restaurant manager had come highly recommended as he'd run events at several well-known Melbourne venues, and he pulled out all the stops to make their day extra special.

After a honeymoon in New Zealand, encompassing rail and coach journeys, they flew home fully refreshed. They'd met up with a young couple who were farming wheat and barley east of the Southern Alps on the South Island, near Timaru, and were determined to keep in contact, inviting them to stay on their farm when they planned to visit Australia the following year.

A short time later, Rose-Louise found she was pregnant. Having learned of Jane's medical history, first with pre-eclampsia then with depression and the debilitating struggle to interact with her precious, much-longed-for baby daughter, Rose-Louise made sure her doctor was told of her mother's complete history and had it recorded in her medical history. She was reassured that if there were any changes in her blood pressure that might indicate pre-eclampsia, she'd be sent straight to the Royal Women's Hospital in Melbourne for assessment and careful monitoring.

Perhaps she shouldn't have been surprised to learn, as her biological father had twin sisters, that she was also having twins! There had been twins in Ewen's family history as well. Felicity was overcome with emotion when she learned their exciting news. From meeting those connected to Barry, who had attended her husband's funeral, there had evolved a whole new family. She felt extremely privileged to be accepted so naturally into all their lives.

Rose-Louise continued to work part-time with her doctor's blessing until she reached the six-month mark.

She remained well, and although she carried a little extra fluid as her term neared, it didn't cause concern. Ewen was immensely proud of her, and even when she found it difficult to sleep towards the end of her pregnancy, she didn't complain. Although they were asked if they wanted to know the sex of their babies, they were both happy to wait until the births.

At eight and a half months, without any complications, Rose-Louise safely delivered two healthy babies—a boy and a girl. A new era had begun, and Rose-Louise and Ewen felt very blessed. A well-qualified obstetrician had joined the Horsham Hospital staff three months before Rose-Louise gave birth, and confidently managed her pregnancy without any need for her to go to Melbourne for specialist care.

*　　*　　*

Anna and Derek were happy to purchase Luke's home from Sally when Derek retired, sold his real estate business in Ardrossan, and decided to downsize. Although the house was smaller, there was ample room on the block to park a couple of caravans if necessary. They felt a special warmth and connection with Luke when they took up residence in his former home. His landscaped garden produced delightful surprises as the seasons changed.

Jenny continued to care for her parents in Wattle Flat until they both passed away within a couple of months of each other. She remained active in the community and regularly hosted overseas students, who stayed for varying periods of time. Jenny enjoyed showcasing her neighbourhood to young people. She remained good friends with Anna and Derek, and they often swapped news of their shared grandchildren.

*   *   *

Felicity could never have envisaged the changes that would happen to her after that dreadful day when she'd been watching the television news at lunchtime and saw the account of her husband's death. As she approached the Clapper farm, returning from her prolonged stay in Horsham after baby Michael was born, she experienced a great feeling of peace. She no longer worried about how she would react when she met up with Peter again. She didn't go straight home. Felicity sighted him in a roadside paddock, stopped the car, and within minutes was secure in the arms of the man she loved.

Peter's wife was relieved when he requested a divorce, and Peter felt positive it was the right thing for both of them.

Soon after Felicity arrived home, Peter asked her to marry him. Two years later, the wedding was attended by Felicity's stepchildren Ken and Rose-Louise, their partners, and their children. Jenny, Anna, and Derek were also wedding guests, along with Peter's two sons and friends from all over South Australia and Victoria.

The ceremony was held in the landscaped garden outside the cottages, where some of the guests were accommodated. It proved to be a joyous celebration of family connections.

*   *   *

The flock of sheep grazed on the clifftop. One wayward sheep squeezed through a hole in the fence on to the old path that led down to where the shallow pool formed at high tide near Clapper's Cove. A roll of tangled barbed wire was partly buried in the tidal pool. The sheep gave it a wide berth.

She'd learned her lessons well. She'd listened to the warnings from her elders and heard how her ancestor had been saved from an agonizing death. Nearly thirty years ago, instead of that sheep remaining trapped in the barbed wire, a farmer had set her free and sacrificed his life for her!

About the Author

Photo by Carolyn B Photography

Helen has lived in country towns, on a farm, and in the city; and has a passion for writing short stories and rhyming verse. Her poems have been produced on a CD and in a book entitled "Homespun Poems from my Heart." After completing her schooling in Western Victoria, Helen trained as a nurse at the Alfred and Royal Women's hospitals in Melbourne and afterwards worked in hospital theatres, or with premature babies.

She also taught and practised Reflexology, wrote a chapter in a Reflexology reference book, and articles in Reflexology magazines, and been a guest speaker at an International Reflexology Conference in Hawaii. She has completed several creative writing courses and a diploma of freelance travel writing and photography. Helen had a dozen pen friends and was a prolific reader as a child, and still reads books at every opportunity.

As her three children are grown up with families of their own, Helen has recently returned to her home town, Portland in Victoria where she lives with her husband David.

Also available from Helen M. Croser

helmarc376@gmail.com

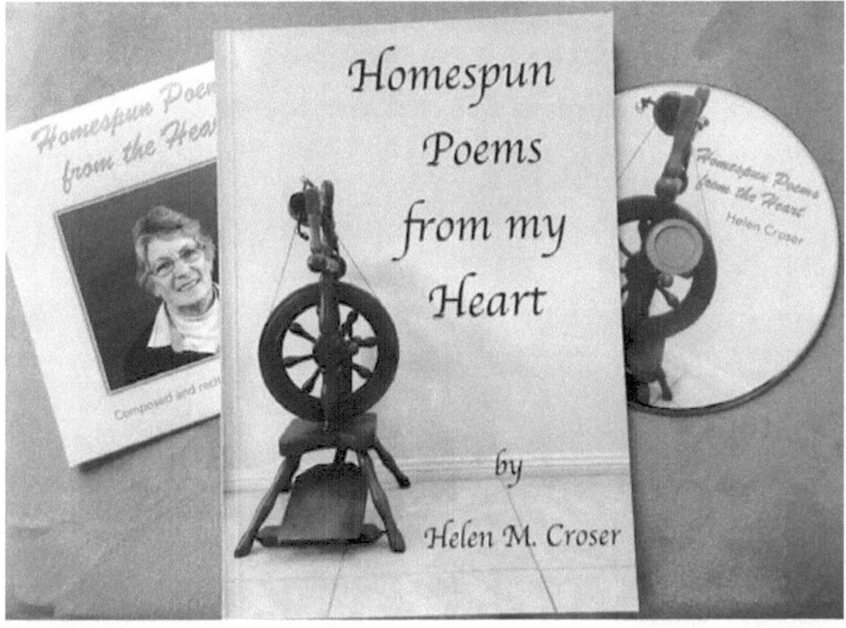